PENGUIN

The Chocolate B[

Gracie Hart was born in Leeds and raised on the family farm in the Yorkshire Dales. She writes sagas with a focus on the wars and her native Yorkshire.

She began her career as a glass-engraver before raising her family. Gracie has now written several family sagas.

Gracie Hart also writes as Diane Allen and averages a 4.5 star review rating across her titles.

The Chocolate Box
Girls at War

GRACIE HART

PENGUIN BOOKS

PENGUIN BOOKS

UK | USA | Canada | Ireland | Australia
India | New Zealand | South Africa

Penguin Books is part of the Penguin Random House group of companies
whose addresses can be found at global.penguinrandomhouse.com

Penguin Random House UK,
One Embassy Gardens, 8 Viaduct Gardens, London SW11 7BW

penguin.co.uk

Penguin
Random House
UK

First published 2025

001

Copyright © Gracie Hart, 2025

Set in 12.5/14.75pt Garamond MT
Typeset by Falcon Oast Graphic Art Ltd
Printed and bound in Great Britain by Clays Ltd, Elcograf S.p.A

The authorized representative in the EEA is Penguin Random House Ireland,
Morrison Chambers, 32 Nassau Street, Dublin D02 YH68

A CIP catalogue record for this book is available from the British Library

ISBN: 978-1-405-96332-9

Penguin Random House is committed to a sustainable
future for our business, our readers and our planet. This book is
made from Forest Stewardship Council® certified paper.

MIX
Paper | Supporting
responsible forestry
FSC
www.fsc.org   FSC® C018179

For my number 1 favourite son-in-law,
Steven Lawson. Love Grumper.

I

York, 1940

Rose Freeman felt the tears running down her cheeks as she held tight to her true love, Ned.

'I don't want you to go – please stay,' she whispered, as she buried her head in his smart RAF uniform and held him close, breathing in the smell of his heavy cologne and not wanting him ever to leave her. 'I know you won't be based far from me, but you might as well be a million miles away, especially when you fly out on a mission.' Rose sighed and felt her heart beating next to his as he bent his head down and kissed her gently on the lips.

'Sssshh, you know I've no option. I have to go. But I'm in good company; we're all friends and we'll look after one another. No harm will come of us, and I can sleep easy knowing you and my mother are looking after each other.' Ned touched his lucky rabbit's foot in his pocket and knew he was lying through his teeth. Elvington Airfield had already lost its fair share of air-crews and now the war was progressing no one was safe.

'I'm frightened this war will take you, just as we've found one another and have plans for the future. Don't go, Ned. Please tell them that you're ill, that your mother needs you . . . anything that makes you stay here.' Rose felt a searing pain in her heart as she saw Ned's friend, Peter, come driving down the road in his open-top car. She glanced down at her diamond engagement ring; Ned's few days on leave had been all too short.

'You know I can't. I'll come home safe. It's only another mission; Pete and I will look after one another. As soon as I can I'll come home and you know that I write to you every day and, like I promised, if I ever fly over the house on my return, I'll cut my engines so you know it's me.' Ned held Rose tight. 'I love you, Rose. Once this war is over we will marry. We will happily live here and bring two, three or even four children up and drive my mother mad with their noise and pestering. Until then I must do my best to protect this country, and you must do your bit by looking after your family and working at Rowntree's until things get better.'

Rose looked up at her man and held him tight, as she always did before he returned to the Elvington Airfield and the dangerous life he'd chosen, even before con-scription had been made compulsory, over the safe and reliable job of making chocolates at the Rowntree's fac-tory. 'I never get used to these farewells; in fact, they're getting harder,' Rose said and kissed Ned. 'You take care of yourself and let me know the minute you return home. Please telephone me at work; they won't mind,' she whispered and ran her hand down his face before kissing him again.

'Come on, Ned, we'll be late!' Peter Lawson called as he opened the passenger door to his co-pilot and best friend, ready to speed back to the busy airfield before the next bombing raid over Germany. 'He'll be back, Rose, don't you worry, and he's got the best pilot in the RAF next to him! We look after ourselves.'

'He's right; they're not going to get us two,' Ned said, wanting to linger in his fiancée's arms forever but knowing he couldn't. 'Now look after Mother, keep the board of Rowntree's on their toes and give my love to your sisters from me. You know I love you.' Then at last he walked across to Peter's car and jumped into the seat next to him in the small open-topped vehicle that was his friend's pride and joy.

Rose stood at the side of the road as both men waved. Then Peter pipped the horn as they drove away, past the perfect homes they were both fighting to protect from the reaches of the Nazi forces that looked like they were to take over the world with their hatred.

'Come on in, love, you can't stop him from going. He's doing what he thinks is right,' Ivy Evans said as she watched the lass that had given her heart to her son.

'I know. I'm proud of him, but every time he leaves now I think will this be the last time I see him,' Rose sobbed.

Ivy sighed. 'He'll be back before you know it. Now, let's have a game of whist to take our minds off him leaving. Else we'll both just sit and worry and that does neither of us any good.' She had been in Rose's shoes when her man was fighting in France in the last war, and she knew all too well what she was going through. 'He'll be back before we know it,' she said quietly again, reassuring herself as well as Rose, and hoping that her words would prove to be true as she shuffled the well-worn cards and held back her own tears.

Seebohm sat down at the highly polished table and looked at his boardroom members, heads bowed, and took a deep breath before announcing the words he had dreaded uttering since the outset of the war that was now plaguing the world.

'Things are not good, my friends. We have got to admit that there is nothing more we can do to keep the war from our doors. We are already missing members of our board, who despite their religious beliefs feel that they have to defend our lands from this monster called Hitler. We are facing shortages of basic materials because of the blockade of convoys and the Ministry of Food guidelines, plus now the Royal Army Service Corporation are demanding the use of some of our buildings. They are requesting the use of this office block and the Card Box department, here on Haxby Road, the Cream Making department, for the manu-facturing of munitions, and the Gum department for the making of shells. I cannot see my way to say no to their request, but we have to balance good against evil. This way we can at least keep our staff in work, albeit the work of the devil.' Seebohm gazed around at his fellow direc-tors and saw disappointment on their faces. As a Quaker firm, it was everything that they did not believe in.

One of the older directors stood up to air his views, looking round at his colleagues. 'We have no other choice, Seebohm; it will hurt all of us. However, if we don't go ahead, Hitler will think nothing of taking over the world; at the moment he's concentrating on the Jews, the Romany and Jehovah's Witnesses, but one day it might be us Quakers. We have to stand up to him and look after our workers. Are there any parts of our business we can save?'

'Yes, we can keep the Black Magic chocolates in production, the newly named crisp bar KitKat will be produced in dark chocolate to save on milk and sugar usage, and the chocolate dragée and Smarties will also continue to be made but in dark chocolate. The other products – Aero, Toffee Crisp and our milk chocolates – will have to be put on hold, along with our new mint product Polo. This is why I think we should say yes to the army's request for some of our buildings – at least that way we keep the good people of York in work. Not that we have much choice in all truth. These are serious times, gentlemen; we either sink or swim, and either way the Luftwaffe might bomb us off the face of the earth.'

'Are all the air-raid shelters now operational on site? We need to protect our workers. And will the army decide who will work for them?' asked one of the younger members of the board.

'Yes to both. The main air-raid shelter, as you know, has been in operation under the factory's orchard for some time, but there is now also one for our workers in the Rose Garden on Wigginton Road.'

Seebohm held his breath. 'I have the army's word that they will not interfere with the running of the chocolate plant and that they will only take the staff who wish to work for them. However, their part of the factory will be called County Industries, to hide their activities here. What you see and hear, gentlemen, will be strictly top secret.' Seebohm Rowntree looked round at the glum faces and hoped they would agree to his suggestions. They had to if Rowntree's was to survive the war that was raging in Europe and that Britain had been dragged into without thought nor deed.

'Then we have no other option, have we? After all, we're fighting for this country's freedom from tyranny. I'm in agreement, Seebohm,' said a board member, who sat back in his chair and looked round at the rest of the board. Slowly a nod of the head and an aye was heard from each member. Rowntree's had no option but to get involved in the war effort, even though it would be doing so reluctantly. None of them believed in fighting or hurting their fellow man.

'Just look at the despair on the king's face. The poor devil got the job of ruling the country when he didn't want it and now he's in the middle of a war.' Winnie Freeman sighed. 'It's always Germany; it wouldn't be so bad but the royals are related to German and Russian royalty; his lot is Saxe-Coburg, not Windsor. They changed their names to show loyalty to this country in the Great War. They always say you can choose your friends but not your family.' She ran her hand over the spread-out copy of the evening's paper and looked at a picture of King George VI and his wife as they viewed some of the bomb damage in London.

'Germany is run by Hitler and his Nazis, that's the problem. They don't care about anybody from what I keep reading,' Rose said as she pulled the belt of her coat tight.

'I know, the world has gone mad. Ned must need his head seeing to leaving an easy job making chocolates to join the RAF and risk his life for the country. I still can't believe that he left you to look after his mother.' Winnie folded her paper and looked at her eldest daughter as she got ready to leave the home that had been hers for twenty-two years for her fiancé's home and mother.

'I couldn't understand at first, but then I realized that his two best friends were serving at Elvington. But it wasn't just them that were encouraging him; he felt he had to join them and protect this country of ours. Besides, he'd have had to join up anyway with conscription coming into play a few weeks later. I'm proud of him, Mam, and it isn't as if Ivy is hard to look after; she's quite independent despite being nearly bent double with arthritis. She keeps cheerful. I could have had a dragon of a mother-in-law if I'd married Larry Battersby. Now, his mother I would not have enjoyed looking after.' Rose stepped forward to hug her mother before she left, hoping she wouldn't catch the cold that had laid her low over the last few days.

'I miss you, our Rose. You're my eldest and the sensible one. I sometimes think my patience is tested to the limit, especially with Annie. She's so matter-of-fact about everything and always pushes things to the limit.

I thought that this fella of hers would just be a whim, but she's still writing to him even after five years. Her father would have a fit about one of his lasses courting a black lad, no matter how polite he is.'

'He'd have been all right, Mam, if he'd have met him; you know he would have been. I can never remember my dad having a bad word for anybody. Annie's happy writing to him. Just as long as he keeps us safe while guarding those naval convoys. There's a sinking nearly every day in the paper.'

'Aye, she'd be broken-hearted if anything happened to him, that's for sure. Now you get back to Ivy – she'll be wondering where you've got to. It's nearly five, so the workers'll be making their way home from the factory and she'll be missing you. It's bad enough that you've had an hour off work to visit me, because I was feeling under the weather. You shouldn't have put your job at risk and upset them at Rowntree's.' Winnie hugged her daughter tight. 'I'm fine and all the better for having you cosset and look after me for a while.'

Rose smiled. 'As long as you are. I'm always here for you, I hope you know? The bosses were all right about me having an hour off. They have more to worry about than me not being there for a while. There are plans afoot that are going to change all our lives; they'll be announcing them as I speak, and you can look forward to Annie, Molly and Connie being right in the middle of it. The whole of York will feel the changes. This damned war and it's only just started,' Rose said, kissing her mam on the cheek.

'Are you not going to tell me what the plans are? It's no good telling me half a story,' Winnie shouted after her daughter.

'You'll find out soon enough, but don't worry. If anything, this house will be better off,' she shouted back to her mother and closed the front door behind her.

She left her coughing and keeping warm next to the fire with a potato and leek hotpot cooking in the oven, a rasher of bacon giving the faintest hint of meat. No matter that rationing that had come into effect; her mother could still make a decent meal.

Rose started to run back to Rowntree village and her soon-to-be mother-in-law Ivy.

It had been two days since Ned had said goodbye to Rose, and Ivy saw the concerned look on her son's fiancée's face and felt for her as she watched her mend and darn her near-worn-through socks. Rose, she could see, was trying hard to hold back her tears, and then she put her darning down and came out with what she was thinking.

There had been no sound of an aeroplane engine being cut as some of the squadrons had returned the previous night. Both women had got used to lying in their beds and holding their breaths while they counted the number of planes returning. There had been two missing and both women knew it.

'I wish Ned had never joined up and gone to the Air Force. This damned war played right into his hands, the idiot. All I do is worry about him.' Rose wiped her tears away. 'I don't know when he's flying or if he's safe. I never know anything nowadays.'

'Now then, Rose. He did what he felt he had to do. Nobody'll be relishing these next few months or years; there's going to be hardship all around us just like in the last war. My Stan and I just put our heads down and hoped every day for better times to come. That's what we have to do now and just stand up to this Hitler. Ned'll be all right. You should be proud of him. Our boys in blue will keep us all safe and we just have to pray for them.' Ivy reached over and patted Rose's hand. 'I'm glad that he put an engagement ring on your finger. I'd always imagined him married and with a baby on the way by now. Instead, just like you, every day I dread a knock on the door and a telegram boy handing over the awful news. But my lad will be safe – I just know he will be. His plane will have come in and will be safe in the hangar and Ned will be fast asleep in his bed if I know him. Back in the last war, eh! They were terrible times them. Nearly our whole street lost their lives; it made you feel guilty if your man or son had survived.' Ivy looked out of the window while Rose felt tears running down her cheeks.

She sniffed and wiped them away, casting her mending to one side. 'I'll make us a drink. And I think there're two biscuits left in the tin, so we'll have them and cheer ourselves up.' Rose tried to smile at Ivy.

'He'll be all right, lass; he knows how to look after himself, does my Ned.'

'I hope he does,' Rose said quietly. 'I hate not knowing what ops he's on or what country he's flying over and if he's all right. I worry all the time. I just want him back here with us. He usually cuts his engine over our house just for a second or two, to let me know that he's returned, but I never heard his plane last night. There were plenty others returning but I never heard Ned's engine signal.'

'We both want him safe,' Ivy replied and squeezed Rose's hand tightly. 'I want to go into York and pick myself out a new hat and outfit and get him married off before I'm put in the ground. He'll be fine; he might not have been on a mission last night.'

'Hopefully not. And don't say that, you're a long way from being dead yet.' Rose tried to smile and hugged Ivy.

Ivy smiled back at her. 'He didn't put that ring on your finger for nothing; it was to give him hope for the future and something to fight for. He'll take care of himself – don't you worry, my dear.'

'My sisters will soon be back home moaning,' Rose said, changing the subject. 'They'll find out later today what's become of their jobs. Rowntree's were going to announce what's happening to the factory this afternoon,' she explained and sighed. 'They'll all have work, but in which department I don't know. At least they're still making KitKats and I've not many changes myself. They still need me to keep an eye on production and keep the boardroom informed of any problems. Especially when it comes to the KitKat bar.'

'I should think not. If it hadn't been for you and Ned wanting to rename it, it would never have caught on so well,' Ivy said and smiled.

'It was my mam I have to thank for that; she remembered a box of chocolates from the 1920s that Rowntree's only produced for a short time, and she said everyone had liked the name. It was a bit daring like the infamous Kit Kat Club in London, so everyone linked it to being a little decadent. So she's the one to thank.' Rose looked at Ivy. 'It's being remanufactured as well, with dark chocolate, and there's talk of it being wrapped in blue not red, because red paper is more expensive to make. 'This war is affecting absolutely everything.'

'Never mind, lass. Now let's have that cup of tea. You'd better make one spoonful of tea do us both and don't throw the tea leaves out – we'll keep them to make a mash later.'

Ivy had lived through days like this before. It was going to be a case of make do and mend and pray for sense to prevail when it came to the war. Her heart ached not just for herself but for the pain she knew everybody was feeling. *The world will never learn*, she thought as she sat back in her chair and watched Rose go into the kitchen.

'Please let my lad keep safe,' she whispered to herself and wiped the one tear that had escaped down her cheek and that she didn't want Rose to see. She had to keep strong no matter what.

2

There had been military-looking people around the chocolate factory and gossip about what was happening at Rowntree's was rife. Part of the factory had been closed, as any products made of milk chocolate had been cut back to the bare minimum, and the workers were starting to worry about their jobs. Everybody had been summoned to a meeting in the main hall and they knew it wasn't going to be good news.

Annie and Molly Freeman, along with Molly's friend Connie Whitehead, listened to the announcement the entire firm had been dreading. Everyone knew things could not continue as they were. Some of the workforce would be continuing in the jobs they were in but most would be offered work making munitions and bombs in the part of the factory the war machine was about to take over.

'Bloody hell, what are you two going to do? The only one who's safe from all this is Rose. Her job's hardly altered and hopefully mine too if Black Magic are still going to be produced, not that I care,' Annie said, looking at Molly and Connie as they stood together after the announcement.

'I don't know. I need my job and Mam will need our money coming in, especially now Rose lives with Ned's mother. I don't fancy making bombs and things, though. But I suppose I'll have to if I want to keep my job.' Molly sighed and looked at Connie. 'What are you going to do?'

'The same as you,' Connie replied, and she looked at Annie as she shook her head. 'I need the money to pay your mam for my keep and I'm trying to save for a place of my own. I've no option but to stay here. Besides, everyone has to help out and sacrifice a little in these hard times.'

'Well, even if my job is safe, I've been thinking about it for a while now. I hate packing chocolates. I'm going to join the Land Army. It's helping the war effort more than packing chocolates. I don't even like dark chocolate and they were trying to get women to join up in the centre of town last weekend, so I'm going to go along and volunteer. Perhaps one of you two will be offered my place in Chocolate Packing,' Annie said, then noticed the dismay on her younger sister's face.

Molly gasped and shook her head, not wanting to believe that her sister could even think of leaving the family home. 'You can't leave home, Annie – what will Mam say? You could be placed anywhere, and you know nothing about farming.'

'We've all got to do our bit, whether we want to or not, and just for once I want to be outside in the fresh air instead of having the smell of chocolate up my nose. I want to be like Josh doing manual work and feeling I'm doing some good,' Annie said. She turned to leave for her department.

'It won't be standing feeding hens and looking after

lambs, you know; it'll be ploughing and mending fences and really heavy work,' Connie said, trying to catch up with Annie as she walked out of the hall.

'I know, but at least I'll not be making bombs to kill people with. I don't think I'd feel right doing that. I'm surprised the Rowntree family has agreed to their factory being used for bombmaking,' Annie said sharply. 'But, as everyone says, we all have to pull together, I suppose – anything to keep the country safe. I hate even the thought of being at war. How can anybody want to kill another human being?'

'Rowntree's have no choice; the War Office will have commandeered it, and us if the truth be told. There's been military and hard-looking businessmen coming in and out of work for weeks now,' Connie said, still trying to keep up with Annie as she stormed out of the building.

'Well, I'm not working for them. I can always send some money back to Mam. Besides, we're short of room; this'll mean you can have my bedroom until I return, now that it seems that you're one of us.' Annie spoke with slight contempt in her voice; Connie had been taken into the bosom of the Freeman family, but every now and again she had to be reminded that she was the lodger and not one of the family.'

'I couldn't do that,' Connie said, glancing at Molly. 'I'm happy sharing with Molly, and the big bedroom will always be yours and Rose's if she comes home again.'

'You and I know that Rose will be getting married once Ned returns – if he returns! The rate this war is going,' Annie said and she stopped with her hands on her hips, looking at her younger sister and Connie.

'Don't say that, Annie! Our Rose would be broken-hearted if anything happened to him. I can't help feeling a bit sick about having to make bombs. Just imagine them being dropped on Germany. They might kill somebody they shouldn't.' Molly looked thoughtful. 'They're bound to hit some innocent people.'

'But one might kill Hitler and then the war would be over,' Connie said with a grin. 'He needs to be stopped, Molly, along with that Mussolini. I'll be only too happy to be making the shells or munitions; I hope one of mine drops right on his head.'

Annie was patriotic but the thought of innocent people dying upset her. 'Don't be daft, Connie; you never do have any sense,' she snapped. 'We shouldn't be making bombs; we shouldn't be at war. The world's gone mad.' Then she stormed off, leaving the two girls gaping and stood in the road.

'Our Annie is always moaning. Take no notice,' Molly told Connie. 'She listens to that sailor boy of hers too much. Although, saying that, I haven't seen a letter from him for a while now. I hope he's all right.' She looked pensive.

Connie sighed. 'Perhaps that's what's wrong. She'll be worrying about him; after all, there are merchant as well as naval ships being sunk every day. Nobody's safe. That's why we have to do this and make these bombs, even if we don't want to.'

'Then we will and let's hope that one of them does

hit Hitler.' Molly put her arm through Connie's and she hoped that they would be kept together wherever they were placed. 'Mam is going to have a fit when we tell her what we're to be doing. She'll not be happy; she'll worry herself to death. Making munitions isn't a safe job. I'm going to dread telling her. Still, we're doing our bit for the country, so she should be proud of us.'

'So, what's been happening at Rowntree's today? Our Rose came round and only told me half a tale, making me worry until you could come home and tell me what was afoot.' Winnie blew her nose and looked at the three girls as they entered the kitchen, chattering between themselves.

'Well, they're struggling to get sugar, cocoa and milk, so we can't make half what we normally do. It's a right mess!' Annie said, and she sat down next to her mother and thought about the state the factory and the country was in. She knew she should stand by her country but some days it was hard to do so.

'It is,' Molly said,' but all we know is that some of the departments are closing and we'll have a chance to work for the war ministry, who want us to make munitions and bombs. Fancy that, making bombs instead of choc- olate – you couldn't make it up! I'm going to feel quite proud of myself.' She put her arms round her mother. 'How are you feeling anyway? You look a bit brighter.'

'I did feel better until you told me all this. Bombmaking? I don't like the sound of that – will it be safe?' Winnie looked at the two girls as they bowed their heads, thinking how much their lives were changing because of the war raging in Europe. However, it was a case of best foot forward, and if that was what her girls had to do, then she would support them as best she could.

'I don't think they had much choice, Mam,' Annie said. 'It was that or we all lost our jobs. Rose will be all right, and I would be I think if I chose to stay.' She hesitated. 'But I don't fancy making bombs and munitions. I'd rather help the war effort some other way. Perhaps now's the time for me to make a change.'

Winnie gasped. 'Oh, Lord, you're not going to sea and following that foolhardy lad of yours? I couldn't live wondering where you were and if your ship was being bombed if you joined the women's navy.' Winnie was aware Annie had been bored for a long time at Rowntree's. She looked at her daughter; she always had to push her luck.

Annie sighed. 'They're called Wrens now, Mam, but, no, I'm not joining them —although it would be a way of seeing the world.'

'Seeing the world and getting drowned or killed, you stick to making chocolates, my lass, it's a lot safer,' Winnie said.

'I thought I'd join the Land Army. I'd be safe doing that and I'd be seeing a bit of a different world, depending on where I was posted. Anything but chocolate while I have the chance,' Annie replied and watched as her mother's face darkened.

'Over my dead body,' Winnie growled. 'You will not go and leave a perfectly good home and a good job to go and live in a barn with a family that we know nothing at all about. The country might be desperate but they're not that desperate enough to take one of my daughters.'

Annie glared at her. 'Well, I'm going. I've made my mind up and I'm old enough, so you can't stop me.'

Molly and Connie said nothing; they knew better than to get involved in an argument between them, and they decided they would lay the table as Winnie swore under her breath at Annie who was standing her ground.

'Why can't your Annie just take things in her stride and accept things? I wouldn't want to go ploughing and milking cows and live on a farm with folk I don't know. She's also the only one of us who has actually still got her job by the sounds of it,' Connie whispered as she and Molly went into the pantry for some bread, out of earshot of the arguing mother and daughter.

Molly passed Connie the bread and looked at the meagre amount of butter that was their ration for the week. Whatever was cooking in the oven would have to be eaten just with bread if they were to have butter on their toast in the morning.

'She never does,' she said. 'She'll be a land girl; I'll bet next week's wage on it. She's not been happy at Rowntree's for a while and now it's her chance to get away. Well, I hope we both get jobs in the munitions. I bet the pay is better and it's still on our doorstep –what more could we want?'

Connie grinned. 'Well, I don't know about you, but I could do with a right good-looking fella coming along and sweeping me off my feet. He's also to have a car, his own house and be worth a bob or two. But there'll be new fellas there, I bet.'

Molly shook her head. 'You don't ask for a lot, do you? I'd just be happy with things going back to how they used to be. Us all at home, secure and working for Rowntree's and not worrying about our house being bombed or if our loved ones are alive or not.'

Back in the kitchen she placed the bread in the centre of the table and looked at her mother and Annie as they both folded their arms. It seemed they had decided it was best if no more words were said in anger over Annie's decision to become a land girl.

'What's for supper Mam? Do we need the butter?' Molly said, sitting down across from Connie and waiting for the storm to pass, hoping calm would greet the supper table once they started to eat.

'It's the best I can make out of what I could get hold of. So don't any of you complain and don't you dare touch that butter. I can't get any more until Friday and that will be if I'm lucky.' Winnie spoke sharply and got up to open the heavy enamelled door of the oven.

'Well, if I was in the Land Army, I could perhaps give you some. I'm sure there must be some perks that go with the job,' Annie said, glowering at her mother as she placed a casserole on the table.

'That's enough. If there's another word said about the Land Army, I really will lose my temper,' Winnie growled. 'Now eat your supper and enjoy your family around you. It's bad enough that Ned has to put his life in danger every day and is away from us.' Then she dished the potatoes and leeks out and tried to divide the small amount of bacon equally.

'And Josh – don't you forget Josh. Or does he not count?' Annie said sharply. She was thinking of her long-distant love in the Merchant Navy.

'Of course he does; all the lads fighting for this country do. But you're not engaged to be married like Rose, and to be fair you've only seen him half a dozen times. I just want you to be safe, Annie, and with us.' Winnie slumped in her chair after filling everyone's plate and looked round at her girls. 'Making munitions will be dangerous enough, but at least you'll be here at home, and I'll be here to look after you.'

'This looks and smells good, thank you,' Connie said, and then she decided to stay quiet as the Freeman family also went silent – least said, soonest mended, she decided. Everyone knew that if Annie had set her heart on the Land Army, they would have a new recruit in her, no matter what her mother had to say.

Connie and Molly lay awake later that evening. It was mid-August and up in their top bedroom it was warm and stuffy.

'Your mam really doesn't want Annie to go, does she? But I can understand why Annie wants to be a land girl. At least she'll feel like she's doing something for the war effort. Although making bombs would be as well,' Connie whispered.

'She wants to see another part of the country,' Molly replied. 'She's always wanted to travel; it has nothing to do with what work she'll be doing. Ssshh, can you hear that droning noise? It's an aeroplane, but it's a way off. I wonder if it's one of ours?'

'It might be Ned and his fellow pilots returning or taking off,' Connie whispered. 'Rose must worry every night and day. Everybody has someone in this war; hearts are going to be broken and families torn apart – your mother's lucky she has three girls and no sons.' Connie then turned to look at her alarm clock and make sure it was set for the morning. The household no longer relied on the knocker-upper. 'I'm dreading tomorrow. What if we don't get a place in either Rowntree's or making munitions? We might have to join up with Annie.'

'Whatever happens, what will be will be.,' Molly said lazily and then opened her eyes at hearing a loud thud in the distance. 'What was that?'

'Perhaps it was the gunners shooting that aeroplane down. It must have been a Nazi. Whatever it was, it was a good way away.' Connie plumped up her pillows and closed her eyes.

'I hope everyone's safe,' Molly said and looked up at her bedroom ceiling, saying a quiet prayer before she too closed her eyes and tried to get to sleep. The war was becoming too real and too close for her liking.

Winnie stood on her doorstep the following morning with the milk that had just been delivered and listened to the news the milkman was telling her.

'Eighty houses and a good bit of York Cemetery hit and in rubble. Those poor folk never stood a chance; there was no way they would think when they went to bed that they'd not be here this morning. Bloody Jerries!'

'Oh my Lord, what if it had been this row? I dread to think. I don't think I know anybody that lives there, but that isn't the point, is it?' Winnie said grimly, and she turned back to go inside to tell her family the awful news, as the milkman wended his way down the street.

'What's up, Mam? You look a bit shocked,' Annie said, as she pinned her hair up, checking herself in the hallway mirror as she did so.

Winnie stood with her hands on her hips and told the girls the news, filling them in with every detail. 'What if it had hit here? Or even worse had hit Rowntree's when it was making bombs? We'd all be blown sky-high.'

'Oh, those poor people, but this is only the start; there will be more yet. I tell you, Mam, I'll be safer in the countryside,' Annie replied and she followed her mother into the kitchen.

'Well, Molly and I are going to help make the bombs if they're willing to keep us both on. Let's give those Germans a taste of their own medicine,' Connie said and gulped her tea down. 'I can't wait to see where I've been allocated.'

'We heard a loud bang and a thud,' Molly said, 'but we didn't realize it was a bomb being dropped. That's the first bomb to be dropped on York. We thought it was a German plane being shot down.' She looked at the kitchen clock. 'We're going to have to get going.'

Winnie blew her nose and wiped her eyes, partly due to her cold and partly from the tears that she could feel welling up. 'Bloody Hitler, this shouldn't be happening again. Give my love to Rose. Tell her that her Ned will be all right; she must be thinking of him after last night.'

Her girls had to be kept safe above all else, but she knew full well that she couldn't guarantee any of them safety no matter how she tried to protect them.

3

'Well, they're not wasting much time this morning,' Annie said.

All eyes watched as the Rowntree's sign was taken down at the entrance and a new sign saying County Industries was put in its place by two men in khaki uniforms. The news of York being targeted by the Luftwaffe in a night raid was also being discussed as they made their way in to work.

'This way please, ladies. Meeting in the NAAFI, and then you'll be given your orders.' A stern-looking man had replaced the usual man at the Blick machine, and he ushered everybody in an orderly fashion.

'NAAFI! What's a NAAFI?' Molly said, following everyone to the main block of Rowntree's and the dining hall.

'It's where the military eat. You're already one of them whether you want to be or not,' Annie said, as they walked there with the hundreds of staff to find out what the future held for them.

'Well, where are you going to be working?' Connie asked. She glanced at the letter she had been given announcing her position in the new firm. 'I'm in Fuse Filling based in the old Box department, and it says I'm expected to work twelve-hour days, and there are lots of orders and guidelines to follow for my own safety as well as that of others. It's not going to be like working for Rowntree's, but I suppose we are helping the war effort.'

'I'm with you in Fuse Filling, whatever that is. I suppose we'll soon find out.' Molly looked quizzically at Annie.

'Well, I'm still packing chocolates in theory, although I'm going to give my notice and go into York this afternoon and join the Land Army, despite what our mam says. You won't get me anywhere near making bombs. I'd prefer my choice to help out. Although I do admire you all in a way.' Annie screwed her letter up and looked across at Rose, who was pushing her way through the crowds towards them.

'I suppose you'll still be working for Rowntree's?' she said to her oldest sister as she joined them to hear what orders they were to follow from the war ministry.

'Well, you thought wrong,' Rose replied. 'I've said I'll work in administration for the board; they needed people in the offices, so I made myself known and I'll be in charge of paperwork. My friend Mary has got my job of overseeing; she needed it with her Joe at sea all the time and she can leave young Joseph in the Rowntree's crèche while she's at work. She'll be safer doing that than working for County Industries.' Rose noticed Annie's angry face.

'Yet your poor sisters are to make munitions? Could you not get us a safer job?' Annie said crossly.

'I had no say in who they put where! I was chosen for the offices because I had typing skills and Mary was recommended for my job upon my recommendation with her Joe already fighting at sea. Anyway, why are you so cross with me?? I know you've still got your job. It's these two who are having their lives completely changed, but it is for the good of the country.'

'I'm not mad with you,' Annie replied. 'I'm just annoyed generally. I thought we'd all be safe in our old jobs. I never thought that our positions as chocolate makers would be jeopardized. Anyway, I've made my mind up: I'm not working here any more. I'm walking into York and joining the land girls. I've had enough of chocolate packing; I'll do my bit and work on a farm rather than make munitions and bombs. Perhaps the Quaker ideals have worn off on me.' She saw the disappointment on her older sister's face.

'Mam won't like that; she likes to keep us all together. But if you feel that's your way of helping out, then we'll all be happy for you,' Rose said to her headstrong sister. 'Did you hear about the bombing last night? I think there've been a few deaths.'

'Yes, we heard it happening at home, but didn't realize what it was at the time. Have you heard from Ned this morning?' Annie's voice had softened. Her sister's fiancé was already fighting in the war and had been for a while now, and she knew Rose dreaded every flight that Ned took from Elvington.

'No. I just pray that he's all right, unlike the poor folk living next to the cemetery. You do what you want to do, Annie, as long as you keep safe,' Rose replied. 'We'll all be fine, God willing.'

'Mam'll get used to us all doing our bit to keep the country going.' Annie hadn't heard from her Josh for months; the last she knew he was sailing with a convoy, protecting it in the North Atlantic. She had to do something more than just pack chocolates, but at the same time, she wouldn't turn her hand to making actual bombs to kill people, no matter which side they were on. Her morals guided her decisions but she would stand by her country and fight in her own way for it. The Land Army was her way to help and that was what she was going to do.

Annie walked into the post office in the centre of York. It was her lunch hour and she was in a rush. She knew it was the first place to go in her pursuit of being a Land Army girl. The office was busy with people going about their business and talking about the war and the terrible events of the previous night that had made it too real.

In the corner of the main office sat a woman in a checked suit with a sign on her table showing her name as Miss L. Saunders, Ministry of Fisheries and Foods. Annie watched as a young girl similar in age to her sat down and started talking to her. She listened in to the conversation as she stood in the queue for a form from the postmistress for her to apply to become a land girl. It seemed the girl was being interviewed; she watched the girl shake the interviewer's hand and smile.

Then finally it was Annie's turn.

'Yes, can I help you?' the postmistress asked.

'I'd like a form to apply to become a land girl, please,' Annie replied and smiled.

'Are you seventeen or over and of good health? If it's a yes to both, here you are. Fill the form in and send it back to the address down in London printed inside or if you're prepared to wait, as it happens, the lady over there is interviewing recruits this morning.' The postmistress handed Annie a green application form.

'Thank you. I think I'll wait. I might as well seeing as she's here and I've already made my mind up.' Annie smiled and looked proud.

'Then please go and wait over there in that leather chair. She won't be long. From what I can see she just asks you the basics and then they do the rest. Next!' the postmistress shouted and Annie walked over to the woman, hoping her mother would forgive her. Her stomach churned as she saw the young woman who had just put her name forward for service shake Miss Saunders's hand and stand up to leave. Was she doing the right thing? After all, she had been given her old position in Rowntree's this morning in a confirmation letter that she'd chosen to ignore. Perhaps she should be thankful that she was to be left packing chocolates, she thought, as she made her way forward to the young interviewer, holding her hand out to be shaken.

'Good morning. Do you want to enrol in the Land Army? Britain and its farmers will be grateful for your help and hard work if so,' Miss Saunders said in a quiet but assertive voice, ushering Annie to sit down.

'I'm not a farmer. I know nothing about farming, but I

am a hard worker. Does that matter?' Annie asked as she sat down in the hard wooden-backed chair and looked at the form that Miss Saunders pushed across the desk. She was giving her the chance to enrol there and then.

'No, it makes no difference at all. You'll learn the tasks at hand as you work. Now, let's start with your name and age. You are seventeen, I hope?' Miss Saunders said, writing down Annie's name and smiling when she replied that she was nineteen.

'Are you in employment and who with?' Miss Saunders asked.

'I work with Rowntree's and I have still got my job packing chocolates, but I'd rather be helping the war effort more. In fact, I'm in my dinner hour now, so I'm in a rush.'

'We must make this quick then. Chocolate cheers the troops up, so you are still helping, even in your present job.' Miss Saunders smiled. 'Obviously we're delighted if you prefer to join us. Now, health – have you any health issues, or know that you're underweight?'

'No to both. I'm quite fit.' Annie had another pang of doubt as she watched the form being filled in and her life changing in front of her eyes.

'Now, what are your measurements, just for your uniform?'

'Thirty-two, twenty-six and thirty-four.' Annie blushed. 'I've large hips.'

'Not at all. Now, can you ride a bicycle, and do you have one that you could take with you?' Miss Saunders kept her head down and concentrated on Annie's response.

'I can ride a bike, but we don't have one at home.'

'Do you think you could adapt to country life? It's a lot different from living here in the centre of York and working in a factory.' Miss Saunders looked at Annie and saw determination in her eyes.

'Yes, I would adapt easily. I prefer my own company and often go for walks in the countryside, following the canal paths.'

'Finally, Annie, is there any part of the country that you would like to be placed in? Would you prefer to be kept in Yorkshire or perhaps a different part of the country?'

'Yorkshire if I can, then I'm seeing new parts of the country but am not too far from my family or perhaps Lincolnshire – that's not too far away.' Annie sat back in her chair as she watched Miss Saunders fill in the last question and sign the form, ready to send to the Ministry of Food and Agriculture for processing.

'Right, that sounds very satisfactory to me. They might ask you to attend a health review, but I've added that you look perfectly fit, so it will probably only be a week or two, but then you can look forward to receiving your orders, train fare, uniform and instructions on where you've been posted. Once you've been given your place-ment the farmer you'll be working for is responsible for paying your wage and giving you living accommodation. Everything will be made clear in the correspondence. Now, is there anything else I can help you with?'

Miss Saunders rose from her chair and extended her hand to be shaken, as Annie stood too, her legs trembling as she realized that she had just changed her life, and perhaps not for the better.

'No, you've told me all I need to know, thank you.' Annie shook her hand and smiled.

She had done it! Now she just had to tell her employers and her mother that she was going to be a land girl and was going to leave the home that she had never before left on her own. She would be doing something to help the war, something that she felt was more valuable than packing chocolates or making bombs.

Annie looked at her watch as she left the post office; she had just enough time to call home before she returned to work. She was grateful that Rowntree's had given her an extended lunch hour when they knew what the purpose of her request was.

She rushed down the street and met the postman with a handful of post from his midday delivery.

'I'm just about to call at your house; here, you can take your letters in with you,' he said, as he hunted through the letters he had for the Freeman household. 'Bills, as usual, your mother will be sad to hear. But there looks to be one for you, Annie.'

The postman, who had known Annie all her life, handed over the small bundle, which did look to contain all bills apart from the handwritten one to Annie that was on the top of the pile.

'Thanks, Walter,' Annie said and looked at the letter, wondering who it could be from. She didn't recognize the handwriting, she thought, as she opened the front door and yelled to her mother.

Winnie stopped using her carpet cleaner on the nearly worn bare carpet that ran down the hallway. 'What are you doing home? Have you lost your job and been sacked?'

'No, not yet. But I have made a decision. Mam . . .' Annie stumbled over her words.

'You haven't done anything daft? You've not really gone and put your name down for the Land Army, have you? You won't last a minute – you're no farmer.' Winnie leaned on her Bex Bissell cleaner and glared at Annie.

'Sorry, Mam, I had to. In fact, I've just filled the form in with a woman from the ministry. I'm sorry, Mam, but I had to do something. Molly and Connie are going to be making bombs in munitions, but I can't do that. Rowntree's count on our Rose, now her fella's in the RAF, but what do I do? Nothing! I just pack chocolates. I need to help more, Chocolates aren't going to help win the war; they're not going to save lives!'

Annie stood in front of her mother, her head bowed, but at the same time she wanted to read the letter that she now could see had a Liverpool postmark on it. It was perhaps from Josh, even though it wasn't his hand-writing, She couldn't wait to read it.

'Oh, Annie! You'll be the death of me. You'll be worked to the bone and happen not even paid. These farmers are renowned to be as tight as a duck's bum. They'll expect you to do all sorts for next to nothing. Do you know where you are going yet?' Winnie walked into the kitchen with Annie following.

'No, they'll write and tell me and give me a uniform

and train tickets to where I'm posted. Here, Mam, there's the post. I met Walter just as I got to our door.' Annie passed over the letters apart from the one that was hers. 'Looks like all bills.'

'Oh, Annie, blow the bills. I've already lost our Rose to her fella and now I'm about to lose you. My lasses, all working for the bloody ministry except Rose, and her fella risks his life everyday for them. There was me thinking with being lasses you'd all be safe.' Winnie caught her breath and spotted the letter in Annie's hand. 'Is that from your Josh? He hasn't written for a while or you haven't mentioned him for a while. He's another, out at sea, protecting the navy and country from those blinking submarines. I never thought we'd have to live through this again.'

Annie glanced at her letter. 'Well, it's from Liverpool, but I don't recognize the writing,' she whispered as she sat down in a chair.

Her mother put the kettle on to boil. 'It's not going to open itself. Are you going to read it?'

Annie put her finger underneath the envelope flap and pulled the one piece of paper from out of the envelope.

Anderson Terrace
Liverpool

Dear Annie,

Josh asked me to write to you in case any bad news came his way. Unfortunately, I have had word that I have lost my much-loved son at sea on the twentieth of July. His ship was hit by

34

a torpedo somewhere in Baltic waters and most of the crew drowned or died from their wounds. The military has not given me many more details, only that.

I'm sorry; I know that you will be upset, as I know you were very fond of each other. He was always talking about you. I would have loved to have met you.

You keep yourself safe.
Brenda xxxx

Annie sat with the letter in her hand and felt tears welling in her eyes and her heart aching. Her stomach churned and her hands shook as she passed her mother the letter, unable to tell her what she had just read. She had loved Josh and now he was gone.

Annie sobbed and cried as her mother sat silent, grimly reading the letter and then raising her head to look at her heartbroken daughter.

'Ssshh, now, my love. He was a brave lad; he went to war when he didn't have to. Ssshh, my love, I know it hurts.' Winnie leaned down and put her arms round her daughter and hugged her tight. 'This bloody war – and it's only just starting; there'll be a lot more tears yet, I don't doubt. I'm sure he loved you. Just remember the good times and then let him go. It's the only way to survive, my lass.'

'He did love me, Mam, and I loved him, despite what anybody said about him,' Annie sobbed. 'I can't face work this afternoon, Mam. I'm not going back in, no matter what.'

'All right, love, you don't have to. We'll let them know

what's happened. I don't think they'll be bothered about you missing so much today. Now, shush, I know you were made for one another. I never said anything bad about him because he was a good soul. It always is the good souls we lose. That's the way of war. Politicians are quick to fight, but it's not them on the front lines. Now stop sobbing – what's done is done and we can't bring him back.'

Winnie kissed her daughter on her head. She'd seen lads go and fight in the Great War and it was happening all over again. When would the world ever learn?

'I'm here for you, Annie – we all are.'

Winnie hugged her daughter tight; she knew the pain she was feeling and she had hoped that none of her girls would have to feel it.

4

Over at Rowntree's Rose was on the rampage; she had tried to keep her sister's job safe and Annie had repaid her by walking out of the meeting. 'Where's our Annie at? I need to have words with her?' Rose said, as she, Molly and Connie met in the corridor between the factories to discuss their lot. They slowly made their way to the dining hall. Their discussions were on what department they were to work in and what was to happen next. None of them felt relieved with the news; they were all filled with hesitance and worry.

'She walked out of the hall when she found out she was to keep her job in the Chocolate Packing department, although her mind had been made up long before that anyway. She'll have gone home, I bet,' Molly said. 'She and you are the lucky ones, although she doesn't think so; she's fed up with making chocolates. I bet she's gone to join the Land Army. Mam and her were arguing over it last night.' She looked at the corned beef stew, scrunching her nose as she was given it, but knew she should be grateful with rationing being so tight. There was no longer a choice of food at dinner time; it was whatever was served to you.

'What? She's giving up a perfectly good job to join the Land Army? She must be mad! No wonder she and Mam were arguing. I sometimes wonder where our Annie gets her ideas from,' Rose said and sipped her tea. 'You two are in the fuse department, aren't you? I saw your names up on the boards in the main office when I had to go for a meeting with the bosses. Will you be all right there?'

Both girls nodded. Rose knew that they'd been put to doing odd jobs around the factory that morning, anything to keep them in work until the announcement. 'At least you've got a job; some have been laid off,' she said quietly, nearly whispering, 'which nobody is proud of in the offices upstairs. Especially when they had to give up the tennis courts and part of the gardens near Wigginton Road for some Nissen huts to be built quickly for the army workers to live in. That's really hurt some of the board, members. They love their sport; never mind that the factory is going to the dogs. They've already appointed an Air Raid Precautions Warden and are talking about making this hall available for any family that gets blitzed. So I'd enjoy that corned beef that you're nearly baulking at, our Molly, while you can. It'll be packed lunches for us all after next week. Poor Mam, she'll have a fit.'

Connie sighed. 'I can't believe all this is happening. We were warned months ago what to expect when war was declared, but nothing's affected us so directly until now. I don't know whether I'm coming or going. There are diggers out there covering bunkers up and army personnel yelling and shouting, and we don't even work for Rowntree's any more. No wonder Annie's joining the

Land Army. I might just join her.' She folded her arms. 'Still, it has to be done to protect old Blighty.'

'You will not, Connie; you'll stay with me and we'll make bombs together. If I'm going to blow myself up, then I'm taking you with me.' Molly laughed and hoped that she was only joking, but she was rather concerned that it might actually happen to them both. 'I'm glad that bomb didn't fall on the Methodist graveyard; it might have hit Dad.'

'Yes, that's what made the ones upstairs talk about making the dining hall into a shelter. It was a bit too close for comfort, wasn't it? Some that live on the road haven't come into work this morning. It's to be hoped that they're still alive.' Rose looked at her engagement ring and thought about her Ned. Every night she listened for the returning planes and especially for Ned's engine cutting out as he flew overhead. The previous night they had sounded more like fighters than the bombers Ned piloted.

Molly reached for her sister's hand and patted it gently as she saw her play with her ring. 'I thought of your Ned, Rose. I always say a prayer for him when I hear aeroplanes overhead.'

'Thank you, Molly. I dread every minute that he's away from home. I don't know how his mother copes; she just takes everything in her stride. She's a tough old stick and I know she worries just as much as me, but doesn't show it for fear of upsetting me more.'

'Our mam seems to be taking it all in her stride as well. Although she's been fighting a cold. The house has smelled of Vicks for days now, but least she's sounding a little better,' Molly said and smiled.

'Come on, Molly, either eat your dinner or leave it,' Connie said. 'We have to get across to the Gum department. We're helping get it ready to make the munitions. Although I don't know the first thing about anything like that.' She looked across at Rose, who still looked drawn and pale.

'You'll have an easy week this week,' said the older girl, 'but make the most of it. You'll already have been told that you're expected to work twelve-hour days. But you're not on your own on that score – so am I. The chocolate production we're sticking with is changing; we have to work longer hours and we'll have to vitaminize the chocolate – most of what we make is being reserved for the forces. The War Office has also asked for them to be supplied with Pacific and Jungle Chocolate that won't melt so easily in warmer climates, so we're all going to be learning for a while. I've also heard that they are thinking of altering the Cream Packing department into a production line for making oatmeal blocks, fruit bars, dried milk and dried eggs. That'll give Mam something to talk about; she already hates cooking with dried eggs. Don't say a word, though, you two. I only know this because I hear *them* all talking. Annie would have been so busy and such a help if she'd stayed working here, if she'd only given it a chance to see what was going to be happening.' Rose watched as Molly held her nose in a bid not to smell the corned beef hash that she hated but was too hungry to waste.

40

Connie grinned as Molly swallowed deeply; she really did not like corned beef.

Then Molly and Connie pushed back their chairs and made their way arm in arm through the dining hall. Rose sighed and thought how lucky the pair of them were, with no worries about menfolk as yet. She'd not slept for fretting about her Ned. With her fiancé in the RAF and future elderly mother-in-law to look after and the onset of twelve-hour shifts, she was feeling under pressure. No wonder Annie felt like running away to the country.

Molly and Connie walked back home after their after-noon shift in the warm summer sunshine, breathing in the fresh air and looking at the flowers and trees in full bloom in people's front gardens. It was particularly nice to see after a day prepping for their new munitions roles and watching their workplace being dismantled and the workings of their new job put into place. Things were definitely going to be different in the weeks to come. No longer would they be making delicate boxes, deco-rating them with ribbons and filling them with wrappers. Even the beautiful rose beds of the gardens had been devastated , the blooms fallen and crushed and the earth mounded up where they had grown. The soil covering the Anderson shelters or levelled out to make room for Nissen huts. Rowntree's had not been bombed the pre-vious evening but it might as well have been the way it looked with all the alterations that the War Office were putting in place.

'I wonder what our new uniforms are going to look

like,' Connie said as they turned the corner on to their street. 'Did you see her that was doing the measuring? She wasn't one for talking, was she?'

'I don't know,' Molly said. 'I didn't really take in what she looked like. I was more worried when I heard somebody say that Gum block and Cream block were the only places safe enough to make munitions because the ceilings were so high. What do you think they meant by that? I couldn't ask because I was moving the Smarties packaging to the part of the building they're going to be using now, and because I wasn't supposed to be listening. I didn't dare listen. I was too busy doing what I'd been told.'

'It must be because we need good light or a lot of air,' Connie replied. 'I'm sure we'll soon find out. I heard that there's going to be eight hundred of us making these bombs. Half of us will work through the day and half through the night, and we'll be switching shifts every week.' After a day of learning new things and feeling uncertain about the future, Connie felt glad that she was where she called home now.

'Didn't you read the letter they gave you first thing this morning? Perhaps you were too busy making eyes at that dark-haired soldier.' Molly grinned.

'Well, you can't blame me. I've never seen so many fellas. All dressed in uniform and looking so smart. I know you had a good look at them as well as me.' Connie grinned back at her. 'I noticed even you were looking star-struck when that tall dark sergeant was showing on his chart where everything had to be moved to.'

'I wasn't. I was just listening hard. They expect every word and action to be done in double quick time. Although, yes, he was good-looking and he did catch my eye.' Molly blushed bright red.

Connie smiled. 'That is one good thing; there are a lot of new men, and some of them are really good-looking. We could have some fun,' she said as she pushed open the front door, only to be met by the unmistakable sound of sobbing from the kitchen.

'Oh no, Mam and Annie have had words,' Molly whispered as they entered the usually welcoming room.

They both stood by helplessly as Winnie cradled the weeping Annie.

'Annie has had some bad news,' the older woman managed to say, drying her own eyes before blowing her nose. 'Josh has been killed while up near Russia with his convoy. A bloody submarine!' Winnie said quietly and looked up at the two lasses who thankfully had no commitments to any man in their lives as of yet.

'Oh, Annie, I'm so sorry,' Molly said, rushing forward to hug her sister. 'You thought a lot of him. You were both always writing to one another, and when he came that Christmas before war broke out I could see he was a nice lad.'

'I'm so sorry for you, Annie,' chimed in Connie. 'Like Molly says, he was right enough. You must be heartbroken?'

Connie felt deep sympathy for Annie, even though she had thought that Annie could have done better for herself. But that didn't matter – poor Josh had died far too young and had broken her friend's sister's heart in doing so.

Winnie stood up and shook her head. 'He'll not be the first nor the last; there'll be plenty more tears to be shed yet, I'm afraid, my girls. Molly, you be there for your sister; she'll need a shoulder to cry on. Now let me get the kettle on. It must be teatime and look at me: I've not got anything on cooking – not that there's a lot in the house. I swear the rations are getting smaller.'

Molly patted Annie on her shoulder and squeezed her hand.

Annie sniffed and wiped her eyes as she looked at her family. 'I don't want anything, Mam, so don't worry about me. Why did it have to be him? Why has it got to be anybody? War makes no sense!' she cried out

'I know, love. I know nothing makes sense any more, but there's nothing we can do about it, I'm afraid,' Winnie said as she filled the kettle and put it on to boil.

'I'm going up to my bedroom.' Annie stood up and hugged Molly and Connie. 'I'll be all right, but I do think that I loved him.'

Molly nodded. 'Would you like me to come upstairs with you and then we can talk while Mam's making the tea?' She held on to her sister's hand as she made her way with her to the bottom of the stairs.

'No, I want to be on my own. I just want to lie down and die,' Annie wailed and started to cry again.

Winnie sighed; she had seen this all before and this was just the start. 'No, you don't, my lass. Josh has already died. This is why we all have to stand together and fight this bloody Hitler. Show him we'll not bend to his ways. Now you go and have a lie-down and one of us will bring up your tea. I've never been prouder of you girls for doing what you can to help in our hour of need.'

'Will she be all right, Mam? There's nothing we can do for her?' Molly whispered, looking across at Connie who was sitting quietly on her own, deep in thought.

'She will, but it'll take time and it couldn't have happened at a worse time. She's just signed up for the Land Army; she'll be leaving us soon.' Winnie stirred the tea, adding a precious teaspoon of sugar into Annie's cup before carrying it upstairs.

'Here, love, a cuppa with some sugar in it to buck you up.' Winnie sat down on her daughter's bed and pulled the discarded eiderdown round her sobbing daughter. 'We live, we love and we lose. That's life, my love, and I can't do anything to stop you being hurt, but I will always be there for you. As long as you hold his memory in your heart, he'll always be a part of you, my love.' Winnie bent her head and kissed her daughter on the brow. 'You have a good sob and remember that we're all here for you and that Josh would not want to see you this upset.'

'I loved him, Mam, and now he's dead.'

'I know my love, and I know you hurt, but no amount of tears will bring him back. Think of the good times you had together and then find strength. After all, you're soon to become a land girl and help to keep our nation fed.' Winnie stroked Annie's hair.

'I should be making bombs like Molly and Connie. I

hate the Nazis! I didn't want to but I do now,' Annie said, and covered her head with the eiderdown.

'Hate gets us nowhere; don't let Josh's death make you bitter. The Nazis will be overthrown; evil never wins. Now you close your eyes and perhaps have a sleep. It'll take time for you to settle your thoughts.'

Winnie rose from the edge of the bed and looked around the bedroom that until a few hours ago had been filled with laughter. Now even the sun that flooded through the windows could not reach the dark corners where despair and grief lay.

5

Molly stood in her underclothes and wished that the medical officer would get on with it. All employees that were to start making munitions were under orders to undertake a medical examination. Memories came flooding back of when she had joined Rowntree's and her first experience of being seen by a dentist. She stood nearly shaking as the medical officer roughly poked and prodded her, taking special notice of her skin and asking her numerous questions. Anyone with a skin condition was immediately rejected; the materials they were going to be handling were deadly and caustic and would cause irritation to anyone who already had a skin condition.

'Right, you seem fit enough. Go and get measured for your uniform and report back in the morning,' the woman in an army uniform said, and pointed her in the right direction.

Molly felt just like a piece of meat as she stood in line shortly afterwards. She was beginning to realize that she was now part of the British war machine.

'What size feet are you?' a man in a serge uniform asked, and on receiving her reply promptly passed her a pair of sturdy shoes with crêpe rubber soles. Then he quickly eyed her up and down and reached for a uniform and turban that he thought would fit her and then a bag on a string to hold any money or food, telling her she must not come to work in any jewellery at all, and if she was married that she was to cover her wedding ring with tape.

It was all in the name of safety; the ones making these changes knew just how dangerous anything that caused friction or which made a spark could be, causing the minute grains of gunpowder floating in the air to ignite. However, they didn't want to tell their new staff everything as that would cause of panic.

'You need to keep them in the locker designated for you in the new changing rooms. There's a clean area where you'll change out of your ordinary clothes and put them in the wire baskets you'll find there, then you'll change into this uniform in the area marked as "dirty". You must never go out of the area or out of the building in these clothes. Do you understand?'

Molly nodded her head.

'You'll also need to cover your face and hands with the cream provided in the changing rooms; this will protect you from the effects of the TNT powder that you'll be handling. Also, the changing rooms are the only place you can eat or drink, but we would prefer you to do neither while you are on your shift. Do you understand?'

'Yes, sir,' Molly said. She felt as if she were back at school and about eleven. She stood for a minute and then the loud-mouthed sergeant shouted, 'Next,' and she moved along to the changing rooms and found her locker along a wall of hundreds. On the walls were posters saying STOP! have you handed in your CONTRABAND? and LOOSE LIPS SINK SHIPS! and warning posters for anyone who talked out of work or decided to take any bomb equipment home with them, although that was highly unlikely, thought Molly, as she looked at her overall with rubber buttons that fastened tightly at the neck and had no pockets. The material was coarse and rough and Molly started to itch just thinking about wearing it.

Connie smiled as she joined Molly in the changing room. 'So you've made it this far as well, have you? Not allowed to eat, not allowed our own clothes – it's more like a prison than a factory!'

A commissioner on one of the doors told Connie to be quiet and for both of them to queue for an identity card to get them in and out of their new workplace.

'You're right, we're going to look like rats in cages – just look what they've done to the Smarties production line!' Molly said as she took in square steel cubicles with toughened-glass windows with two holes in them for their arms to reach for the TNT, which was to be weighed on a set of scales, poured carefully into small cylinders that acted as the shell of the bombs. It was a strange new factory for everyone who had known it previously.

'Maybe your Annie has done right. Twelve-hour shifts, itchy uniform, no dinners and treated like robots. Do you think we'll last?' Connie said as they were ushered to receive their identity cards. 'We had a rough idea that it wasn't going to be a picnic, but I don't think we realized just how different and perhaps even dangerous our new job would be.'

The following day, along with five hundred other employees, Molly and Connie stood in small groups of novices, learning from a man from the war ministry how to handle the munitions. They'd already endured searches for contraband and anything that might cause the slightest hint of friction and all those who had any skin exposed were covered with face powder and a thick skin cream on their face and hands. The TNT was poisonous if exposed to the skin, so there they all stood, hair brushed under the khaki turbans and their serge uniform tightly fastened with rubber buttons up to their neck with white hands and faces as they watched the conveyor belt that had once moved Smarties from one stop to another carry a box of ten shells to be assembled by the new workforce. A face mask had been given to everybody as the process was explained. In every compartment there was a red brass bucket filled with sand to dampen and absorb any accidental blasts, which hopefully would never happen. However, precautions for every danger while handling the TNT had to be put in place, the word 'bomb' never mentioned so as not to cause panic. They only referred to 'shells' and 'detonators', leading to confusion among a few of the girls as to what they were making.

The instructors stood over groups of girls and showed each how to go about their jobs. A set of brass weighing scales ensured that the correct amount of

TNT was weighed, while a wooden box holding all the parts needed came down the production line. The outer shell was held tight, then a measured amount of TNT was poured into each shell from the box at each workstation before adding the detonator parts and sealing it. Molly and Connie watched carefully and noticed small particles of the TNT floating in the air, as each intricate component was screwed into place and then travelled along conveyor belt to be taken to a new underground store that had been made.

The instructor finished her demonstration and folded her arms and sternly looked at her trainees. 'Do not at any time drop what you are making or knock it on the shells' red sides once packed. We do not want any messy accidents.'

A silence went around the room. All the trainees knew that their work was dangerous, but perhaps not to the extent that their instructor was telling them.

Molly went through the actions in her mind, making a note of every component and every part in detail, especially taking note not to drop anything, most of all the shell when packed and finished. 'First the shell, then the brass disc, then add gunpowder, the paper disc, the safety shutter and then the detonator, and then that's my job done. I don't think I'll ever manage to do this,' Molly whispered to Connie. 'It's too complicated and dangerous.'

Connie grinned. 'Don't be daft. There looks to be only a few bits to it. Just think about the way you add bits to the chocolate boxes. Main body, then the TNT,

then the detonator thingy and all the bits in their turn . . .
Just don't go and drop the bloody thing.'

Then they all moved forward and were given their
individual positions all doing the same thing with the
trainers moving between them. Connie and Molly made
sure they were working next to one another. Their work
space made it hard for communication between the
friends as they concentrated on putting the right component in the right place, following a diagram that had
been placed in their small workstation.

Molly, no matter how carefully she tried, struggled
to pour the TNT accurately; it was so fine there was a
cloud of dust around her. Not only that but the smell
was sulphurous and went straight through her face mask.
She looked around as she finally finished her first shell,
making sure she and Connie had done the same thing.
They looked the same, so Molly started on her second
one and breathed a sigh of relief. Connie was right: it
was like making a chocolate box, and all would be fine,
she thought, as she fairly quickly reached for her third
shell. But twelve hours of this every day was going to be
hard, and there were to be no long breaks or luxurious
dinner breaks like at Rowntree's; a quick meal and a toilet
break when really needed was to be the norm. How easy
and lucky life had been making chocolates. No wonder
Annie had opted to be a land girl.

Her hands shook as she measured and poured the
black grains into the bottom of the shell casing and she
stuck her tongue out of the side of her mouth, concentrating, as she placed the next components together.

When she looked up to the blacked-out skylight she saw the small particles of gunpowder floating in the air. They were actually making bombs. The only thing that they were not adding was the fuse; that would be added before the bomb was ready for dropping. If the factory's location were given away, they would be a sitting target for Jerry.

Connie started humming the latest song, presumably to block out the reality of what they were actually doing. Molly thought that she'd not sleep that night for worrying about the seriousness of her new job. Then she remembered Annie's tears over Josh. She had to do it, to stop Jerry from killing innocents like Josh and to keep the men in the army, navy and RAF safe. If she wasn't to fight, then this was the least she could do, and she picked up another shell and followed the instructions yet again. By the end of the week, she hoped she'd be putting the components together as if she'd been doing it all her life. It was her way of contributing to the war. She put any thought of detonations and blasts out of her mind and got back to the job at hand.

The first fortnight had flown. The twelve-hour days had been long ones, filled with learning and trepidation of the new work. Two weeks had felt like two months and already they were feeling the strain of their responsibilities.

Connie and Molly walked home with the other workers. They had both changed back into their civilian clothes and felt more at ease out in the evening air, with the smell of TNT clearing from their noses and the coarseness of the rough serge against their skin no longer bothering them.

'I'm so tired,' Molly groaned as they turned the corner for home. 'To think we have to do this for another four days and then, after the weekend, change to working through the night! I don't think I'll wake up in the morning and be able to drag my feet back to that place.'

'I'm just ready for something to eat; my belly thinks my throat has been cut. I hope your mam has got something nice and warm for supper.'

'Poor Mam, she's in a bit of a state. And Annie's mourning for Josh and she says while we're doing this job she lives in fear of us and half York being blown sky-high if Jerry finds out where we're making the shells for the bombs to be dropped on him. She's worrying about us all, including herself while she's making her chocolate.'

'I know,' Connie said. 'She was in a right fluster this morning, but at least her cold is mending; she's not coughing any more. What I wouldn't do for a lovely slice of roast beef or even corned beef stew.' She grinned.

'No, never, I hate it, but I do miss the dinners we were served. That measly cracker out of the bag we're made to wear round our necks isn't enough to keep me going. I'm never going to complain about a meal ever again.'

'Oh, can you smell that, Molly? I don't know what your mam's got on the go for us, but it smells good.' Connie had opened the front door and been instantly hit with the smell of cooking from the kitchen.

'I've bothered about you girls all day,' Winnie said, smiling at both girls as they entered the kitchen. 'Every time I heard a bang or a noise I imagined it was an accident at Rowntree's. It's been a terrible few weeks. How are you both? You look tired. Annie's been back from her last week working packing chocolates for ages. She's famished as I've made her wait until we can all sit together and eat,' she babbled on as she took supper out of the oven.

'Yes, I've had to wait for you two,' Annie moaned. 'I'll be glad when I've gone and left Rowntree's. I'm fed up of being asked to log in and for them to check who I am every time I go in. I'm only making bloody chocolates. All because of you lot that are busy making bombs.'

Molly gave Annie a look of disdain. 'For once in your life stop moaning. You should be us, checked every minute of the day, no dinner, no pockets in our uniforms, have to step into clean or dirty areas just to have a rest, and handling stinking TNT that smells like rotten eggs,' she replied crossly. She was tired and hungry and hadn't got patience for Annie's moaning, even if she was feeling the loss of Josh.

'Now, girls, stop arguing and sit down round the table and enjoy this.' Winnie had brought a beautiful pie in her favourite white enamel dish out of the oven and put it, steaming, in front of them on the table.

'Oh, just look at that,' Connie said and felt dribble sneaking out of the side of her mouth. 'A lovely steak pie! You must have chatted old Bill Allen the butcher up for that. It is truly worth the wait.'

'Sorry, Connie, it's not steak; I only wish it was,' Winnie said. 'It's called Woolton Pie, and the recipe is recommended in *War Recipes Made Easy*. I lined up outside Allen's for an hour, but he'd run out of everything, so I made it to the market and the veg man. It's full of parsnips, carrots, potatoes and anything else I could get my hands on, with a potato and oatmeal crust; it'll be good!' Winnie saw the expectant faces fall as she cut into the pie and passed them each a piece.

'Well, at least if I'm to work on a pig farm in Lancashire, there'll not be a shortage of bacon, I hope,' Annie said as she prodded the vegetable pie with her fork.

Molly, who was thankful for the meal in front of her, gasped. 'You've been told where you're going already?' 'It seems like you've only just applied'

'Yes, Pendle Farm in Clitheroe, a pig farm. I got my orders and train tickets this morning. I can't say I'm enthralled with having to look after pigs all day, although the letter says they have other stock as well. Though anywhere is better than Rowntree's.' Annie sighed. 'I did want the open countryside and it's not that far from home. It's the pigs that I'm not so keen on, but I'm sure I'll enjoy it.'

'You'll not be thinking that when you're cleaning them out. They stink. I think I'd rather be making shells,' Molly said, then looked longingly at the last piece of pie left in the dish.

Winnie smiled as she pushed the dish to her youngest daughter. 'Go on, you have it, Molly. Thankfully I also have a spotted dick steaming on the stove top with custard. I have to fill you up somehow after these long shifts.'

'Do you fancy going halves, Connie?' Molly asked.

'No, I'll pass, thank you. I'm not so keen on parsnips, but I'm going to savour every mouthful of your mam's pudding. Now that will stick to my ribs.' Then Connie grinned as Molly ate what was left straight out of the enamel dish. 'It's hard work is fuse filling.'

'I can see that. Now, let me untie this muslin cloth and dish my pudding; the currants are few and far between but it'll fill you, up,' Winnie said, then blew on her fingers to cool them down. She dished up her much-loved pudding, smothering it with custard. 'Now that's what I like at the dinner table: peace and happy faces,' she said a moment later. 'Make the most of it, my girls – we'll not all be together for much longer.' Winnie pulled her handkerchief from up her sleeve and wiped her eyes.

Molly looked up from her pudding. 'Don't cry, Mam. At least we've not been called up and are relatively safe. If we were lads, we would have had to have gone to fight. We're all right, so stop worrying.'

'Yes, we're all right, Mam, and if I'm allowed home occasionally, I'll bring back some bacon or something and help out if I can. I know Rose is hardly here – she's busy now she's part of the management at Rowntree's and looking after Ned's mother – but we'll all be just fine.' Annie spoke quietly and tried to wipe thoughts of Josh from her mind for a brief minute.

'I know. I love you, my girls. You must make the most of each day that comes now war is upon us. Do you hear?' Winnie looked at the three young girls and hoped that they would all stay safe.

'Yes, Mam,' Molly and Annie replied, and Connie nodded her head as she thought about Billy, her baby half-brother with his adoptive parents in Montana. She missed him, but at least he was safe over there away from the war in Europe.

'Now, how about a game of whist before bed?' Winnie said. 'Perhaps not then,' she said, as all the girls shook their heads. 'Well, I'll go round to Elsie's instead, and you do as you like.'

Molly and Connie lay in bed not long after – it was only just dark but they were exhausted.

'It's dangerous what we do, isn't it? Sometimes when I think about it I imagine one little spark and the whole place and us being blown sky-high. They never really told us that when we were training; it was as if we should have known,' Molly said quietly as she looked at her alarm clock.

'Everything and everywhere is dangerous at the moment, Mol. It's like your mam says, we have to make the most of each day. Saying that, there's a dance on Saturday in the Rowntree's hall. Should we go, just for a laugh?'

Molly yawned and closed her eyes. 'Yes, as long as we're not too tired. Night-night, Connie. I'm shattered.'

6

Molly looked in disbelief at the colour of her pee as she got up from the toilet in Rowntree's. It was a reddish colour and a feeling of uneasiness came over her as she flushed the toilet and unbolted the door in a panic, which a fellow worker noticed via the washroom mirror as she reapplied her protective cream.

'I'm sure I'm turning yellow. Look around my hairline. I've a yellow cast and my pee is pink! You don't look as if you've any problem with your skin, but by the look on your face I take it your pee has turned pink?' she asked kindly.

'Yes it has. Are we all ill? And why are you going yellow?' Molly said, recognizing that everything was perhaps not fine.

'It's the TNT. It gets into our bodies. We'll be shining as bright as the sun itself in another month or two. That is if you don't prove to be too allergic. The girl next to me came out in a terrible rash on her first day and had to be taken off her job,' the older woman replied. 'My sister's been doing this for a while down in Birmingham; she's as yellow as a canary, and that's what us that work with the TNT will be called after a while, bloody canaries, because even our hair will turn yellow in time! I bet they didn't tell you that when you signed those forms.

I still decided to work here – the pay is good and at least I'm doing something for the war effort.' She held out a hand. 'I'm Betty, I worked in the Smarties department . . . not that you can tell that's what we were making here a few weeks ago.' She sighed.

Molly introduced herself. 'I was in the Card Box department. I think I've seen you before in the dining hall'

'Oh, don't mention the dining hall. I so miss those dinners. How do they think we can work twelve hours on a tiny snack or an odd drink of tea? They're even wanting us to stop drinking tea. This morning I heard they want us to only drink milk. That will be to stop our pee turning pink, I bet!' Betty sighed again.

'I didn't know all this was going to happen. It's quite worrying,' Molly whispered.

'It's better than fighting on the front line. My old man is somewhere in France. Lord knows if he'll ever return to me. Not that I'm that bothered. He's a bit of a bastard and I'm enjoying myself while he's away,' Betty said, as she applied bright red lipstick. 'Got to look a bit glam; this cream and uniform does nothing for a girl. Are you going to the dance on Saturday night? I am. I'm going to make it my job to win over that bolshie sod that searches for so-called contraband. I'm sure when he pats me down every day he's looking for more than anything to do with bombs. I'll warn him that when I light his fuse, there won't half be a bang.' Betty grinned, smacked her lips together and hid her lipstick behind the mirror. 'Put some on if you want, love; just make sure you hide it.' With that, she winked and left Molly shaking her head at the married woman who was playing the field while her husband was fighting for the country. She hadn't even a boyfriend, she thought, as she looked at herself in the mirror for any signs of yellow. She never would get one if her skin was going to change yellow; that would be a disaster.

'Do you think I look all right? I could have done with a new dress, but there's nothing in the shops and besides I haven't had the time to buy one.' Connie looked at herself in Annie's wardrobe mirror as Annie and Molly sat on Rose's now empty bed and watched her preen herself. By the following week the bedroom would be empty and Annie gone, leaving Connie thinking she might be able to commandeer the empty room.

'You look just fine, but I would have perhaps chosen a lighter lipstick – the shade that you have on reminds me of the woman I was talking to in the works toilets, and all she was after was a man to replace her husband.' Molly lay back on the bed and flicked through a copy of *Woman's Own*, looking at the tips on how to make do and mend, including a picture of a toy tin man made out of a colander and various pots and pans, along with another character made out of cotton thread and bobbins holding a pair of scissors.

'What do you mean, Molly? Do you think I look a bit loose and easy? I'd hate for anyone to think that,' Connie said. She puckered her lips and inspected herself again.

'No one would ever think that. How could we?' Annie

grinned and nudged Molly, who was still absorbed in the magazine that was shared by everyone in the family home but somehow always to be found in Annie's bedroom if lost.

'No, of course not,' Molly said. 'The colour reminded me of her, that's all. You look lovely, Connie – you're sure to attract somebody at the dance tonight.' She returned to the magazine, noticing on the next page there was an offer of free frock and coat patterns from Best Way Fashions, advertising wartime renovations to existing clothes. That made Molly suddenly think of the treadle sewing machine that was hardly used by her mother or anyone else in the family. It was in the corner of the front room with a pot plant upon its case.

'I think I'm going to send for these patterns. I remember when our nan used to make our frocks and all sorts. Mam never uses that sewing machine, but I think I could reinvent some of the few clothes that we have.' Molly tore the advert out without thinking and folded it into her pocket.

'Ey, I haven't read that yet. I hope there was nothing on the back that I was interested in.' Connie slumped in between Molly and Annie and looked at the front of the magazine, which showed a young woman with a fresh complexion holding sheaths of corn with a broad smile on her face. She smirked. 'So that's why I never got a look in. You've been hiding it away, Annie. *My life in the Land Army, a special supplement*. That doesn't look like you, Annie; you'll be surrounded by pig muck.' Connie put her arm round Annie.

'You can make fun all you like but at least I'll not be turning as yellow as a dandelion,' Annie replied, trying to break loose of her grip . 'I'm not going to the dance; I'm going to pack. Besides, I don't feel like joining you. It wouldn't be right after losing Josh.'

'Oh, Annie, come with us, please. It'll do you good,' Molly said, looking at her sister with concern.

'No, I don't feel like it. You two go. Everyone's been talking about it; there'll be a lot there. I just feel that since I left Rowntree's I'm no longer part of it.' Annie felt her feelings bubble up inside her and started to cry. 'I'm sorry. Everything's changing and I don't know if I like it.'

'Oh, Annie, dry your tears. You'll be all right. You can always come back home, I think, or hope, if you don't like it – and we're not going anywhere.' Molly hugged her sister and Connie put her arm round her too.

'Well, as long as bloody Hitler doesn't go and drop a bomb on us, or Molly and I don't drop a fuse or two and blow Rowntree's up.' Connie kissed Annie on the cheek – she may not be her sister and they may often have had spats, but Annie never, ever cried and of late she had done so a lot.

She checked herself out in the mirror one last time and frowned. 'I look like a right hussy. Can I borrow your lipstick, Molly? You're a lot more sedate than me.' Connie had realized that she looked a little too daring in her low-cut dress and bright lipstick. Though that was what she had wanted: she was out to have a good time now she was earning decent money, having been given more responsibilities, and having not so far turned the yellow that everyone was warning them that they would.

It was soon evening and one of the Local Defence Volunteers was on hand later that evening to welcome them to the already noisy and busy Rowntree's hall.

'Evening, ladies. Make sure you get into the dance hall quickly; we don't want to let any light out when you open that door. You've got your gasmasks as well as your handbags, I hope?' He looked the two young women up and down in the darkness.

'Yes, we have and we'll be quick,' Molly replied, as she unhooked her arm from Connie's and opened the heavy door and then walked between the huge blackout curtain and the hall that was full of the noise of the band that was playing and the hum of people enjoying themselves.

'They might be trying to keep the noise in but, Lord, Hitler can surely hear that back in Berlin,' the LDV proclaimed to his colleague, as he shook his head and muttered that enjoying life so much when there was a war on was totally wrong.

'Orange squash, is that all they have to drink?' Connie said with disgust as she made her way over to the long trestle table where drinks were being served. 'Well, we are certainly going to go home sober tonight!'

'I'm not bothered. I'm not keen on drinking anyway,' Molly replied, taking a glass of orange and then folding her arms while she looked around her. 'There's a lot of people here, and just listen to the band, aren't they good, even if all fairly old?'

'I suppose so but they're a bit steady for me. It's all

right if you have someone to waltz with or even do a foxtrot with, but I wouldn't mind doing a rumba, always think that's slinky and sexy, or a cha-cha – that one's a bit faster.' Connie looked around the large hall; all the windows were tightly covered with blackout blinds and the lights were dimmed. The room was filled with Rowntree's and War Office employees. Union Jacks adorned the walls, along with wartime advice posters issued by the government. 'Hey, look, Mol, there's that good-looking lad that checks our identity card every morning. I think he's really dishy.' Connie smiled like the Cheshire cat as she tried to catch the eye of the young man that said good morning to them on their arrival to work.

'Yes, I see him,' Molly replied. 'I also see that he's got either a girlfriend or a wife; she's passing him a drink now and putting her arm through his.' There weren't many young men and what there were seemed to be already spoken for. She also noted that the Rowntree's bosses were there, keeping an eye on their employees even when it was their weekend away from work.

'Now, I do like this one. Come on, Molly. I'll lead, you follow and we'll dance together.' Connie grabbed Molly's arm and pulled her to the dance floor. 'Go on, grab my hand and waist and then we'll go.'

Molly hesitantly placed her arm round Connie and blushed as they both started dancing around the room.

'Mind my feet,' Connie said, as she led the way, following the music and trying not to bump into other couples. 'There, you see, we can have a good time without a man – we'll have to.'

'Yes, I must admit you can dance, although I'd feel more comfortable with a man leading,' Molly said, concentrating on her steps.

'Well, you might just might be in luck. Look what the wind has just blown in?' Connie nodded her head towards the swish of the blackout curtain behind the main door and the entrance of six young men all dressed in army uniform. They had heard the noise from outside and had decided to see what the party was about. They hadn't been invited but the LDV had been persuaded to let them in providing they didn't cause any bother.

'Oh my, don't they look handsome? But they'll not give us time of day,' Molly said as Connie pulled her across the dance floor and danced gracefully and effortlessly past them.

Connie grinned. 'They will if they have any sense. Bagsy the dark-haired one with blue eyes. Isn't he dishy?'

'If you say so? I'm not particularly bothered,' Molly replied and spotted William Allen, a friend from her school days, watching her with interest. She threw him a smile as Connie dragged her over to the drinks table.

At the table Connie stood posing, trying to attract the attention of one or all the soldiers that had just entered the hall. She was blatantly showing that she was interested in drawing their attention to them both.

'Hello, Molly, I haven't seen you for ages.' Molly turned to see William Allen standing beside her, offering her a drink of orange, as Connie threw flirty looks at the group of young men.

'William, I only just spotted you – in fact, I had to look twice. You've changed since we were at school,' Molly said quietly, hoping she hadn't offended him.

'You mean, I'm not the piggy-looking person that I was?' He laughed. 'I know, I was nearly as round as I was tall, but working for my father soon put a stop to that. Miles on that boneshaker of a delivery bike soon knocked pounds off me. I'm now as fit as a butcher's dog, because I'm just that.' William smiled warmly at the lass that had always been kind to him at school. 'You've altered and all, Molly. I know we don't live far apart but with both of us working full-time we never get to see one another.'

Molly sighed. 'Yes, and that's all I'm going to be doing now I'm working twelve-hour shifts in munitions. I'm going to have no life.' She watched as Connie plucked up the courage to walk across to the group of soldiers that were still standing together with hands in their pockets looking around the dance floor.

'You're working in munitions at Rowntree's? Blinking heck, Molly, you are brave – well done, you. Tell your mam to mention it next time she's in the shop; my father will put a bit of something special to one side for her under the counter. Is she working with you and all?' William asked and nodded his head towards Connie.

'Yes, she is. We both started recently and our Annie is to leave us on Monday; she's joined the Land Army and is to travel to somewhere called Clitheroe in Lancashire.' Molly tried to concentrate on William but couldn't help but see that Connie had got herself a man and was being escorted by him around the dance floor and had a huge smile on her face.

'Wow, you Freeman girls are something to be admired, and Rose is doing well too, I hear, getting into management at Rowntree's. They don't have many women working at the top. But for you to work in munitions is something to be really proud of.' William looked at Molly with admiration. 'Do you fancy a dance? I'm not right good – I've got two left feet – but let's give it a go?'

'Oh, all right. I'm not that good either, but I'll dance better with you than I did with Connie; we both giggled more than danced.' Molly took William's hand as he led her on to the dance floor.

'She looks as if she's happy with a soldier on her arm. Us local lads don't stand a chance what with men in uniform catching all you girls' eyes.' He placed his arm at the small of Molly's back.

'Oh, I don't know. I don't think much of soldiers; I'd rather dance with someone I know,' Molly said as she watched Connie fluttering her eyelashes and flirting with the soldiers now gathered round her.

Across the other side of the room, she saw Betty running her hands down the lapels of the man she told her she was going to seduce. She was dressed in her finery with bright red lipstick to lure her prey. When her husband came home, if he ever did come home, there'd be hell to pay, Molly thought, as she put her arm on William's shoulder. Her life had changed completely. She was making munitions for the army and now dancing with William Allen, who was surprisingly light on his feet and had changed from being the pudding of the class-room to quite a good-looking young man.

Several hours later, Molly and Connie lay in their beds – it was after midnight and the rest of the house was deadly silent, but the two girls were still talking.

'Well, you were spoilt for choice. I saw you with all those soldiers round you, but I also noticed you didn't end up with the one you said you fancied,' Molly whispered.

'No, he was a right bossy so-and-so. I can live with-out that, but his little blond friend was nice. I had the last dance with him.' Connie sighed. 'Who was that you were dancing with? You were with him all night. I didn't recognize him.'

'That was porky William, the butcher's son, although he's no longer porky. I know he lives only a few streets away but I haven't seen him for years. He used to always be teased because he was fat and what with him having ginger hair that made him catch it even worse, poor lad.' Molly sighed. 'We were cruel at school when you think about it. He was always nice to me but I never hardly bothered with him. He's a good dancer and I never noticed the colour of his eyes before; they're bright green, really unusual.'

'Will you be seeing him again?' Connie asked, yawning and pulling her pillow round her.

'No, he never said anything, although he did offer my mam a better service when she went to their shop, so perhaps the night was worth being spent with him.' Molly closed her eyes. 'I thought that warden was going to blow his top when he asked us to quieten down as we came back down the street.'

Molly smiled as she remembered walking back home arm in arm with three of the visiting soldiers, all smiling and laughing down the darkened streets until they had met an ARP Warden who had lectured them about the time of night and that they should be making less noise. 'Are you going to see your blond soldier then?'

'No, I don't think so. I don't even know his name. The one that first caught my eye was called Richard, but the nicer one never said who he was. They're only visiting; they're helping put up the barrage balloons along the Ouse. They said they'll be back in their camp at Catterick next week.' Connie looked up at the ceiling and thought about the kiss he had given her.

'Did you see that Betty?' Molly asked. 'What a hussy! She was outside the hall with that horrible man that checks us every day. They were like two dogs on heat, and she's married!' Molly harrumphed and plumped her pillow up.

Connie sighed. 'Yes. She's certainly making the most of her man being away. I couldn't be like that; I saw what having another man in your life does when my mam shacked up with Bill Tyler. We'd better get to sleep, Mol; we've just another night in our beds and then we start our night shift. Six in the evening until six in the morning. I'm not looking forward to that.'

'No, me neither. I don't know if I can do it, but we're going to have to. I don't know whether I'll be coming or going.' Molly breathed in and squeezed her eyes closed.

Night shifts and Annie leaving was not going to make it a good week, and that was even without any news of the war being thrown into the mix.

'I know, but we'll have to cope. Night-night, mind the bugs don't bite,' Connie said and she closed her eyes, thinking of the dance that she had enjoyed and trying to blot out thoughts of the coming weeks.

7

Annie looked at her mother as she stood next to her on the busy platform in York's huge railway station. The platform was crowded with troops and service personnel, and both Annie and Winnie felt as if their world was falling apart when the guard shouted, 'All aboard,' and made his way down the platform slamming the doors of the train that was soon to pull out of the station.

'I've got to go, Mam. I promise I'll write. And don't you worry about me. I'll be fine.' Annie hugged her mother tightly and held back her tears. 'You've got my address. I love you, Mam.' Then she turned quickly and stepped on to the waiting steam train just before the guard shut the door, stood back and blew his whistle.

Winnie stood on the platform, hanky in hand, and felt like crying. None of her girls had hardly been away from home before and now Annie was going to Lancashire and all they knew about it was that it was a pig farm. She waved as the train started to move.

'I promise I'll write!' Annie yelled as the train built up steam, filling the station with white smoke and making her mother nearly invisible. Annie leaned out of the train window for as long as she could before pulling on the leather window strap and closing it to settle in her seat.

'Leaving home?' an elderly gentleman who sat across

from her asked, noting the lass wiping her eyes with her handkerchief and pretending that it was just the smoke as she brushed a tear away.

'Yes, I've joined the Land Army,' Annie replied. 'You have to do your bit, don't you?' She concentrated on the picture of Scarborough Beach filled with sun worshippers when times were better that was placed above the luggage rail.

'You do, my girl. Well done, you. Have you farming in your family?' the man asked.

'No. I've not been to a farm in my life, but I'm a quick learner,' Annie replied, and smiled.

'You'll have to be, my lass. Farmers have no time for softness and laziness, but once you know your job, you'll be all right.' Then he picked up a paper and started to read.

Annie read the headline, british troops go on offensive in El Alamein, and wondered where El Alamein was and worried that she didn't have a clue about farming. Perhaps she should have joined one of the forces, but Lancashire was far enough away from home for her, never mind being posted in some far-flung country or serving on a military base miles from home. At least the Freeman family were doing something, especially Molly and lodger Connie, who didn't seem to have realized just how dangerous their job was. She decided to enjoy the view and watched the countryside open up around her, the flat fields of corn and wheat gradually turning rougher as the train passed Leeds and trundled its way down to the hills and eventually to the moors

74

of Lancashire. She marvelled at the mills that made Lancashire the industrial powerhouse that it was, but above the grey-smoked towns there were rolling hills and green fields that provided Lancashire with its food.

At every stop were soldiers going to and from their bases with their sweethearts and wives kissing them goodbye. Hearts were breaking. It was a sad train, she thought, as a soldier in full uniform joined her and the friendly man in the carriage.

Annie looked at him and thought of her Josh; she had loved him, even though they had not seen each other often. They had written of their love to one another in their letters.

'Are you all right, love?' the soldier asked. 'Off anywhere nice? I'm back to my billet at Preston and then we'll be heading to France.' He struck a match on the soul of his boot as he spoke and lit the Woodbine that was hanging out of his mouth.

'I'm going to Clitheroe. I've joined the Land Army,' Annie said, hoping to avoid further contact with the good-looking young man in his khaki uniform.

He drew a long breath and then sat back. 'Oh, aye, where are you going in Clitheroe? It's the next stop by the way, so you'd better make yourself ready.'

'A place called Pendle Farm; it breeds pigs from what I understand,' Annie said, reaching for her small suitcase stowed above her head and trying to keep her balance as the train went over the points of the railway line.

'What a coincidence! You'll be all right there, for it's my uncle's farm, would you believe? He'll expect you to work hard, but you'll get fed well. Tell him Mike sends his regards and that I'll give Hitler his best regards when I meet him too.'

Annie looked up in surprise but there wasn't time to ask more as the train drew to her stop and she stood to pull back the compartment door. 'I'll be sure to pass that on. And good luck to you in France,' she managed as she struggled with her bag.

'He'll have you tattie picking, I'll tell you now, and that is back-breaking work. Take care, love.' Mike grinned, watching the dark-haired girl alight from the train. She was a bonny lass. Pity he was off to war; he'd have asked her out given half the chance.

Annie stood on the busy platform; it was more rural than she had thought, and she'd been told it was a market town not a mill town, like some she'd passed through on the train. She picked up her suitcase and followed the crowds across the wooden crossing to get to the main station building where she hoped that her new employer would be waiting for her as promised. She listened to the locals talking and realized that their accents were a lot different to hers and she hoped she would soon get used to it. Her heart beat fast as her train ticket was checked before she left the sturdy Victorian station and stepped out on to a street that had more horses and carts than cars upon it than York. She looked around and saw a shabbily dressed man holding his horse's head and stroking its mane while he talked to it.

'Excuse me, are you Mr Farrington? Pendle Farm?'

Annie said and hoped that he would say that he wasn't after looking at the state of his dress and noticing the pungent smell that came from him. 'I'm Annie Freeman.'

'Aye, that's me, lass. You must be our new lass. Tha' doesn't look much of a farmer; we'll have to feed you up else you'll be worth nowt to us.' Bernard Farrington looked at the lass he'd taken on as cheap labour and immediately thought that it was going to cost him more to feed her than he'd get in work out of her. 'I said I'd come and meet you, as we live a bit out of the way at Pendle Farm. Which is a good job some days; we wouldn't want posh Clitheroe moaning about the smell of our pigs.' Bernard grinned and took Annie's case. 'Now then, climb yourself up next to me and we'll be away. Time waits for no man.'

Bernard put Annie's suitcase in the back of his trap and watched as Annie struggled to lift herself on the seat next to him because of her tight skirt.

Bernard grinned as at last Annie managed to sit next to him. 'I hope you've brought your breeches; you'll be no good in clothes and shoes like that. My pigs will wonder what the heck's going on.'

'Yes, I've my uniform in my suitcase, along with some boots, so you needn't worry,' Annie said, feeling awkward as Bernard flicked the horse's reins and they set off down the road, passing under the railway bridge and heading out into the countryside.

'There's a bike come for you at the farm, so you'll not have to bother me if you want to come shopping into town and the missus has made a bed up for you with the other lass that's staying with us in the old part of the house. It'll get a bit cold in there in winter, but it all might be over by then and, besides, it's only August. Owt could happen yet.'

'You've another land girl working for you?' Annie enquired, wondering what she was like and where she was from.

'Aye, she's from down south. Permed blonde hair and painted nails. Arrived yesterday. She'll be in for a shock when she starts working tomorrow. Mrs F says she'll be all right after a week or two but I've doubts myself. My nephew used to help us along with another lad, but they've both been enlisted.'

'Is that your nephew Mike? He was on the train with me. He told me to tell you that he was going to give Hitler your best regards.'

Bernard laughed. 'Aye, that'll be the cheeky bugger. It's to be hoped he doesn't get that close to Hitler, or else he'll not be coming back to help me with my tattie harvest in another month. I told him he must be desperate to get away from me if he'd rather enlist than feed my girls and pick my tatties. Bloody Hitler, he needs stopping. Although I'm not complaining. I've never had things so good, selling bacon here, there and everywhere. By the way –' Bernard turned and looked seriously at her – 'what goes on at Pendle Farm stops at Pendle Farm, do you hear? There's somethings this War Ag doesn't have to know. They like to know what goes on at every farm so that they can tell the Government who's farming what and what they can expect in their coffers. Nosy buggers'

'Yes, yes, of course. I'm not a gossiper. It's none of my business anyway.' Annie didn't have a clue what he was trying to tell her, but she presumed all would become clear once she'd started working for him.

'Aye, well, just thought I'd tell you now and then we start out on the right footing.'

Annie sat quietly next to her new boss and watched the fragrant summer hedges go past her and admired the scenery, especially the brooding hill that raised its head to her right. She gazed up towards it.

'That's Pendle Hill, famous for its witches. It's a dark place even in summer. We live just under it and have done for centuries; it's the family farm. There's no witches now. I don't think there ever were, probably just some harmless old women that folk took a dislike to. That will be it,' Bernard said.

Annie felt a chill down her back as they turned on to a rough path that had a hand-painted rough sign with Pendle Farm written on it.

Annie still felt uneasy as they pulled up at the top of the farm track, blackberries and roses overhanging the lane, and on the other side of the hedge she could see and smell pigs, hundreds of pigs, roaming around with piglets at their feet.

'Those are my girls, my moneymakers, especially now this war is on. Then there are my tattie fields in the valley bottom in the richer soil. I hope you like bacon and mash because that's what we get a lot of. My old lass will make sure you're fed if nothing else,' Bernard said. He pulled on his horse's rein as they stopped outside a long, white-painted farmhouse with windows that were rotting and a door that opened to reveal a ruddy-faced woman with an apron made of a flour bag tied round her waist.

'I thought you'd found another woman, Bernard, you've been so long. So is this our new lass?' Lizzie Farrington said, watching as Annie alighted from the cart and stepped back at a hen running round her feet, chasing a fat worm that had been turned up by the cart's wheels.

'Aye. This here is Annie. She needs fattening up, Mother; I think she's thinner than the other,' Bernard said as he passed Annie her case and smiled at his wife.

'Well, come on in, lass. We don't bite and there's a drink waiting for you. Now, your papers say that you're from York – never been there. I've never been out of Lancashire. I asked this other lass why would I need to leave such a grand place as this; there's everything you could wish for just here.' Lizzie Farrington pushed the old front door open and let Annie pass her into the low-ceilinged kitchen. It had a flagged stone floor and long wooden dressers on each wall filled with pots and orna-ments, with a large wooden table in the centre.

Next to the lit fire was a very pretty blonde girl with a cat on her lap in a wooden spindle-backed chair. She looked up at Annie and smiled, but the minute Lizzie Farrington looked away to place Annie's suitcase at the bottom of the stone stairs that led to the bedrooms and the older part of the house, she shook her head grimly.

'Now then, the kettle's just boiled and there's tea in

the pot, although it's been reused about three times. If my Bernard could grow tea, we'd make a fortune.'

Annie watched as Lizzie poured the weakest tea she'd ever seen into brown-stained mugs and passed one to her with the smallest amount of milk that was possible.

'Thank you,' Annie replied as Lizzie looked her up and down.

'There's a chair over there. I'll just move all the rubbish that's on it; it's only Bernard's overalls that he puts on when he mucks out the pigs,' Lizzie said, bending over to move a newspaper and a heap of clothes that dislodged the foulest smell Annie had ever smelled. She found herself feeling sick as she tried to swallow her drink.

'You'll have to get used to,' the blonde girl whispered as Annie placed the stinking overalls outside the front door in the sunshine. 'Everything stinks,' she added quietly, before smiling at Lizzie Farrington as she came back in.

'This is Helen. She's from Tottenham in the middle of London, would you believe, and she's decided to farm. It'll take you both time to get used to what we do, but it's a grand life: plenty of fresh air and sunshine and you're safe from bombs up here,' Lizzie Farrington said, not noticing the smirk on Helen's face when fresh air was mentioned. 'Bernard will show you your jobs and I could do with some help sometimes in the house. You'll both be fed well and you've both got your own bed; Helen will show you yours, Annie. The War Ag has given you both a bicycle. They're in the barn and you'll have to use them if you need to get into Clitheroe. It's five miles, though, and you can only have Sunday off along with evenings, but I'll not entertain young men visiting at any time.' Lizzie drew breath as she stood in front of them and went through the rules of their new home. 'I'll need your ration books and you'll get paid for your work by us each week. Now, if you happen across something that we do that might seem strange, there's no need to tell anybody, especially those from the War Ag, when they visit. Not everyone needs to know our business.' Lizzie blushed. 'Now, I think that's everything, so we'll have to see how we go on.'

'Thank you, Mrs Farrington, you've made everything clear, and I only hope that I can help you here at Pendle Farm,' Annie said soothingly.

'Aye, well, so do I, lass, because we need all the help we can get and my fella won't take lightly to feeding a lass that can't pull her weight,' Lizzie muttered, looking across at Helen. 'Now, Helen, show this 'un your room and then it'll soon be time for supper. Tomorrow you both make a start, and you'll be jiggered by the end of it, mark my words.'

Helen brushed the cat off her lap, stood up and smiled. 'Yes, Mrs Farrington, I'm sure we will. Come on, Annie, I'll show you our bedroom; we have a beautiful view right across the valley.'

Annie looked at Helen; she seemed about the same age as her but was more well-built and had make-up on, even though she wasn't going anywhere. She also talked in a strange accent, and as she walked to the bottom of the stairs she moved as if she were on a catwalk her skirt was so tight. Annie knew there and then she'd be no good working out in the fields dressed in anything like that.

'C'mon, ducks, I'll show you the palace that we're to live in. It is right cosy, ain't it, Mrs F?' Helen said and grinned.

Lizzie Farrington looked at her and sighed. 'It's as good as any other room in the house.'

'That doesn't say a lot,' Helen whispered, grabbing hold of Annie's suitcase and nodding for them both to go upstairs.

Annie followed Helen up the worn stone stairway and along a landing where the floorboards creaked and dark brown wallpaper hung off the walls.

'What a bloody place we've been sent to! I imagined a bloody big posh house in the country and instead I get posted to this pigsty –a pigsty inside as well as out-side. Thank God I brought my perfume; the whole place stinks!'

Helen walked round a corner and opened a dark var-nished door into a room under the sloping eaves of the farmhouse. Old oak beams supported the ceiling and on either side of the room were two single metal beds with bedding that had seen better days.

'Welcome to Buckingham Palace. I've already taken the bed the furthest away from the window. So if we're still here in winter, you'll be the one to freeze, because there are more gaps in the frame than there is wood.'

She put Annie's case down on this bed and then sat on the other and crossed her legs as she reached for a box of cigarettes and matches from the small table nearby. 'Put your uniform in the wardrobe along with mine. They'll not stay clean long, though; everything around here is filthy and stinks!' Helen drew a long deep breath of her cigarette and exhaled.

'It does smell. I must admit I wasn't quite prepared for this,' Annie said as she sat down on her bed and looked around the bedroom. There was more faded wallpaper on the walls, a washstand between the beds and a tall old dark brown wardrobe.

'Wait until you see the pigs. Lord, do they smell! We've to muck them out in the morning and feed them, and old Farrington says that they bite. They wouldn't think twice about eating a dead body if they came across one. He put the fear of God in me yesterday when he showed me around. And he's an old letch; I caught him catching a load of my bottom when I was leaning over a gate. Mucky old man and mucky farm – we could have done better for ourselves, gal.'

Annie smiled and opened her case, taking out a photograph of her and her sisters and her mother, placing it on her bedside table. 'Well, at least we're safe here. There's no likelihood of pigs being bombed.'

'That's the only good thing. The old smoke is taking a pounding. That's why I'm here; anywhere's safer than London at the moment. Bloody Jerries. Where are you from then? You sound different to how they talk here, but not that much?' Helen took another deep drag of her cigarette and watched the smoke hover in the air of the small room.

Annie looked across at Helen, deciding she was even more common than she had first thought Connie; at least Connie's hair wasn't peroxide blonde. 'I'm from York. Further over to the east and slightly north. I've been working in the Rowntree's factory, but they have turned to making munitions, not chocolate, and I didn't want to be part of that. So I volunteered for the Land Army. You have to do something to help.'

'I didn't know where Lancashire was; it was either here or picking apples in Somerset. I wish I'd chosen that now. Anyway, now you're here we can have a good time, as long as we don't stink of pig. Life's too short. And Clitheroe looks to have a bit of life, I noticed, when old dirty drawers picked me up.'

'Yes, it looks quite a big town. It's got a market and a castle that I spotted as we drove out. We'll have to make the most of it, I suppose. At least we'll be well fed,' Annie said, trying to make the best of the situation they found themselves in.

Helen sighed. 'That is, if you fancy eating anything. I went into the pantry and there's only a flitch of bacon hanging up on hooks by a string and potatoes in bags. Everything is so rough here.'

'Yes, but we're safe, and that's the main thing, and we're helping the country. My youngest sister is making munitions and my other sister's fiancé is in the RAF, so all she does is worry about his safety. I think we can count ourselves lucky.' Annie reached to the bottom of her suitcase and took out a photograph of Josh smiling and looking smart on board the ship that he had sunk to his death upon. She placed it next to the one of her family and tried to hide her sadness.

Helen looked at the photograph of the young black man in his uniform. 'Is that the boyfriend then? I'm surprised!'

'Surprised! What, that I have a boyfriend or that he's black? It made no difference to me –' Annie breathed in – 'and it definitely doesn't now, now that he's gone and I'll never see him again.'

'Gone? What do you mean "gone"? And I meant no offence – he looks a nice lad,' Helen said quickly.

'He was killed in action a few weeks ago at sea. I've brought his picture with me.' Annie hesitated. 'I miss him so much, even though we didn't have time to get that close.'

Helen moved next to Annie and put her arm round her. 'I thought we were never supposed to have to go through this again, or so we were promised after the last war, but this time it's even worse –they come and bomb us in our homes! I lost my aunt and uncle in a bombing raid. So, yes, you're right: at least we're safe here. We'll stick it out together and, pigs or no pigs, we'll make the best of it. Now, my gal, stop feeling sorry for yourself. You and I are going to have some fun in this mucky backwater if it's the last thing we do.'

8

Rose stood at the garden gate and looked up to the bright blue skies overhead. She couldn't stop the tears from flowing as she thought about the hastily written letter that she held in her hand that Ned had managed to send to her without his superiors knowing. It read:

Going on a mission into Germany tonight, my love. Can't say where and please don't give Mother my news, but, God willing, we will return safely. If something goes wrong and I don't, please remember that I will always love you. And promise me that you will take care of Mother. I love you, my darling Rose. Don't worry. I will do my best to be safe and return to your arms.

Your ever loving Ned

Rose looked at the note yet again, before folding it up and putting it in her pocket. The young lad on the bicycle that had delivered it to her had whistled and acted as if nothing were amiss as he had given it to her, not knowing that its few words would send her world into turmoil. How could she not say anything to Ivy when she knew he was risking his life that evening? She couldn't bear the thought of having to stay calm until she heard the familiar drone of his aeroplane above the house as he made a detour back to the airfield at Yeadon, just to let her know that he was safe.

She wiped her eyes and breathed in, returning to the house after answering the door.

'Who was that and what did they want, Rose dear?' Ivy asked. She turned down the radio and waited for a reply.

'It was just an errand boy delivering some leaflets about another war effort scheme. Nothing to worry about,' Rose replied. Then she smiled and tucked the light blanket round Ivy's knees.

Ivy sighed. 'They like to keep us all in line and tell us what to do. As if we haven't enough on our minds with our brave boys fighting. I don't know what this world is coming to. I'll get back to my radio show – at least it gives me a bit of light in the darkness. It's Tommy Hadley in his show *It's That Man Again*; he has a wicked sense of humour. He makes me laugh and you've got to keep the spirits up.' Ivy turned the sound up on the ageing Marconi wireless and sat back in her chair.

'Ivy, would you mind if I went to see my friend Mary? It's been a while since we had a talk and if you're happy listening to the wireless, then I'll just visit for an hour. If that!' Rose hoped that she would agree.

'Yes, get yourself gone. I'm quite content. Just make sure you're home before dark, and don't forget your gas mask just in case . . .' Ivy sat back, already smiling to herself as Tommy Hadley made a joke at the expense of his fellow actors.

Rose reached for her headscarf. 'Yes, I promise. Do you need anything before I go?'

'No, go on, it will do you good. You look a bit pasty – a breath of fresh air and a catch-up with friends are good for the soul. Now shoo.'

Rose breathed a sigh of relief as she pulled the front door shut behind her. She couldn't have kept her secret to herself all night and she knew if she visited Mary at her father's house near Dean's Gardens she'd be able to talk freely. The distraction of Mary and Joe's baby son would take her mind off the mission that Ned was flying that night.

'Rose, now you are a welcome sight. Do come in. I've just finished bathing young Joseph; he's about to have his night-time bottle and then be put to bed.' Mary smiled at her young son whose hair was still damp but who was warmly dressed in winceyette pyjamas with the sweet smell of baby powder all around him as she held the door open and welcomed Mary into their home.

'Doesn't he grow so fast? And he's the image of his daddy!' Rose smiled and tickled young Joseph under the chin. She felt quite broody at the sight of the love between mother and son. Joseph gurgled contentedly and Rose felt a gush of love for the bonny baby.

'Everyone says he's like his father. I must admit Joe's been away so long I've nearly forgotten what he looks like! Still, mustn't complain. I'm not the only one who has a loved one in the forces. Here, do you want to hold Joseph? I'll just go and get his bottle while you and him sit together; it's warming in the kitchen.'

Mary handed him to Rose to take and Rose realized just how solid he was as she struggled briefly with his weight. She bounced the little boy on her knee and made cooing noises as he looked up at her.

'Dadda, Dadda,' Joseph said when his mother came back into the room.

'What a clever boy! Won't your daddy be proud of you now you can say his name? Now, come on, leave Aunty Rose alone and come and have your bottle.' Mary spoke gently and took the young child from Rose's arms and sat with him to give him his bottle. She watched with love and care as Joseph drank the milk quickly and then his eyes started to close, content that he was secure in his mother's arms and that his stomach was full.

Mary sat back with the child fast asleep in her arms. 'There, hopefully that's peace for the night, providing he doesn't get woken by anything. I'll put him in his cot after you've gone, but I love to sit with him for a while at this time of night. I see so little of him when I'm at work and he's looked after by the nurses there. Although I'm not complaining. Rowntree's are wonderful in allowing us mothers to work and having the facilities for our children to be looked after. There aren't many firms that would do that, even if there is a war on.'

'I'm just glad that you were allocated to the Jungle Chocolate production. Making munitions is not for mothers, although I daren't say that in front of our Molly or Connie. Both are worried that their skin is turning yellow from the dust,' Rose said, and she tried not to think about why she had come to see Mary.

But Mary could see that something was bothering her best friend. 'Is Ned all right? You must worry about him all the time too? I don't know how you do it, working with management and looking after his mother, as well as keeping an eye on your own family.'

'I just have to get on with it, don't I? As you say, everybody's in the same boat.' Rose looked down at her hands and tried to hold back the tears, but found herself weeping uncontrollably as she remembered the note that Ned had sent her. 'I'm sorry. I didn't come here to give you my worries; you have enough of your own. It's just that Ned is on a bombing mission tonight. I don't know where, but it's over Germany somewhere; he can't tell me. The long and short of it is, I'm afraid that he won't come back, as he told me tonight's mission was a dangerous one. He's never done that before.' Rose blew her nose in her handkerchief and wiped her eyes.

Mary looked at her best friend with sympathy, holding out her hand to her and squeezing hers tight. 'He'll be all right, Rose. His crew will all look after one another; he'll be back before you know it.' Mary hoped her confidence wasn't misplaced. 'I never know where Joe is. He could be anywhere at sea, although he's part of the Home Fleet. All I know is that he's on HMS *Hermes*; that's all I'm allowed to know.'

'I know I'm being selfish telling you my troubles. Hopefully, as you say, he'll return home as fit as a fiddle. It's just that he never tells me as a rule what he and his crew are doing, so he must know that it's going to be bad. And when he asked me to make sure his mother was looked after if he didn't return, then I couldn't help but worry.'

'Yes I can see why that's worried you. This rotten war, it is really telling on our nerves! Does his mother know he could be in danger tonight?' Mary moved her arm as Joseph's weight started giving her pins and needles.

'No, I never said anything; I left her listening to her favourite radio show. There's no need for her to worry as well as me. I shouldn't have said anything. You have your own worries.' Rose sighed. 'I wonder how our Annie is settling in on her farm. None of us ever thought that she would turn her hand to farming.'

'No, it did surprise me a bit as well, although happen it will do her good after the bad news she received about her friend. Though I don't think I would have turned my back on Rowntree's. She'll need work when the war is over . . . if it ever comes to an end,' she finished mournfully.

Rose looked down at the sleeping Joseph. . 'I know, but you know our Annie; once she sets her head that is that, and she was heartbroken over Josh's death. She might make herself a new life down in Lancashire, you never know.' Rose realized that Mary probably had jobs to do or at least needed some time on her own while Joseph was asleep. 'I think I'll be on my way before it gets dark, else Ivy will only try to pull the blackout curtains and fall.' She got up. 'I'll see myself out. You put that little one to bed and thanks for being a friend, Mary.'

'If we can't help each other, then who can we help?'

said Mary. 'I'll perhaps see you at work tomorrow. And don't worry —Ned will come back safe and sound.'

Mary looked up at the dejected Rose. She knew as well as she did that being a pilot in the war was dangerous; more airmen were killed than in any other service. At least her Joe could swim to safety if he had to. She looked down at her precious child and stroked his cheek as she heard Rose close the front door and whispered, 'Please keep your daddy safe tonight and your uncle Ned.' She kissed him before taking him up the stairs to bed.

Rose walked quickly through the centre of York; it wasn't quite dusk but the streets were empty and people were already pulling their blackout curtains as she turned towards home.

'Evening, miss, going home, are you? I would before it gets too dark,' an ARP Warden said as she rounded the corner not a hundred yards from Ivy's house.

'Yes, I'm nearly there. I just live down this road,' Rose replied and thanked him.

But just then, to her horror, the air was filled with the piercing noise of air-raid sirens , giving the warning of an aerial bombing.

'Hurry, miss, get to a shelter; it must be York's turn to be hit tonight again. Here let me take your arm,' the warden said, moving towards her.

'No, no, leave me. I must go and make sure my mother-in-law-to-be is safe. We've our own Anderson shelter in the back garden that we share with our neighbours.' Rose pulled away from his grip and ran without looking back at the warden, who was already busily directing people out of their homes to the safety of a communal shelter up the road.

Rose pushed open the front door and ran into the front room where Ivy was still enjoying her radio play. Ivy had a habit of dismissing the air-raid warnings, saying her old bones weren't worth saving

'Ivy, the air-raid sirens are sounding! We're in danger of being bombed! Come on, take my arm and let's go to the shelter in the back garden. I bet the neighbours are already there.' Rose spoke urgently, hoping that Ivy would get a move on.

'Wait, I need my blanket,' Ivy said as she stood up from her chair, 'and I could do with a cup of tea, Rose. I'm going to miss the last few minutes of Tommy; can't I just stop and listen to him out?'

'No, I'm sorry. Now come on, take my hand and let's get to the shelter. You can listen to Tommy another time, providing we don't get bombed, and I'll make a cup of tea once the sirens give the all-clear.' Rose took Ivy's arm and almost pull her through the house to the back door, the older woman complaining all the time.

'You go. I don't like that tin box under the ground, and the Fletchers think themselves something special. What if I need a pee? I'm not showing myself up while I'm in there with them.' Ivy continued to resist as Rose walked her down the garden path to the shelter that Ned and Peter Fletcher had built for moments just like this before he had gone to war.

'It'll be all right. Look, the door is open! They're yelling for us to get in, and just in time by the sound of it,' Rose said, as she helped Ivy over the threshold of the half-buried Anderson shelter that was covered with earth just as she heard the first bomb drop and the drone of German bombers overhead.

'Oh heavens, I never thought that they'd bomb us here!' Ivy caught her breath and sat down hard on the metal bench next to Susan Fletcher. 'What's there to bomb here? The airfield's a good few miles away —not that I want them to aim there, of course.'

'Well, they've obviously got their eye on something. Let's hope that it's not Rowntree's, else we'll all be blown to kingdom come,' Susan replied and she felt her stomach churn as she heard another explosion and the sound of aircraft fire overhead. 'They're risking all our lives with that munitions site being where it is. My Peter is on the night shift there. I only hope he's safe.' Susan put her arm round her young son Robert, holding him close as she gazed into the gloom of the blacked-out Anderson shelter. 'It's all right, we're safe here,' she said and patted his head.

'My sister's there too; she started the night shift this week. And I hope my mother is all right; she'll be on her own, but she's got good neighbours.' Rose held Ivy's hand tightly as another bomb fell and the drone of the bombers and the sound of fighter aircraft chasing them with attacking fire could be heard.

'You should have gone to look after your mother. I'd have been all right,' Ivy said, and squeezed Rose's hand.

'Listen, that'll be our Ned showing those Jerries what for; he'll get the devils.'

'Ned's a pilot in bombers, Mother, not fighting planes; he's in a Halifax, so it won't be him tackling the Jerries,' Rose replied, not saying that Ned was probably doing the same as the pilots above to families deep in Germany. Her heart beat fast as she heard the combat overhead and prayed that her family and friends were safe.

After an hour of living in dread Ivy sighed. 'I know. I just get muddled up sometimes. He's brave is my son, and all the lads are that are keeping us safe.' She paused. 'It's gone quiet – listen! They've fought them off, but somebody somewhere has had a pelting this evening.'

The three women sighed as the air-raid siren eventually sounded giving the all-clear and they all looked at one another and hugged Robert as he wiped away a tear in the darkness. 'Do you think it's fit to go out? They didn't drop bombs directly on us else we would have felt it more,' Susan Fletcher said as she edged towards the doorway, feeling her way along the ridges of the corrugated-iron hut.

'Yes, let's get out. I don't like in here. The sooner I'm out, the better; it's quite claustrophobic.' Ivy stood up with trembling legs as Susan opened the door to the darkness of early evening and the smell of aviation fuel in the air. 'Well, our houses are still standing, but somebody's isn't, poor souls.' Ivy took hold of Rose's hand and Rose could feel the old woman shaking. 'I never thought I would live to see the likes of this.'

'Come on, Ivy, let's get you back home and settled for

the evening. We shouldn't have to endure another attack today,' Rose said quietly.

'My lad and his mates will show them. What they give they must expect to receive. Some poor souls in York will be shedding tears because of their doings tonight. Did you think it sounded as if they were bombing the railway station? They'll not have dared touch the Minster; Churchill wouldn't let them!' Ivy mumbled, as she made her way back to her chair and covered her legs with her blanket. 'Have we enough milk for a mug of Ovaltine? Or am I to do without again before my bed?' She looked up at Rose.

'I can make Ovaltine, but half milk and half water, else we'll have no milk for the morning,' Rose replied, wondering if Ivy was right in thinking that it was the railway station that had been targeted. She hoped that nobody had been killed or injured, and couldn't help but think of her old boyfriend Larry; he'd have been at work cleaning the trains' boilers, she thought, as she watched the pan of milk and water come to the boil before stirring it into the amber grains of the Ovaltine. No doubt the attack would have brought heartache for somebody. She sat down with Ivy and tried hard not to think of her Ned flying over Germany.

Later that night Rose tossed and turned in her bed, looking up at the ceiling and counting the minutes on the bedside clock. She couldn't sleep, she wouldn't sleep, until she heard Ned's signal above the house.

Daylight spread its claws along her bedroom ceiling when it was four a.m. but still there was no signal from

Ned that his plane was back. Where was he? Had he forgotten to tell her that he had returned or, worse still, had he been shot down somewhere over darkest war-torn Europe?

Rose buried her head in her pillows and cried. *Please God, please God, let my Ned be safe and back home.*

9

The talk inside the munitions factory at Rowntree's the next morning was of the previous evening's air strike and the fear it had spread among the workers when they'd heard the siren. The spotter who was placed right on the top of Rowntree's main factory roof had sounded the works alarm before the main siren went off and it had caused panic in the workforce.

'Lord, I'm tired. I don't like working nights and I was so frightened last night as we rushed across to the shelter in the Rose Garden. Still, everybody kept their spirits up with singing, but if it had hit here, we would all have been goners. But it's so claustrophobic. I hate it in there; we are all packed like sardines.' Molly yawned and changed out of her overalls and into her day clothes and closed her locker behind her before she went to be patted down by the guard who was working his way through most of the women, all of whom had romantic designs on him.

'I wonder where they hit. They definitely bombed somewhere; you could hear it even though we were underground. It was frightening.' Connie frowned and batted the guard's hands as he did his job a little too intently. 'Dirty devil, I'll report you. I'm not that sort,' she said, causing the guard to glare at her before catching up with Molly, who was waiting for her just outside the main door. 'He gets far too familiar, does that one. He should know us two are not trollops, unlike some I could mention.'

Gone were the nerves that the girls used to have when the security men had first appeared in their military uniforms. They were just men to them now. It was the girls and women that they worked alongside that they should respect, as they handled explosives everyday. Girls like themselves. 'Well, it looks like everything around here is still standing,' Molly said, as she breathed in the fresh morning air and linked her arm through Connie's. 'I'll be so glad to get into my bed and sleep; I hope Mam has got some porridge on the go.'

'I don't think I want anything. I just need my bed, to crawl under my sheets until late afternoon and not to even think of filling another shell,' Connie said, and then she went quiet as they reached the end of the street and saw Winnie talking to her next-door neighbour.

She spotted them coming down the road towards her. 'Have you seen our Rose this morning, you two?' Winnie asked, as soon as they stopped next to her.

'No, Mam,' Molly replied. 'She doesn't start work until eight, and besides we don't mix any more; we're not allowed.'

'Gladys here tells me that it was the railway that took the hit last night. None of the trains are running today, but, worse still, she says the bomb landed on the engine sheds and killed four men. I was just wondering if one of the fellas could be her old flame Larry Battersby. It's to be hoped not; he was a good lad. It's a terrible shame for whoever it was, though.'

Molly sighed and rubbed her eyes. 'I hope not too, but there's plenty that work there; it could have been anybody.'

'It frightened us to death in the factory,' Connie chipped in. 'You've never seen any of us walk so fast to that shelter. We would all have run if we were allowed, but we have our orders.'

'They could have blown the whole town up if it had hit those munitions. I'm surprised at Rowntree's letting them commandeer the place what with their beliefs.' Gladys crossed her arms and scowled.

'Now, Gladys, we all have to do our bit. We'll be safe, stop fretting. Right, girls, let's get you two fed and to bed ready for your next shift. And let's hope that it isn't bad news for the Battersby family. I might not be that keen on them, especially the mother, but I'd not wish them any heartache.'

'We'll soon know, I suppose,' Connie said. 'It'll be in the papers. At least we don't get hit so often, not like some places in the country. York doesn't have anything important enough to be bombed. Or at least didn't until the munitions factory came to Rowntree's.' She followed Winnie inside for her breakfast and much-needed bed.

'So at least they got you all into the shelter on time. It will have been good practice if nothing else. My heart goes out to anyone living in more built-up towns down south. I couldn't live with the threat of being bombed every day,' Winnie said, as both girls finished their porridge. 'Get yourselves to bed and I'll yell for you when it's time to get up for your next shift. Your nights and days will be all mixed up by the end of the week, but it can't be helped; we all have to do our bit.'

'Thanks, Mam; I am so ready for my bed.' Bleary-eyed Molly bent down and kissed her mother on her head. 'I didn't think it would be like this. Perhaps our Annie got it right. Hopefully she'll write to us soon.'

'Yes, I can't help but wonder how she's going on; it's strange without her here. I only seem to have half my family now with Rose not living here.' Winnie sighed and thought of better times when all her girls and her husband had sat round the kitchen table. Those times had well and truly gone, and the days were long and just a little empty now if she was to be honest with herself.

'Never mind, Mam, you've still got me and Connie, although you don't see a lot of us nowadays.' Molly followed Connie up the stairs and left Winnie on her own with her thoughts and the dirty breakfast pots.

She would wash up later, Winnie decided, as she went and sat in the front room in the comfort of one of the easy chairs where she would close her eyes for just twenty minutes or so. After all, she'd not slept much the previous night either, as fear had ruled her head, and she too had thought like Gladys that they would all go up in smoke and a loud bang if the Germans aimed wrong. The mantelpiece clock ticked steadily and Winnie found herself falling asleep, grateful that hopefully all her girls were safe for another day.

'Oh my Lord!' Winnie woke with a start. The banging

on the front door made her jump up and look at the time, which made her panic given it was eleven thirty and nearly dinnertime.

She rushed to the front-room window and pulled the net curtains back to see who was making the din at her door. Her hair needed brushing and she was only half awake as she realized that it was Larry Battersby's mother and that she looked as stern as ever. Knocking on the window to get her attention, Winnie signed that she was coming but to give her time to get there.

'There's no need to knock my door down, Maude Battersby. What brings you here? Tell me quietly instead of hammering and shouting, because I've two lasses asleep upstairs after doing the night shift at Rowntree's,' Winnie said in a rush before she took in that the usually hard-faced woman had tears running down her cheeks. 'What is it? Is it your Larry? I heard that the bomber had dropped its load on the railway yard and I did worry he might have been there.'

Maude nodded. 'He was; he was cleaning the engine out when the bomb dropped. The engine smoke box shielded him a bit, but he's in a terrible state: burnt from head to toe and only just alive. However, alive he is, and I'm thankful. But, Winnie, all he's asking for is your Rose.'

Winnie looked at the woman who had been partly responsible for the break-up of the romance between their two children and couldn't help feeling sorry for her. 'Aye, come in. Our Rose doesn't live here any more. She lives with her fiancé's mother down in the new

Rowntree's village, but she's at work at the moment. Sit yourself down and I'll make you a brew, and then I'll go and see if I can get her out of work for you.' Winnie looked at the uncleared table and thought that was of little worry as she heard the hardened matriarch of the Battersby family sobbing. 'He'll be all right, pet. The doctors are good nowadays.'

Maude shook her head. 'No, he'll not. He's delirious and he keeps calling out for Rose. I'll not stop for a drink. Please just see if you can get her and tell her that he's loved no one else since she left him. He keeps whispering under his breath that he has to make peace with her. He's in York County Hospital, Ward Nine, and please tell her to have some pity for him and me. I'm going to lose my son and I might not have been right with your lass, but I pray that she'll be right with my lad for just one last time.' Maude took hold of Winnie's hand and looked at her with pleading eyes. 'Go for her please.' Then she left in as big a whirlwind as she had arrived, leaving Winnie standing at the sink with a half-empty kettle.

Winnie shouted after her down the garden path. 'I'll go and she'll come. Ward Nine. We'll be there as fast as we can.' Then she got her thoughts together, put her coat and hat on, and ran out of the house, leaving a note for the sleeping girls on the kitchen table and hoping that they would wake in time for their next shift. Then she ran to drag Rose from her work whether she wanted to or not.

*

Rose ran up the stairs to the ward that Larry was in, her heart beating fast. All heads had turned when her mother had burst through the doors to the meeting that she was attending at Rowntree's – much to the alarm of the secretary that was guarding the room from intrusion. She thought at first that she had brought her news of Ned. And, truth be told, she was relieved when she heard her mother say Larry's name, although she soon felt ashamed of that.

She stood at the doors of the ward now and plucked up the courage to enter the bay where she could see nurses and doctors concentrating on their patients and where Larry's mother and oldest brother stood. Rose felt her stomach turn as she approached the man that she had once loved.

Maude Battersby saw her approaching and held her hand out, pushing Larry's brother out of the way. 'He's been waiting for you; he wants to tell you something,' she said, wiping her eyes and taking in Rose's look of sheer horror and revolt at the burnt skin and disfigurement on the face and body of her boy.

'Are you the girlfriend he's been calling for?' the doctor said. 'We're doing all we can to save him, but he's very weak. He'll be glad that you have come; he's asked for you constantly.' He motioned for Rose to sit down next to Larry.

'Rose, is that you? I'm so glad that you've come,' Larry managed to say quietly with closed bloodied eyes and scars on his face.

'It's me, Larry. Oh, what have they done to you?' Rose sobbed and pulled out her handkerchief.

'It doesn't matter about me, but before I go I need to make my peace,' Larry said even more faintly.

'Ssshh, save your strength,' Rose whispered, and despite the scars she took hold of his left hand and held it.

'Rose, I just want you to know that I love you and that I'm sorry for . . .for you know what . . .what happened. I wanted to marry you more than anything else in the world,' Larry said quietly and then seemed to struggle for breath.

Rose swallowed her tears, knowing her words were important. 'I know, shh. It's in the past. I love you too.' She knew she was lying to help a dying man. 'I forgive you, my love.' She wiped a tear away and tried to forget the night that Larry, in his anger, had tried to rape her. He had loved her; it was true – he'd loved her since they were at school together –and perhaps he was right when he had said that she had ideas above her station.

Rose looked up at Larry's family; they were preparing for the worst and so was the doctor, who asked her to leave.

They had made their peace with one another and now the battle was on to save Larry's life.

'I don't know why you rushed to Larry Battersby's bedside. I thought he was in the past,' Ivy Evans said as Rose sat down across the kitchen table from her mother-in-law-to-be. 'There's my Ned fighting the Hun and you're at another man's bedside. Not to mention the money he'll have lost you with taking time off work.'

'He asked for me, Ivy; we've known one another a long time. But I don't love him; I love Ned and only Ned. I was just comforting a dying man and, believe me, he is dying – or it would be better if he did die, given the state he's in.' Rose had to bite her tongue to stop herself from saying more. She could understand Ivy standing up for her son, but Larry still had a small place in her heart and she could not have rested without making peace with him.

Ivy sighed. 'As long as you are faithful to my lad. He's all I've got and I was so glad when he took a fancy to you. I just knew you were meant for one another.' She looked at Rose. 'Is it just Larry that you're thinking of or is there something else on your mind? You've not been right all day, not even this morning before you set off for work.'

Rose looked down and held her breath as a tear rolled down her cheeks. 'I didn't want to say anything, but I never heard Ned's plane return last night . . .I know he was on a mission because he sent me a note to tell me, and he said that it was a dangerous one. I'm beside myself with worry but I didn't want to trouble you . . .'

Ivy stilled, her eyes filled with pity as well as concern. 'Oh, my lass, and you went to go and see that lad as well, not knowing where Ned was! You might have missed hearing Ned's return, you might have dropped off to sleep and missed his plane, or happen he went straight back to the airfield instead of circling.' But despite her reassurance Ivy looked concerned; she knew Rose always listened out for him when she knew he was flying. And it must have been a dangerous mission if he had sent her a note.

'Perhaps I'm fretting too much and the sight of what can happen when you're bombed has unnerved me. Ned will probably walk into this house the minute he gets leave and tell us both off for worrying,' Rose declared, deciding not to show Ivy the note.

Rose sipped her tea and held back her tears. Seeing Larry so badly burnt had upset her, but Ned perhaps not safe at his base obviously troubled her even more. The true face of war was beginning to show itself and it was not nice.

The following morning Rose got up and went to work as usual, though she had hardly slept and the bags underneath her eyes told of the worry that she carried. Waiting outside the Rowntree's entrance stood Molly, also looking half asleep, and Rose couldn't help but notice the beginnings of a yellow sheen to her skin that was more noticeable in the summer sunlight.

'I'm glad that you're here, Rose. Mam said I had to wait for you and that if you wanted to come home with me, to tell you to do so. She would have come herself, but she thought it better coming from me.' Molly reached for her sister's hand. 'Maude Battersby called round just before I came to work yesterday evening. I'm sorry, but Larry died about an hour after you left him; there was nothing they could do for him.'

Rose hung her head, feeling like a small piece of her heart had just died. 'It's for the best. Poor Larry, he would never have returned to anything like his old life or been able to work. I did really love him at one time. Do you know when the funeral is? I'll have to go, but I'll feel uneasy.'

'No, she never said. They won't have arranged anything yet. Mam says to come home for a while if you want, and to tell them in there what's happened; they'll understand.' Molly nodded her head in the direction of the factory and let out a huge yawn.

'No, I'll be all right; it's better to keep busy and I've Ivy to see to at dinnertime.' Rose looked with concern at her youngest sister, who had suddenly grown up into a woman. 'You get yourself home. You must be shattered. You needn't have waited for me; you could just have left a message.'

'It's all right. I've been sitting in what's left of the Rose Garden, enjoying the sunshine and fresh air, and, besides, our Rose, I've been admiring the new lad that checks us all in and out. He's so handsome; better than the other one. Connie has her eye on him too, so I made it my business to talk to him just a little this morning. Just to say hello and isn't it a beautiful day. I didn't get far, though.'

'Molly Freeman, are you showing an interest in boys?' Rose said, smiling at her sister. 'Make sure that you get a good one, otherwise they'll only break your heart.'

'Well, you've got a good one in Ned, and look what would have happened if you had married Larry. You'd have been a grieving widow,' Molly said grimly.

Rose sighed. 'Oh, I might be a grieving fiancé anyway,

Molly. I never heard him return the night before last, but nobody has come to tell us anything.'

Molly leaned forward and hugged her sister who she could see was close to tears. 'He'll be all right, Rose; you'd know by now if there was anything wrong. Somebody would have sent word.'

'I know I'm just being silly. Now, you get home and tell Mam I'm fine, and I'll get to work. Don't tell her about Ned, else she'll only come round and natter with Ivy and the two will send me crackers.' Rose kissed her sister on the cheek and then turned and smiled at her. 'Lovely sunburn you've got –you look almost radiant!'

'Get to work, you cheeky devil; you know I'm not sunburnt. Love you, Rose. Try not to worry.'

'Love you too, little sister. Now get to bed.'

10

'It's a sad day for York, losing those railway workers, and I'm sorry that your old beau lost his fight. But, as you say, perhaps it's for the best if he was to be left scarred and in pain.' Ivy was calling through to Rose as she washed the evening meal's dinner pots up and put them away.

'Yes, he would never have been the same,' Rose replied, and then she took off her apron and joined Ivy on the settee, only to stand up straight away as she heard a car pull up on the driveway.

Her heart pounded. It sounded like Ned's best friend Peter's car! It had to be the pair of them, she thought, as she raced to the doorway and saw the shape of a flight cap through the window.

'Is that my lad? I told you that he'd be safe and home soon,' Ivy shouted, as Rose opened the door, only to find Peter standing alone on the doorstep looking serious and glum.

'Peter, are you on your own? Where's Ned?'

Rose felt rising panic as she peered over Peter's shoulder, hoping that Ned was about to get out of the car and that all would be well.

Peter took his cap off and looked at his best friend's intended and dreaded telling her the news that he said he would personally deliver to Ned's family. 'I'm sorry, Rose.'

'He's not . . .he's not dead, is he?' Rose felt her legs go weak as Peter took her arm and helped her inside and into a chair next to Ivy.

Both women looked at Peter, fearing he was about to tell them the worst.

'Oh my Lord, my lad, he can't be!' Ivy held a handkerchief to her mouth and took Rose's hand.

'No, we don't think that he's dead. I saw him bail out just before we reached the coast of France. Bloody Jerries were on our tails and Ned had a new inexperienced crew with him. Their plane caught the worst of the flak after our bombing of the Tempelhof Airfield near Siemensstadt, Berlin. He thought he was going to make it and he nearly did; he could just about see Blighty when his engine caught fire and they had no option but to bail out.' Peter went silent and looked at both women as they cried.

'I think I saw him gather his parachute and run for cover in a nearby copse, but I could have been wrong. It was hell up there; we were being fired on and you didn't have time to hang around He was alive I think. The Resistance will hopefully find him and get him home, or if the Jerries do capture him, he'll be a POW, but alive, that's the main thing.' Peter fiddled with his cap; he had been dreading telling Rose and Ned's mother, but he knew he had to as Ned's best friend and the one who had convinced him to join up.

'He told me he knew it was a dangerous mission. He

asked me to look after Ivy and to remember that he always loved me,' Rose wailed.

'Yes, you two meant the world to him and still do, so don't despair. If I know Ned, he'll be keeping himself safe and he'll be back with us as soon as he can get himself across the Channel and home. We fulfilled our part anyway; there won't be many planes taking off from Tempelhof for the time being. We saw to that. But it was bad; we were lucky to get out with just the casualties that we sustained. Ned was heroic. He led the bombing raid – I wish I'd been part of his crew; he might not have got hit then.' Peter dropped his head low and didn't look at the two women; he felt that he had let his best friend down.

'It isn't your fault, and I'm glad that you've come to tell us both,' Rose replied and blew her nose. 'As you say, he's not dead, and we all know Ned has fighting spirit; he will return to us.' Rose squeezed Ivy's hand. 'He will, won't he, Ivy?'

'Aye, he will if he can, pet,' Ivy replied, and she hoped that she was right.

The night Ned bailed had been one of the utmost fear but now, exposed to the elements two days later, his heart was beating faster than ever. He lay low in the trees that hid him from the Germans. In the distance he could see the wreckage of the Halifax and a group of soldiers gathered round it. Luckily, he had buried his parachute when he had landed and there was no visible trace of him, unlike the tail gunner who had landed not far from the plane, breaking his leg and who was now being pushed on to an army wagon to be taken away as a prisoner of war.

Ned turned on his back and breathed in deeply, looking up at the sky through the rustle of poplar tree leaves and closed his eyes. He was lucky to be alive, and his hunger over the last few days told him he very much so – he had foraged on what he could find in the French countryside. The bomber had hole after hole in its fuselage; they should not really have made it out of Germany, let alone this far into France. If only they had managed another thirty miles, they would have made it to the south coast and at least have landed in England, even if not anywhere near York. His young co-pilot had died instantly when a piece of shrapnel had hit him as the Germans had thrown all they had got at them. He had tried to keep him alive but failed as he fought with the controls of the plane. It was the first time anyone had died in front of Ned and the image haunted him as he lay thanking God he was alive. The rest of the crew had bailed out as soon as he had given the order, knowing that the plane was not going to make it, and he hoped that they had made safe landings and not been found by the Germans like the tail gunner.

He thought of Rose and his mother back home; he had known it would be a mission fraught with danger and was glad that he had sent the note to Rose telling her that he loved her. He lay still and listened – he could hear the engine of the wagon being started and the German soldiers shouting at one another. '*Schnell,* ' he heard being yelled loud and clear, and he hoped that none of them would come near him and discover him. Every muscle in his body relaxed as he heard them drive away down the nearby road. *Poor Johnny Tyler, what would become of him?* he thought, closing his eyes and wondering the same about himself as sleep and exhaustion took over his body.

Ned awoke sometime later to a poking in the ribs and a sudden shake and the sound of two French voices discussing his presence under the tree, wondering if he was dead or alive. The farmer and his young son jumped back and threatened him with their pitchfork as Ned moved and opened his eyes.

Ned put his hands up and looked at them both.'*Français*, are you *Français*?' He held his hand out to be shaken, but they both stood back. 'Do you speak English?'

'*Oui*, a little. Are you the pilot? The Germans will be looking for you,' the older man replied, and then summoned his son to offer Ned a drink from the flask that hung round his neck.

Ned accepted it gratefully

'We will take you to our home; you must not be seen or it will be the worse for all of us.' The farmer spoke in broken English and his son helped Ned to his feet and indicated for him to follow them. 'The Germans are everywhere; they will shoot us all if we are found. Hurry, my farm is just through those woods. You can hide in the barn until I can contact somebody to help you.'

'Thank you. I am grateful and I know you are risking your lives,' Ned said as he followed quickly and took in the wreckage of the plane that he had so nearly died in, before heading into the cover of the woods. 'Can I ask your name?'

'My name is Pierre, and this is Jacques, my son – that is all you need to know. Now keep quiet and try to walk quicker; the Germans will be looking for you and your crew.'

Ned nodded but said nothing as he followed the two men through the small trees until they came to a clearing and a rustic-looking farmhouse with farm buildings surrounding it.

'I will put you in the barn, up in the loft behind some bales of hay,' Pierre said and summoned his son to run into the house to tell his mother what was happening. 'You should be safe there, but if they come and find you, I beg you not to say we have helped you.' Pierre pulled the heavy wooden doors open and ushered Ned into the barn, which was covered with straw and had a horse stabled in the corner, making it feel warm and welcoming, smelling of the countryside. 'You climb up those ladders and pull the hay round you. Some food will be sent to you and something to drink.'

'Thank you. I really can't thank you enough,' Ned replied sincerely, before taking the first rung up the ladder and to safety as the farmer closed the large doors, leaving Ned in near darkness apart from a shaft of light from the forking hole that showed the dust of the stable dancing in the air like fairies.

Once hidden in the hay and with his stomach filled with bread and cheese and slightly light-headed from the wine that Jacques had brought him, Ned lay back and allowed himself to think of home. Would he ever return and see those he loved again? He was now at the mercy of anybody who could help him.

11

'I don't know. Larry Battersby died and now Ned is missing, and our Rose will have to be strong,' Winnie said, as she sat and took tea with Ivy. 'You must be bothered to death. Your children mean more to you than life itself if you're anything like me.'

'He's everything to me, is my Ned. He was there for me when his father died and he'd made himself into something at Rowntree's. He should never have enlisted in the RAF, but I'm still proud of my lad and I only hope that he's still alive and looking after himself.'

Winnie looked at the folded newspaper on the table. 'At least we know that he was last seen alive, unlike some of these they have listed here; their mothers will be truly broken-hearted.' She picked up the edition of the *York Courier* and looked at the report of the missing and dead airmen from the local airbase at Elvington Airfield. 'They knew they'd perhaps not come back, flying that far into Germany. Rose said he'd sneaked a note out to her to tell her as much. She must have been worried to death when she didn't hear him return as normal.' She sipped her tea.

'Aye, and she never said a word to me; she'd promised not to worry me. And I was sharp with her for going and sitting with her old fella as well. I felt terrible; her head must have been all over the place. She's a good lass. Ned and Rose are made for one another. I pray that he returns.'

'Rose will wait for him no matter how long it takes for him to come home.'

'Are you all right that Rose stays with me, Winnie?' Ivy said after a pause. 'I don't know what I'd do without her; I'm a bit lost on my own.' Ivy spoke quietly and hoped that Rose had not mentioned coming home.

Winnie smiled and patted her now good friend's hand. 'It goes without saying, Ivy, and, besides, she's promised Ned she'll look after you and us Freemans never go back on a promise. You sleep easy, Ivy; you're part of our family now. You'll be looked after by all of us. Now ought we to have a game of rummy to try and cheer ourselves up?'

'Aye and a nip of sherry, just to keep our spirits up. Medicinal, of course.' Ivy winked as she indicated where the sherry was kept. She was glad that Winnie had come round to see her, otherwise the day would have been long with Rose returning to work. A drink and a game of cards would put the hurt and loss she was feeling for her son to one side and stop her thinking the worst, imagining him lying wounded or perhaps dying somewhere in France. It was all she could think of since Peter had called to tell them the news. She prayed someone would help her son and get him home safe and sound.

Rose sat in front of the Rowntree's board and explained about Ned being missing in France. She hadn't meant to break down in front of Seebohm Rowntree but found herself sobbing now as he stood next to her and gently put his hand on her shoulders.

'He's a clever man, Ned; he will return, I'm sure. It sounds as if he landed safely; I'm sure he will try and make his way back home. I've heard that a lot of the French are fighting against the German regime and are helping the Allies in whatever way they can. He's got brains; he'll keep low and make his way back home as long as the Germans haven't captured him.' Seebohm looked at his board of trustees. 'This should never have happened; the world should not be at war.'

'Thank you, sir, for your kind words. I didn't mean to bring my troubles to work,' Rose said quietly and she blew her nose before rising from her chair. 'I'll go back to my work now. At least that keeps me occupied. When I go about me job, especially when I oversee the packaging of the Jungle Chocolate, I know that it's going to our troops who are fighting for all of us.'

'That's the spirit. Every bar of that chocolate brings a smile to a soldier's face and hopefully somebody in France is doing the same for your Ned, giving him shelter and food and drink. Now, our way to beat the Hun is by not weakening and doing our jobs. So, gentlemen, let's get back to it and, Miss Freeman, I hope that you get positive news shortly.'

Rose walked quietly out of the boardroom, leaving the men still talking; it was still a man's world, even though they did encourage women employees to take part. But only when needed; they regarded women as the weaker sex. It was usually an all-male board and they had all looked embarrassed as she had broken down in front of them. She breathed in deeply and walked quickly to her post, her head down and tears in her eyes.

Mary put her hand out to stop her. 'Oh, are you all right? It must be awful what you're going through. I've only just heard about Larry. You must be feeling so down. You should have told me. I always knew you could do better, but he wasn't a bad man really.' Mary put her arms round her best friend and held her tight as she burst into tears on Mary's shoulder. 'That's it, let it all out. Don't keep it in. I'm here. Come on, they won't miss us for ten minutes. Come and have a tea in what's left of the canteen and tell me everything.'

Rose sniffed. 'I shouldn't. I've just updated the board and Seebohm Rowntree, and he was telling everyone to get on with their jobs, although he was very kind.'

'Yes, and if I know them, I bet most of his cronies are still sat round the table, enjoying a glass of brandy. Now, come on, a cup of tea and then you can get back to chocolate making.' Mary put her arm round Rose's waist and they walked down the corridor to the canteen.

'Now tell me, how are you feeling? And don't hold back, because I can take it. I often lie awake at night wondering where my Joe is and if he's safe or whether he's been torpedoed and left to drown. At least from what I hear Ned was alive the last time Peter saw him; it could be worse.' Mary shoved a cup of over-stewed tea under Rose's nose. 'Now drink and calm yourself.'

'Oh, Mary, I just feel as if my world has fallen apart. I didn't think I had any feelings for Larry Battersby, but when I saw him in such a state I remembered how it used to be between us before it went wrong, and how he used to hold me and tell me he loved me. I felt so bad about the way I turned my back on him. And then, as if by rough justice, the following day I learn about Ned and that hurts so much. I love Ned more than anybody or anything. I want him back safe and sound, and all I can think about is him being injured as badly as Larry. Maybe Peter was mistaken about seeing him make it from his plane. Even if he did make it out safely, he's in France and it's crawling with Nazis; they could shoot him on sight or take him to a concentration camp and I'll never hear of him again.' Rose took a small sip of tea and cradled the teacup in her hands as she thought the worst.

'Rose, we're all the same: anybody whose husband, boyfriend or son is in the forces wakes up every morning just praying their loved one is alive. The best we can do for them is to be there when they return and to fight the Nazis in any way we can. Don't fret. Ned will come home safe and sound, I'm sure of that. The RAF will have connections to get him out once he's been located. Now you stop worrying.'

Rose sighed. 'Sorry, I'm being selfish, I know I am. At least I've no children, although I do have Ivy to look after.'

'She's probably harder work than any child. Old folk are set in their ways and she must be fretting something terrible.'

'My mam's visiting her today, so the sherry will have been taken out of its hiding place. I know what them two get up to behind my back, yet they'll both look so innocent when I get back.' Rose for the first time in days smiled.

'That's better. Now, don't worry. There's nothing we can do about our lot, except be here for one another.' Mary rose from the table. 'I have to get back, else somebody is bound to have a dig and say I'm fraternizing with management.' She grinned. 'Although everybody will have sympathy with you.'

'Yes, and I'll stop feeling sorry for myself. You are right – you've got to get on with life. Everybody is putting their lives on hold to fight this evil. They can't be seen to be winning.'

'That's it. Best foot forward,' Mary said, and for a brief moment wondered who was in charge of who.

'It is about bloody time they gave us a bit of happiness in this place,' Betty said and grinned across at the new man in her life – the guard that frisked her every day and made a meal of it – and winked. Music from the radio started to blare out from the tannoy that had just been fitted in the fuse-making room. 'Anything to make life a bit more bearable is gratefully accepted. Eh, girls?' Betty said, and she kept on filling her share of shells, everyone could do it in their sleep by now.

'I don't know if I'll be able to concentrate as well with this playing, but I must admit it's better than listening to idle chatter or silence,' Molly said to Connie, and she concentrated on her job as the hourly news was read out over the tannoy.

A cheer went around the room as news time ended at the number of German planes that had been shot down by the British. It was the morale boost that everyone needed: realizing that the long hours and dangerous work were worth all their effort and giving them a purpose.

'Those might not have been shot down if it wasn't for us. I'm proud of what we're doing. My skin might be yellow, my hair going ginger where my fringe comes out from my turban, but we're protecting our lads and this country. Just like any soldier.' Connie spoke quietly and then flashed a grin at Molly as a popular song came on the tannoy. 'Ey up, it's "Ragtime Cowboy Joe"! I love this song. Come on, Molly, sing along. The music makes our job a lot better.'

'I will in a bit once I've got used to the noise and can concentrate,' Molly replied, as she filled another batch of shells, and glanced at Betty and Connie singing along and making the most of the new facility.

'We are the Cowgirls Union. Molly, join in!' Betty yelled. 'The more members, the better.'

Molly wouldn't be bullied, even though for the first time in weeks she had a smile on her face as the next tray of shells came her way.

'Sshh, did you hear that on the tannoy? They're asking for us to take a soldier's washing home with us if we can. There are thousands of soldiers based around York, but we never get a chance to meet them. Perhaps if we take some of their washing home with us, we could get to meet them. Surely they'd come and thank us, wouldn't they?' Connie said. as the music was interrupted with a Rowntree's announcement 'When would we have time to wash and iron it? Mam would end up doing it, not us, and she'd only moan at us,' Molly replied. She sighed, thinking that the tannoy was just adding complications to her life.

'Well, I'll ask her this morning when we get home. It could be her chance to help with the war effort.' Connie grinned. 'Speaking of soldiers, have you got any closer to altering clothes to make us dresses? I saw you lugging the sewing machine down to the front room the other day, but I haven't heard you using it.' Connie was thinking that doing washing for a soldier might bring romance in her life and she wanted to look her best.

'I've got it working, but the clothes that I could alter are so worn and thin.' Molly sighed. 'You can't get anything that you need nowadays.'

'Do you want some cloth, girls?' Betty said quietly. 'Would parachute silk do? I've got contacts on the black market and I can get my hands on some used parachute silk, but you say nothing to nobody! It's no good for the job it was intended for but it makes lovely dresses, so don't feel guilty about using it. Just dye it the colour you want and it'll look grand. And if you want stockings or lipstick, just drop me a nod. I have contacts who can get most stuff.' Betty winked at both girls.

Molly and Connie looked at one another and smiled. They had both heard on the grapevine that the guard dabbled in all sorts, including the black market. Now it was clear why Betty was all over the burly guard. It wasn't just lust; maybe she was friendly with him for what she could get out of him too. It couldn't be his looks or his chatty ways because he had neither

The weeks of nights on and then days off were starting to take their toll.

'You two look tired this morning. Night shifts don't do anything for you,' Winnie said as both girls entered the kitchen and slumped at the table.

'Yes, well, they're blasting music and news at us over a

tannoy and somebody did more singing than fuse filling last night. I kept watching her shove the detonators in as she sang along and I thought, *Any moment now there's going to be an almighty bang and all that would be left would be Connie's shoes.*' Molly yawned and looked across at Connie, who seemed more exhausted than usual.

'Don't be daft. I'd not blow anybody up; they have to be activated first,' Connie said with an innocent look on her face.

'They don't, you idiot. Once you put that detonator in at the top, it would blow up if you dropped it or if you knocked it by accident on the red-painted side. Why do you think I concentrate so much? I thought that you must have forgotten that, else you wouldn't be wiggling your hips to the music while filling them.' Molly couldn't believe that Connie hadn't realized that every day since they had started work there their lives had been at risk.

Connie gasped. 'Oh, Lord. I didn't think they would explode until they were taken down into the main magazine. I never heard them tell us that when we started. Do you mean I could have killed myself nearly every day I've worked there?'

'Yes, you idiot, although I can't remember being told that either. I've just worked it out watching them in charge. I don't think a lot of people do. We weren't told how dangerous the job was in case we wouldn't do it.'

'I'm shocked. I honestly never knew,' Connie said, chewing on a piece of bread that was nearly stale and then deciding it wasn't worth the effort and that bed was a better place to be. She left the table without another word.

Winnie folded her arms and looked at Molly. 'She must be tired and a bit thick. Even I knew you could blow yourselves up and I don't know half what you do. Even if you didn't put the detonator in, gunpowder's not to be played with. I'm surprised they've put music on, I am!' She sat down and looked at the partly eaten crust. *Bread and butter pudding tonight*, she thought – *waste not, want not*.

'Mam, they were asking on the tannoy if anybody could take a soldier's washing home with them to help the war effort. The army camps drop it off at Rowntree's, with the soldier's name tag on and you return it the following week to pick up his next lot. Do you think Connie and I should volunteer?' Molly said quietly.

'What you're asking is if you bring some washing home, will I do it?' Winnie smiled. 'Camps are springing up all over the place around York. I wondered how they were going to keep up with basics. It's just like Rowntree's to get involved in the practical side of war instead of fighting,' she said. She looked at her daughter. 'Yes, you and Connie bring whoever's uniform you're given and I'll wash it and iron it. Though I hope they're not too fussy, because I'm not the world's best at ironing.'

'Thanks, Mam. It's just another thing we can do to help. We all cheer when we hear how many German ships and planes have been destroyed, though the people in them are just the same as us, aren't they?' Molly said and yawned. 'There'll be a German Rose waiting for her loved one to return and she'll hurt just as much as our Rose. War makes no sense.'

'No, it doesn't, love. Now you get to bed; it'll soon be time to go back to work. I'm proud of you, Molly – you're a grand lass.'

'Thanks, Mam. I love you too.' Molly hugged her mother and then made her way up to bed.

'Are you able to take a bundle of washing home?' the overlooker asked Molly as she clicked out of her night shift the following morning.

'Yes, I can and so can Connie; my mam says she doesn't mind taking in some washing,' Molly said. She watched as the overlooker passed her a bundle of clothes tied up with string and labelled with the name of the soldier that they belonged to. All Molly could think was that her mam would be glad to see that there were no white shirts and that she wouldn't have to buy some dolly blue to get them white.

'It all needs washing and ironing, and has to be back by next Tuesday when another set will be given to you.' Then the overlooker moved on to the next worker volunteering.

Both girls tucked their bundles under their arms until they were out of sight of Rowntree's and back on their home street.

'Well, whose have you got? What's his name?' Connie looked at the brown label with her soldier's name on it and read out loud. '*Corporal Michael Grady. Yorkshire Fusiliers.*'

'I've got Sergeant Burt Bradley, also of the Yorkshire Fusiliers. I wonder what they're both like. Do you think they'll be young and handsome or old and stuffy? I bet mine is the latter; he must be if he's a sergeant and he's called Burt.' Molly tucked the washing back under her arm.

'Well, I'm going to think of mine as dark-haired and handsome, and if he's in the Fusiliers he will ride a horse and look romantic.' Connie went off into a dream, thinking of her perfect man.

'Well, whoever they are, they're going to smell of Mam's carbolic washing soap and have their clothes well-scrubbed. We can dream about who the men are every week when we get their washing, because it will be the nearest we'll get to a man,' Molly groaned. 'I could do with a night out or even a walk down the streets of York for a change.'

'We'll have to try and only sleep till dinnertime on Saturday, and then we go and have a look around the shops and perhaps go to the pictures. We can always catch up on sleep on Sunday.' Connie hoped Molly would agree.

'Yes, let's do that. I haven't been into the centre of York for weeks, and I could perhaps try and find some material for us new dresses. Although material's like hen's teeth nowadays, and I don't think we will have enough ration tokens yet.'

'You don't have to bother, Molly. I've got that in hand. Betty's going to get us some of that parachute silk and some stockings through her mate. But we can buy some dye so that we don't look like we're dressed in parachute silk. Although she was also going to see if he could get his hands on some cotton material. Seemingly he can get his hands on anything you want if you're willing to pay for it.' Connie spoke with a glint in her eye. 'We're going to club together and buy some.'

Molly looked at her best friend with disgust. 'But it's from the black market; we shouldn't buy anything from him. It's wrong, Connie.'

'Everybody else does it and, besides, we can afford to now we're working all these long hours. I'm not putting my life on the line for nothing; we might as well get some pleasure from putting our lives in danger.'

'I still think it's wrong, but I must admit a new cotton dress would be nice, and I've got some lovely patterns that I got from the *Home Front Pattern Book*. They were free and look so good and easy to make.' Molly went quiet and then decided to say what she had just thought of. 'You told her that we didn't want any material that's yellow or orange, I hope? We're yellow enough without showing it off.'

'Oh, stop worrying about your skin. It'll go back to normal after we stop making those blinking munitions. Besides, everyone knows what we're doing for our lads and they're proud of that; we're admired by everyone.'

'They might, but I'm still embarrassed. My skin used to be so perfect. I don't even like being called one of the canaries that work at Rowntree's. It sounds like I'm a caged bird.' Molly opened the door to the home, hoping her mother would have breakfast in hand – she could eat a horse, although she knew it would be whatever rations would allow them.

'Stop your moaning, Molly. Think of those that are fighting for us all. Think of our Rose worried to death about Ned. We're the lucky ones,' Winnie said as soon as she heard her daughter complaining. 'Now eat your fried bread and be thankful you've got that to eat. Then I'd get your sleep; you sound tired to me.'

'I am, Mam. I could fall asleep at the table,' Molly said. 'Here, this is the washing for the soldiers. Thanks for doing it for them.' Molly passed her mother the bundle, sat down and decided she was better not saying anything else seeing as she was just moaning.

'We'll go and have some time to ourselves come this weekend. That will make us both feel better. All work and no play isn't good for us,' Connie said. She looked at her slice of fried bread – she could have done with an egg and a rasher of bacon with it, but those days had gone.

'Yes, the pair of you go and enjoy yourselves. Get out and do something, no matter how tired you are,' Winnie agreed, looking at the exhausted girls who were doing their best to keep the wheels of the war machine turning.

She was proud of all her girls; they were doing their bit, especially Annie who must be that busy that she had not yet found the time to write to her, and now she would help a little by washing the soldiers' uniforms. She looked at the labels and the clothes in neat piles and she too wondered what the owners looked like and if they were soon to go to war. They were training now at various camps around York but soon they would be fighting for their country.

The following Saturday Molly was relieved that she and Connie had some time to themselves. 'All we've done lately is go to bed, go to work, get up again and do the same again. It's so good just to have a walk down here past the Minster and through the Shambles and the market.' Molly breathed in the late-summer air and looked up at the blue skies that were clear of planes and noise. 'You wouldn't think there was a war going on, would you? People are still looking in shop windows, even though they haven't the means to buy anything, and all the teashops are open.'

'You wouldn't if you took no notice of the safety tape on every window and the barrage balloons around the Minster. The good thing is all the soldiers that aren't training and who have time on their hands are wandering the streets; some of them look so dishy. I wonder if the ones that your mam is doing the washing for are as handsome as the one over there. He looks like Clark Gable. Isn't he gorgeous?' Connie sighed and almost swooned at the sight of a group of soldiers gathered by a bench just outside the cathedral entrance. She couldn't take her eyes off them.

'Well, they didn't look at us two, so you needn't start puckering your lips or running your fingers through your hair. Not with us dressed as drab as we are and glowing yellow.' Molly looked across at the group of young soldiers and had to agree that they were indeed a handsome bunch. However, she pulled on her friend's arm as she saw two of the soldiers look at them and laugh. 'They're laughing at us, Connie. I told you they would, given we look like we do. Come on, let's get to the picture house. At least we'll be in the dark there and nobody will notice us.'

'Don't be daft. They're not laughing at us. Look, two of them are coming our way and one of them is the Clark Gable lookalike. Pretend you're looking in the shop window and ignore them.' Connie pulled her handbag on to her arm and put her nose in the air and started talking about the pair of shoes that had caught her eye in the shoe shop earlier.

'I don't want to talk to them,' Molly moaned.

'Yes, you do, Molly Freeman. They're our chance of a good day out. Now don't you say a word and leave it to me,' Connie whispered before speaking in a louder voice. 'Come on, Molly, we're going to be late for the mid-afternoon matinee; we'd better get a move on.' Putting her arm through Molly's, she set off in the direction of the cinema.

'Er . . . excuse me, ladies, my friend and I couldn't help but overhear,' the smaller of the two said. 'Are we right in thinking that you're going to the pictures? We were just thinking of doing the same thing.' He looked at Molly with a smile.

'We are,' Connie replied. 'I was just saying we were going to be late and I have set my heart on watching

Vivian Leigh in *Waterloo Bridge*. I hear that it is so romantic and I loved *Gone with the Wind* when I watched it the other year.' She fluttered her eyelashes at the soldier she had likened to Clark Gable.

'We wondered if we could join you? We don't know York; we've just been stationed here before going to join the lads over the Channel and we're at a loose end.' The soldier waited for a reply as the girls looked at one another. 'I'm forgetting my manners. I'm Danny Baxter and this good-looking dark-haired gent is Matt Drummond.' Danny held his hand out to be shaken and grinned while his friend Matt smiled and looked down at his feet.

'Well, I don't know, but I can't see any harm in it. Can you, Molly?' Connie said, and she nudged Molly with her elbow.

'No, please do join us,' Molly said quietly.

'There, you see, I knew you'd be welcome. I'm Connie, Connie Whitehead, and this is Molly Freeman. We're pleased to meet you both.'

'And you both work in munitions; we could tell that as soon as we saw you both, but no disrespect to you. Without you girls working like you do, the cause would be lost. You're to be admired as much as any of us soldiers,' Danny said, as he slipped his arm through Connie's.

Matt looked at Molly but didn't do the same; he just walked beside her. 'Are you both from York? Danny and I are from Lancaster. We're here on a training exercise before we're sent over to France.'

'Yes, we live with my mam and work at Rowntree's,'

Molly said, and straight away she knew should not have told him about Rowntree's. 'I shouldn't have said that,' Molly blurted. 'Loose lips sink ships and all that.'

'Don't worry – we know that part of Rowntree's are making munitions. We're not going to say anything; it's bloody Jerry that you've got to worry about,' Matt said and then grinned. 'We wouldn't want good-looking lasses like you two losing your lives, so we'll go along with you still making chocolate there.'

'My sister is. She's overseeing all the departments making Black Magic, Jungle Chocolate and KitKats. We used to do that as well,' Molly said as they walked towards the picture house and stood in the lengthy queue.

'So I know where to come if I need some chocolate,' Matt said. He stood next to Molly just behind Connie and Danny.

'Here, girls. Matt and I will get the tickets for us all, since you've been good enough to keep us company.' Danny stepped forward to the ticket booth and placed his money down.

Connie smiled, but Molly said, 'That would be very kind, but we should pay for our own tickets.'

'No, we both insist.' Danny smiled and paid for the tickets. 'Now come on, girls.' He took Connie by the arm and marched into the darkened picture hall. He led them to the back row, moving two young women along in order for them all to sit down together.

'I apologize for Danny. Once he gets something in his head that's it. I hope the back row is all right for you?' Matt said, as they sat down, having noticed Molly looked uncomfortable and awkward, knowing as she did that the back seats were used by courting couples.

'I'm fine. I can't wait for the film to start,' Molly said and smiled as Matt gently put his arm round the back of the seat and moved closer to her.

'Yes, Vivien Leigh is one of my favourite actresses. Can't say that the content will be that good; the bombing of London is a bit too close to home,' Matt said and slunk into the seat as the lights went low and the curtains opened. 'I suppose we'll have a publicity film to show our brave lads fighting and giving us advice on how to turn potato scraps into something good, or something along those lines.' He smiled at Molly in the dim light. 'You're very beautiful; I bet you have a boyfriend.'

Molly was taken aback by the directness of the question. 'I don't. I haven't the time for one,' she replied, taking in how handsome the lad was; he was rather like Clark Gable, Connie was right. Connie would have something to say to her. Although at the moment Connie could hardly be seen – to her shock Molly could see Danny was already kissing her passionately and Connie was not complaining one bit.

'It's lucky I met you then today.' Matt reached tentatively for Molly's hand. 'Don't worry, I'm not like Danny. Let's just enjoy the film. He thinks he's Romeo, but girls get fed up with him – he's far too intense! He gets slapped regularly.'

'They do seem to be entwined,' Molly said, and she tried to settle down to watch the film of fighting in

France while getting Danny's elbow in her side. 'I'm surprised at Connie.'

'He lives for the day. He thinks once we get over in France we'll not be coming back. I have other plans. I aim to come back and settle down to a nice peaceful life,' Matt said quietly, and tried to ignore his friend's antics. 'It will all end in tears before the film ends, believe me. He will try and push it just a little too much.' Matt smiled at Molly. 'Ey up, the film's starting, not that them two will know.'

Molly watched as the opening credits of the film played and thanked God that she had the quiet sensible one next to her; Matt seemed a nice lad with morals, unlike Danny and his wandering hands.

'Well, that was good, but perhaps a little bit depressing, and Robert Taylor is no way as good-looking as Clark Gable, but Vivien Leigh was as beautiful as ever. She made a lovely ballerina,' Molly said as she stood up, trying not to look at Connie who was tidying her hair and making herself decent as the lights went on and people got ready to leave their seats.

'Yes, he was going off to France, like we will be shortly' Matt said, his eye on Danny comfortably sitting next to Connie, who looked slightly annoyed with him.

'When do you go? Do you know?' Molly asked as they made their way along between the rough velvet and wooden seats and smiled at the usherette, who escorted them out into the foyer.

'In a fortnight. I can't say I'm looking forward to it.'

Matt stood and looked back towards the door to the screen. 'Looks like we've lost those two. I must say your friend Connie didn't look that impressed.' He smiled.

'That's because she missed nearly all the film, but it's her own fault; she should have told your friend to stop,' Molly said, and then she went quiet as Connie and Danny came bustling through the doors, neither looking that happy with one another.

'Come on, Molly. I'm ready for home. Some people just have no manners,' Connie said, and scowled at Danny.

'I never heard you complaining,' Danny said sharply, sniggering as she put her handbag on her arm and made her way down the steep steps and waited on the pavement for Molly to join her. He lit a cigarette and grinned at the girl he had tried to have his way with.

'Looks like we're going,' Molly said, looking up at her handsome date. 'You were right. Thank you for your company and I hope that you keep safe in France.'

'Thank you, Molly. But before you go can I ask for your address? And may I call on you perhaps one evening next week?' Matt asked as he held her hand tightly.

Molly blushed. 'Yes, you can, but my mam might have something to say. She couldn't believe that the handsome soldier was asking to call for her.

'Surely you're old enough to make your mind up? However, if it's going to cause problems, how about we meet next Saturday afternoon outside the Minster, and I'll not bring Casanova with me.' Matt nodded at his friend, who was now chatting to the usherette.

Molly smiled and tried to ignore Connie's impatience.

'I am old enough. I'm seventeen. But meeting outside the Minster would be better and, yes, I'd like that.'

'Then I'll see you at two o'clock next Saturday and I'll act like a gentleman, unlike someone we know.' Matt smiled as he watched Molly run down the steps and look back at him as she put her arm through her best friend's arm and they walked off.

'You're wasting your time there, mate. You'll not get anything from that one,' Danny said and passed his friend a ciggie.

'Unlike you, my friend, I believe there's more to life than getting my leg over,' Matt replied. 'Besides, I like her and she's pretty.' He lit the cigarette and took a deep drag on it.

'More fool you, mate; you should be getting it while you can. Another fortnight and we both might be six feet under.'

Matt grinned. 'Yes, but I might need something to remind me what life is all about, so I'll take my chances and maybe I won't get my face slapped like you do on a regular basis.'

'Then it's your loss, mate. All I'm saying is, get it while you can.' Then Danny winked at the usherette and ran down the steps.

'How, come you got the gentleman and I ended up with *him*? There was no controlling him,' Connie said, as she looked at Molly, clearly jealous.

'You had your choice and you didn't look to be complaining until the lights went back on. Did he really have his hands where I thought they were? I looked across and couldn't help but notice,' Molly asked, concerned.

'He would have put his hands everywhere if I'd let him. By the time the film was over I was glad to be able to get up and give him a piece of my mind. I'll not be seeing him again in a hurry.' Connie sighed and checked her reflection in her compact mirror as she tried to feel less used. 'Did I hear you're meeting the handsome one again? At least he behaved himself.' Connie grinned.

Molly smiled back at her best friend. 'I am. We're meeting at the Minster next Saturday. Did you actually get to see any of the film?'

'No, not a lot,' Connie replied. 'It's a good job you can tell me the plot, else I'd not have a clue what it's about.'

'Well, at least you didn't pay for your ticket,' Molly said and couldn't help but think of her tête-à-tête with Matt.

Connie sighed. 'Oh yes I did, but not in the way I should have done. The dirty-minded devil. Never again. Well, not until someone takes my fancy.'

'I give up with you. But it's all fun so we should enjoy it while we can,' Molly replied, thinking about her handsome Clark Gable lookalike.

Saturday couldn't come fast enough.

It was the end of the working day and Rose walked home feeling subdued. The days were long and although everyone tried to put on a brave face, an undercurrent of worry was everywhere. She was glad to be home as she opened the garden gate and made for the front door.

Ivy called out as soon as she heard the front door

open. 'Oh, Rose, am I glad you're back. I couldn't wait for you to come home.'

'Why, have you and my mother run out of sherry? What juicy gossip have you dug up between you?' Rose said sarcastically as she closed the door behind her and hung her coat up. 'I presume my mother's still here since Molly and Connie are working the nightshift this week?'

'Yes, I am, and you can hold your cheek and get yourself in here. We have some news for you, something that will put a smile on that face of yours for the first time in days.'

Rose went in the front room, where Winnie grinned the biggest grin she possibly could, partly because of the sherry and partly because of the wonderful news that they had been brought.

'Here, lass, sit down next to me.' Ivy patted the seat next to her. 'We've had Peter here this afternoon. He wanted to come and see you, but I told him we'd tell you rather than take you out of work.' She held her breath and looked at her daughter-in-law-to-be.

Rose looked at the two older women. Was it going to be good news? Fearing the worst, her eyes filled with tears. 'He's dead. He was shot down and they've found his body.'

'Nay, anything but! Ned's been found and he's alive and unscathed. He's fine, lass. Now he's just got to get back home.' Ivy pulled Rose to her and squeezed her tight. 'It's going to be all right, lass. He's being looked after and everything's being put in place to get him home. But it will take a while; you'll have to be patient.'

Winnie looked at Rose as she sobbed with relief and Ivy held her close. 'Aye, he's in safe hands, Rose. They're looking after him well. The Resistance have got him in a safe house. They're risking their own lives to hide him, but as long as he doesn't get found they'll be fine.'

'Quiet pet. He'll be back with us,' Ivy said. 'My lad'll keep his head down and get home, it's to be hoped, so you can hold your tears.' She looked across at Winnie and hoped that she was right.

'I can't believe it. Did Peter really say Ned was all right? Where is he in France? And how does Peter know?' Rose pulled away from Ivy's arms to blow her nose and look at her mother.

Winnie smiled at her daughter. 'The Resistance has been in touch with RAF Intelligence; they have his name, squadron and everything. Peter volunteered to come and tell us. He's alive and all right, so stop crying. He'll be back to wed you, so don't you worry.' She tried to hide her fear that even though Ned was safe with the Resistance he was still in danger.

Ivy took over: 'A farmer and his son found him not far from where his plane crashed. They took him back to their farm, fed him and looked after him until members of the Resistance could take him off their hands. He's in a safe house on the coast, at a place called Plouha in Normandy, just across the Channel. As soon as it's safe for a boat to go and collect other refugees and service-men, they'll go for them. They say they'll use a small motorboat and go under the cover of darkness.' Ivy couldn't hide her jubilation.

'In Normandy.' Rose sighed. 'And he's safe. God bless those that are looking after him.'

'Aye, they got in touch by wireless, but they have to be careful not to be caught. I think Ned's living somewhere behind a false wall, out of sight of the Germans. But that doesn't matter, does it, lass. He's alive and he'll be back with us soon it's to be hoped.'

Ivy refilled their sherry glasses and poured a drink for Rose. 'Something to celebrate, my girl,' she said, as she and Winnie took a long sip.

'Ned's alive and is to come home. I can't believe it.' Rose wiped away a tear and sat back on the settee. She didn't need a drink; she was full of the joy of knowing her Ned was safe. And even though there would be a long and dangerous road to get him home, for now nothing could outshine the happiness that was glowing inside her.

It had been a hard week at work, Molly thought, as she got ready for meeting Matt. Connie had never shut up about her experience with the sex-mad soldier and had kept digging at her for getting the better man. Betty and Connie had been wheeling and dealing with Betty's guard and now two lengths of parachute silk were waiting for Molly to make into something wearable with the help of her grandmother's sewing machine when she had the time. It was to be worn with two pairs of stockings that had been bought from Betty on the understanding that no questions were to be asked about where they had come from. There had been no German bombers in the skies above York that week, unlike other places in the country that had been pounded. The ports and railway stations were especially being targeted, and the RAF was being kept busy defending their homeland. The newspaper had nothing but reports of fighting in Europe and rationing was starting to hit everyone hard. There was not a lot of joy in life, Molly thought, as she puckered her lips and added a liberal coating of lipstick, still noticing her yellowish skin before anything else.

'Oooh, look at you: lipstick on, hair brushed and that knitted blue cardigan on that you always favour. I hope he's worth all the effort,' Connie said, as Molly made her way downstairs and picked up her handbag.

'You look lovely, pet, but remember what I told you: tell him to behave himself and keep yourself safe,' Winnie said, looking at her youngest with a hint of worry in her eye.

'I will, Mam,' Molly replied, 'and he's not a bad lad.' She wanted to add 'unlike his mate', but thought better of it as Connie gave her a warning glance.

'That's a good lass. You go and have a good day then, and don't be too late back. It looks like rain as well. Have you got your coat?' Winnie shouted as she watched her daughter go, leaving her and Connie alone in the kitchen. Winnie sighed as she heard the front door close and turned to Connie. 'She's not listened to me. She's in such a flap, she's not taken her coat! Is this soldier she's going to see all right, Connie? He's not, you know . . . I only ask because sometimes they live every day like it's their last.'

'No, Mrs F, he's all right; he's steady and he's really handsome. I'm envious really.' Connie sighed and picked up the latest copy of *Women's Weekly* and hoped that she would not ask anything else.

Molly's stomach churned with excitement and self-doubt. Was she dressed right? Would he recognize her? Hopefully that awful Danny would not be with him. She sat on a bench outside the Minster where they had agreed to meet and watched people coming and going. She folded her arms tightly. There was a sneaky wind blowing down the street and the tall spires of the Minster were framed by dark rain-filled skies. She listened to the Minster chimes tell her that it was two and that her date should be with her. She scanned all the converging streets but there was no sign of her dashing soldier. At quarter past there was still no Matt as drops of rain started to fall. Molly pulled her cardigan round her and wondered what to do.

Half past came and there was still no sign and Molly sat like a drenched cold rat. Matt wasn't going to come; she'd been stood up and now she had to face Connie's jibes. She had stood up to go home when a troop wagon came up the street and squealed to a halt just in front of her. She looked as the tarpaulin covering it was pulled back at the rear of the wagon.

Matt jumped out of the back and a group of soldiers jeered as he walked up to her.

'I thought you would have gone,' he said. 'Look at you – bless you, you're soaked. I'm so sorry I'm late, and the worst of it is I can't stop. I didn't know how to get a message to you. I don't even know where you live, but we're being deployed early. It cost me a packet of fags for them to make this detour, but it's worth every smoke just to see you,' he said with a tender smile. 'We're going to France tonight, but here's the address for my regiment. If you want to write to me there, they'll forward me your letters. I hope that I can have yours. too.'

'I thought you weren't going yet. When will you be back?'

'They need us over there and I don't know when we'll be back, I'm afraid. I hope that you will write to me?' Matt reached out and took her in his arms while all his fellow troops cheered.

'Go for it Matt' she heard the distinct voice of Danny shout.

Matt kissed her quickly and took Molly's breath away as he held her at arm's length. 'Promise you will write me your address and I'll write back to you!' he yelled as he ran back to the wagon, leaving Molly standing in the rain, tears running down her cheeks mixing with the cold rainwater.

'Yes, I'll write. Take care. Please take care,' Molly called back as he was pulled by his colleagues into the back of the wagon, and then she stood and waved until it disappeared down Micklegate and all too soon out of her sight.

Molly stood in the rain and wondered if it was the end of what she had hoped to be a romance, but perhaps it could be the beginning if she and Matt were lucky. She would write, she decided, as she folded the piece of paper with a pencil-scribbled address on it and started to walk home. Now she could see why Danny was living for the moment – it was to avoid heartache – and she had a feeling that perhaps that was the best thing to do with war raging.

13

Because of the pail, the scraps were saved.
Because of the scraps, the pigs were saved.
Because of the pigs, the rations were saved.
Because of the rations, the ships were saved.
Because of the ships, the island was saved.
Because of the island, the empire was saved.
And all because of the housemaids' pail.

Helen lay on her bed. 'I'm absolutely exhausted, and look at the blisters on my hands. If I never see a shovel again, it will be too soon.'

Every day since they had arrived at Pendle Farm had been one of mucking out the pigs, feeding the pigs and mending fences and gates that they had rutted under and disturbed.

'And the smell. Do you know I've breathed it in so much I've got used to it now? I hope we don't smell like them.' Helen sat up and pulled her green wool jumper over her head and sniffed at it. She pulled her buckle open on her sturdy brown breeches, un-fastened her side buttonsand sighed. 'I didn't know I was signing up for this, else I'd have thought twice about it. Oh well, we're in for a treat tomorrow, so old Bernard says.'

'It's Mr Farrington, and don't you forget it. He keeps

telling me. Some treat, picking up swill pails from all the houses in Clitheroe. I'll be lucky if my stomach doesn't churn and empty my contents into one of them,' Annie said, lying down on her bed in her cami and knickers and looking up at the crack along the ceiling that seemed to grow a little each day.

The whole house was in a dilapidated state, but the Farringtons didn't seem to be worried. The pigs and the tattie harvest were all they talked and bothered about, and every penny counted, especially when it came to the pigs that were hidden up the fellside and were being reared without the ministry's knowledge for sale on the black market through the butcher in Clitheroe.

'Never mind that. He says he goes to the pub and that we can make our own amusement for an hour while he has a natter with his old cronies. It'll give us a chance to have a look around the shops.' Helen leaned back on her bed. 'I hope Lizzie will give us some of our wages. I don't know if she'll let us loose with our ration books. Have you seen the way she locks them up in that battered roll-top desk? You'd think they're worth millions.'

'I'm not saying anything,' Annie said, laughing. 'They feed us as well as them, after all. Though we just get bacon, eggs and potatoes. But we shouldn't complain; we're never hungry like a lot of people. In fact, I'm sure I'm putting on weight.'

She and Helen, despite their differences in lifestyles, were starting to get on well. But both of them missed their families and both were often heard sobbing in the middle of the night.

Annie yawned and decided to get ready for bed. 'Have you heard from your parents today? I've not had a letter for a while, but I know they're all busy. Molly is still making munitions, Mam is doing soldiers' washing and Rose is worrying to death about her fella Ned over in France; nothing really changes with mine.'

Helen wished she'd had a letter from home. It had been a fortnight since she'd heard from her mother and she was concerned. It might be quiet in the countryside of Lancashire, but in London it was a different world altogether, with bombs falling regularly, especially around the docklands. 'I haven't heard a thing. I'm worried about them. I miss the radio and with the Farringtons not getting a newspaper, at least when we go into Clitheroe I can get caught up with the news. It's like being in the back of beyond here; there's absolutely nothing here. It would be better if I could find some entertainment somewhere. I used to love going to the nightclubs and coffee shops in Soho. I had such good nights out. Now look at me: not a bit of perm in my hair, broken nails and stinking of pig shit.' Helen smiled but behind the bravado she could have cried.

'We should make more of our spare time before winter comes. After all, it's September now – in another few months it will be absolutely freezing here, I bet,' Annie said as she climbed into bed. 'We could always go on the bicycles; we've never used them yet. I'm that tired of an evening I can't be bothered.'

'We could but I've never learned to ride one. There was no need for one in London; we had the underground and buses passed our door every day. Besides, it isn't ladylike.' Helen laughed. 'Mind you, looking after pigs and mucking them out isn't either when I think about it. So perhaps I'll give it a go. It will get us away from this place at least one day a week.'

'I'll teach you, and then we can go where we want. There must be something going on in these villages round about. It's do that or go quietly mad like the Farringtons. Now, I've got to go to sleep else I'll never wake up in the morning. Night-night, Helen, mind the pig bugs don't bite.'

'Come on, girls, get your bums moving!' Lizzie Farrington yelled. 'Bernard's waiting for you; you've got to be quicker feeding the pigs than this when he's going into Clitheroe!'

Helen and Annie rushed across the yard and started to take off their strong leather boots in the porch of the farmhouse, hoping to find time to change into more appropriate clothes than their Land Army uniform.

'Nay, there's no need to take them off. Go as you are. You'll only get the pig slops spilt on you and that'll mean another load of washing. I've enough on with what washing I get off you both. Now go on, he's waiting round at the barn – the horse will be getting worked up if it's to stand any longer waiting for you.'

'We need some money,' Annie said and carried on unlacing her boots.

'Bernard has some for you, though there's not a lot that you'll want. Now go on, get a move on, else he'll start cursing.'

Lizzie looked as black as thunder as Annie hesitated and then thought better of taking off her boots off and relaced them quickly.

'I hope I don't stink!' Helen tugged her jumper up to her nose to check and pulled a face. 'And I hope he has got some money for us, else it's not going to be much of a trip out. It's already clouding over and blowing a cold wind.'

Annie and Helen climbed on to the back of the flat wooden wagon that had two big metal containers on it and a growling Bernard that was holding the reigns.

He set off as soon as the girls had wriggled their bums on to the backboard. 'What have you been doing? You knew we were off to Clitheroe! You've got a lot of doors to knock on today, not to mention the stallholders for their leftovers, not that they have a lot left over for my girls nowadays.' Bernard shouted this over his shoulder to them both as they sat tight and looked at the country lanes and hedges that were starting to be filled with rosehips and wild blackberries.

Today was the day the girls would knock on most of the household doors in Clitheroe asking for scraps for the pigs back on the farm. Every scrap counted to fatten the pigs up and for the householder to perhaps benefit when the time for butchering the pigs came round.

Annie nudged Helen. 'We can walk this far and pick them one evening. They'd be really good with cream.'

'Them, out of the hedge? Do you think so?' Helen looked in disbelief and then tried to drag Annie back as she jumped off the back of the cart when they next passed a trailing briar with berries upon it. She watched as she picked a bunch of the glistening black jewels and then ran to catch up and jump back on the cart with them in her hand.

'Here, try them. Mam and us used to have a walk out into the country when we were young and collect them. I'd forgotten.' Annie passed the few she had in her hand and watched as Helen hesitantly tried the first one and then smiled as she saw her enjoyment.

The black juice trickled down her lip and she licked it away. 'God, they're lovely. Will we be going blackberry picking? Is there anything else we can scrounge from the hedges?' Helen said when she'd finished the rest of the berries.

'Hazelnuts in another few weeks. They're tasty,' Annie said and was glad for her mother's enforced walks when she was young.

'Food for free, now that's good.' Helen sighed; there were some good things to be said about the country-side, but she was a town lover at heart, no matter how beautiful the countryside was. She looked up at the dark foreboding shape of Pendle Hill and thought about the stories of the Pendle witches. As she watched the scud-ding clouds throw shadows over the rolling large hill, she could well believe the happenings there and shivered.

'Are you cold? I could have done with my coat,' Annie said.

'You two will soon be warm running back and forth in Clitheroe, collecting scraps from folk's waste bins. But be aware also that there are some who're my special customers; they're the ones who've invested money as well as scraps. Those ones will give you a lot more scraps for my girls because they part-own the pigs that are in the top pens. You'll soon know who I'm on about. They'll ask after the pigs' welfare; they always do. Make sure you're right with them. They'll be wanting their meat in another week or two with no questions asked. If they ask when the pig killer is coming, tell them the first Saturday in October, as arranged, and brass for payment will be expected promptly.' Bernard drew breath. 'Have you heard that, lasses? But you say nothing to anybody else; they have to take their chances and queue with their ration books at the butchers like everybody else.'

'Yes, Mr Farrington,' both girls replied.

But Helen, seeing a chink in Bernard's armour, was quick to ask, 'Have you some money for us, Mr Farrington? We could do with some for our dinner and perhaps a postcard to send home.'

'Aye, I'll give you some brass, enough for fish and chips and a postcard home. Aye, your folks would like that. But it'll come out of your pay. That's due at the end of the month. I've not forgotten. I like to keep things on a monthly basis and then I don't forget when you're paid. No matter what these ministry men say, weekly doesn't work for me.'

'We'll look forward to that, Mr Farrington, thank you.'

'Aye, well, you're not a bad help, although my nephew Mike used to do it in half the time it takes you two. Why the silly bugger enlisted I don't know.' Bernard muttered on while both girls looked at one another, knowing all too well why Mike had been so desperate to make a break.

Clitheroe was thronging with people; it was market day and, even though there was a war on, country people still tried to carry on their trade. The vegetable stall had turnips, carrots, cabbage and potatoes.

Bernard got down from his wagon and slapped the long thin stallholder on his back and produced a packet of something wrapped up in newspaper from under his jacket, which he passed to him in exchange for a bag of vegetables before the girls even had time to climb down from the cart.

Bernard put the bag down next to his seat and turned to talk to the stallholder. 'These are my land girls. They'll take your turnip tops and any rotting stuff off your hands. My lasses at home will enjoy it as usual and you know your share will be ready in a fortnight. Our tatties will be ready for lifting next month. Are you still all right with our little understanding?'

Annie and Helen listened to the conversation that was just about in code between the two men, as they loaded a pile of unwanted rotting vegetables on to the cart.

Bernard was a wheeler and dealer; if he could make a penny, he'd be happy but even better if there was a shilling in it.

'Right, then. Good to do business as usual. I've got to get off. I've got to call at my usual stops and then I hope to have a pint in the Brown Cow before we get ourselves home.'

He ushered the girls to sit back on the cart as he climbed up to his seat. 'Now then, lasses, we're going to go street by street. Them that have a pail outside their door with scraps in, just pour them into the big metal buckets. My pigs love their Friday treat; it's amazing, even though there's rationing on, what folk throw away. I sometimes look at it and think I could eat that myself. You'll have already found out that Lizzie is a bit limited in her cooking skills, but it's not worth complaining. I'll not alter her now.'

Bernard sighed and then flicked his horse into action along the busy main street and towards the backstreet cobbled terraces of the mill workers' buildings. Outside most front doors was a small pail filled with the house scraps for the week, each one to be emptied into the large tall buckets and replaced back on the householder's step.

Annie took one side of the street and Helen took the other. Occasionally a door would open and a voice would shout out and ask Bernard if everything was all right and going to plan, and he'd nod his head and shout back, 'Aye, not long now.' Some even passed offerings from their garden to him, a bunch of string beans and a boiling of beetroot. This was no-money commerce and Bernard was king of it.

After the backstreets they stopped off at the hotels and emptied their slop buckets. At the Railway Hotel, the manager came out and spoke to Bernard in a whisper that both girls could just make out.

'Half a porker and a flitch of ham when you've cured it. Here's the money we agreed upon and not a word else we will both end up in the clink.'

'You know me, Reggie: soul of discretion. There'll be no more rabbits for a while, so chicken will be off your menu.' Bernard grinned; he knew the chef had been passing herby rabbit off as chicken in his restaurant. 'Mike's gone into the army and I'm no good with a gun.' Bernard looked at the envelope that was nearly bursting with money and put it in his inside pocket. 'That'll keep my old lass from moaning. I'll deliver the pork once it's been butchered, but the ham will have to dry out for a while. That is if I can get my hands on the saltpetre that I need to cure it. Shouldn't be a problem, though. I've sorted it at the chemists with a bit of under-the-counter dealing.'

'You be careful, Bernard. The ministry takes a bad view of black-market dealing. I wouldn't be in your shoes if they heard about it . . .'

'Aye, well, nobody's going to say owt because everybody's getting what they want and that's the main thing. You'll have pork chops on the menu in three weeks, don't you worry, but now after seeing the chemist I'm off for a pint at the Brown Cow and then home to my old lass.' Bernard patted his jacket pocket and winked before climbing back on the wagon.

'Remember, lasses, loose lips sink ships, and I'm not going to have this ship sinking,' he yelled over the top of the nearly full and stinking metal pails. 'Now, while I have a jar or two, you go and get yourselves some dinner and have an hour around town. I'm feeling flush, so two bob each should get your dinners and have something left over for yourselves. Three o'clock, back of the Old Brown Cow, and don't be late.'

Bernard pulled the wagon to a standstill at the top of a cobbled street that on one side had a castle that had been protecting the market since medieval times and reached into his breast pocket to pull out a handful of silver, counting it into equal amounts of two shillings. 'Three o'clock and behave yourselves; the pub's just down here on the brow of the hill.'

Annie and Helen watched as Bernard made his way down the street. They were thankful to be away from the smell of the slops and Bernard and to have an hour on their own in the market town with two shillings in their pockets. The shillings were to be treasured, although they would have seemed like pennies in Helen's old life. But she was grateful today; she could buy a newspaper and send a postcard home, and get a fleeting glimpse of a past left behind as the girls looked in shop windows and realized that Clitheroe was quite a wealthy farming community despite the back-to-back mill houses and the likes of the lowly pig-farming Farringtons, who didn't seem to have much money.

'I can't get over that chippy not having never heard of jellied eels; we always ask for them back home,' Helen said as she tucked into her fish and chips wrapped up in an old newspaper.

'He didn't look impressed when we just asked for a 2d fish and 1d of chips, but I want to keep some of this money in case I see anything I fancy. Besides, that's the going price in York for fish because there are more fish and chip shops competing for your money. These are so good; it's so long since I've had fish and chips, and I swear if I eat another bacon sandwich, I'm going to turn into a pig.' Annie grinned and relished every mouthful.

'Mmm . . . I can't eat mine fast enough. Look, nearly finished,' Helen said and showed Annie her near empty newspaper wrapping, and then she stopped, pulled the papers back and unfolded the greasy bottom page of the daily newspaper and held her breath. 'Oh my God, London has been bombed relentlessly. Look at this. Hitler has been bombing my home patch.' She smoothed out the newspaper, looking at the date of the fifteenth of September and reading what she could as she leaned against the fish and chip shop wall.

'This was over a week ago. Is that why I haven't heard from my mother?' Helen shook her head and held back her tears. 'I hope they're all right. This is down the East End, not far from the Docks, but it sounds as if all London is ablaze. Thank heavens my ma doesn't live there – just look at the terraced houses that were on fire and the firemen fighting it, the poor devils.' Helen held her breath and looked at Annie. 'They say there are at least four hundred and thirty dead, and look at the head-lines: BLACK SATURDAY, AS GERMANY TAKES REVENGE FOR THE ACCIDENTAL BOMBING OF BERLIN. I knew nothing of this. All we do is work eat and sleep. I've not heard the news or read a paper for weeks.'

'Surely they have bomb shelters and air-raid warnings. It's no good worrying until you've heard different and somebody would let you know if something had hap-pened to your family.' Annie quietly put her arm round the usually confident Helen. 'They'll be all right, I'm sure they will.'

'Look at it! They won't, I know they won't! Where I live we have a lot of Jewish people and the Germans have proved their hatred against them, so Tottenham will surely be in their sights, although they seem to be targeting the Docks and power stations more. Let me go and get today's paper and see what it says. I pray that it's stopped now.' Helen spotted a newspaper stall across the road and, with her stomach churning and feeling sick from thinking that her family might be one of the many casualties, she weaved her way between cars and horses and carts. She had to find out what was going on at home.

BLITZKRIEG LIGHTNING WAR STRIKES LONDON FOR THE TENTH NIGHT, she read, her hands shaking, while Annie went inside the shop to pay for the paper and talk to the shopkeeper who had seen the distress that Helen was in.

'Look at this,' Helen said when she came back out. 'I've walked down this street hundreds of times; it's only yards from where my ma lives. All London is ablaze because of the bombing, no wonder I've not heard from her.' Helen sobbed as Annie put her arm round her. 'Bloody Hitler, I hope he rots in hell.'

'He will do if our brave lads have anything to do with it. Look, it says the Spitfire pilots are shooting his bomb-ers down as fast as they come over. They should have thought twice about trying to get the better of us.' Annie tried to sound positive but the news had shocked her too. She'd not heard much about the war either since arriving and, in fact, had relished the peace of the farm and the busyness of her days had stopped the everyday worry that had consumed her in York.

'I fear the worst, Annie. My lot might be dead and I don't even know. There seem to be so many dead and injured. I should go home. I'll have to ask the Farringtons for a few days off and see if my home is still standing.' Helen wiped away her tears and folded the newspaper. 'We should be thankful that we're up here and safe.'

'The shopkeeper asked if you were all right when I told him you were from London. He said his heart went out to you. He said he doesn't sleep a wink at night even here because his son works at a nearby airbase making the Halifax bombers. But he says the Germans won't get the better of us all. The lads in blue won't let them.' Annie tried to sound confident.

Helen sighed. 'They already have got the better of us by the looks of it. All those innocent people . . .'

'They'll not win. Churchill won't let them and we as a nation won't. I hope your family will be safe but, as you say, best that you go and see them, and then you can put your mind at rest. It's blowing a chilly wind and looks like rain. Let's go and grab a drink of tea at that cafe, and then we'll see if Mr F is sober enough to take us back to the farm.' Annie put her arm through Helen's, but no amount of words would suffice and she knew that if it had been her family in London there would have been no way of stopping her from returning to them.

*

'Bloody Hitler, the bastard,' Bernard ranted, as he pushed his old horse back along the lanes towards the farm. The slops spilt over the side of the large pails as he urged his horse on. Bloody rain and all; we're all going to get sodden.' Bernard was not a happy man when he had had more than three pints as the girls were finding out; they hung on to the cart for dear life and looked at each other thankfully when they eventually turned up the farm lane.

'And the bloody landlord at the Brown Cow has put his prices up,' Bernard growled. 'I told him he'll not be getting any sausages from me, or bacon, no matter how much sour beer he gives me for my lasses.' Bernard pulled up in the yard and rolled out of his seat on the wagon, going straight to the outside lavvy next to the house with some speed, leaving the horse still tethered and the slops untended.

Lizzie opened the farmhouse door and stood with her hands on her hips. 'Every time I let him go into Clitheroe he does this. I take it he's pissed, else he wouldn't be running into the khazi like he has done. Stupid old fool! And just look at you two – if he'd got himself home on time, you'd have made it home dry. I bet you had to wait for him. He'd be busy putting the world to rights with his cronies,' Lizzie grumbled and took the reins of the horse.

'Leave it be, woman. I'll see to it now,' Bernard shouted as he came out of the lavvy, pulling his braces up over his shirt and tucking it into his breeches. 'I only needed a pee. Can't a man even have a piss nowadays?'

'Right you are then. You see to it. I'm not wasting

my breath on you when you're like this . . .' Lizzie said sharply. 'Come on, girls, you leave the miserable devil to it and go and get changed into some dry clothes. He can see to it all; you'll have had to put up with him for long enough. I hope he remembered to get me some flour; I gave him our ration books.'

Both Helen and Annie looked at one another as they went inside; there had been no mention of getting any shopping.

'You've forgotten, haven't you? I ask you to do one thing and you can't remember that. You are bloody useless, Bernard Farrington; all you think about is your pigs,' she yelled as she followed both girls into the kitchen.

'Ah, go and boil your head!' Bernard shouted back.

'It'll be yours I boil, along with the pigs in another fortnight; it'll make good brawn and nobody would miss you!' Lizzie shouted.

The two land girls made themselves scarce, not wanting to get involved.

'Well, what a welcome back. Bernard can't hold his drink.' Annie pulled her wet woollen jumper over her head and hung it over the back of her bedroom chair.

Helen sighed, took her jumper off and shivered. 'It's quite funny, but I don't feel like laughing.'

'It'll be all right, don't worry.' Annie wanted to convince Helen that things would be all right for her and her family, but she knew she might be offering her friend false hope.

14

Helen went down to the farm kitchen in a sombre mood the following morning. The Farringtons had argued all evening and their voices had even been heard from their bedroom, meaning neither girl had fallen asleep until they put pillows over their heads. No matter what the mood, Helen knew she was going to have to ask for time away from the farm to see how things were at home.

Lizzie Farrington seemed even more in charge that morning. A pan of porridge was already waiting for the girls as they sat at the kitchen table and watched the extra-stodgy helping be dished out with a sharp slap of the spoon.

'I'm sorry if you heard us two arguing; there's no making sense of my man when he's had a drink and to make things worse he's asked everyman and his dog to the pig killings in a fortnight. We're supposed to keep things quiet if we butcher our own pigs. Not advertise it.' Lizzie folded her arms and watched both girls stare at the porridge that was so thick they could stand their spoons up in it. 'Well, are you going to eat it or what? It'll keep you warm all day will that, because autumn is on its way, that's for sure, and it's pouring down again this morning.'

Annie and Helen looked at one another. There was

not even any sugar to add to it, but they didn't dare do anything other than eat it given the mood Mrs Farrington was in.

Helen breathed in and decided she had to ask for leave now. Her heart was aching and until she knew if her family was safe she would not rest.

'Mrs Farrington, I'm going to have to ask . . .' Helen started.

Lizzie moved to the fireplace while listening to her.

'I need to–'

'You need to what?' Lizzie turned with letters in her hand. 'I forgot to give you these yesterday I was that mad with that man of mine. They came with the postman while you were out. I'm sure he waits until he's got enough to make his journey up our lane worthwhile. There's two for you, Helen, and one for you, Annie. I told him now we've got folk staying they need their post more regular, but it was like talking to someone deaf. He doesn't like it here, can't do with the smell of the pigs, funny devil, but I never notice it.' Lizzie passed the letter over and then went into the pantry.

'Thank heavens for that – two letters!' Helen grinned and opened one and immediately started to read, the relief increasingly evident on her face as she did so. 'My parents are with my Aunt Dorothy; they're stopping with her in Dorset, the bombings have been that bad. Our house is all right, she thinks, but neighbouring streets have been hit. My father has joined the Home Guard and Mother is darning and knitting socks for the troops.' Helen sighed and looked at Annie. She opened her second one. 'And this one was written earlier, telling me that they were going.'

'That's good news for you then. I'm so glad.' Annie looked at her letter and decided to read the contents while disguising the taste of the porridge between gulps of well-stewed tea.

Belgrave Street
York

Dear Annie,

I hope that you have settled in. I don't blame you for going to the country; I think I could be tempted to join you.

It's taken us until now to realize how dangerous the job is. It really is nerve-racking filling the shells and making sure you don't accidentally drop them. One lass nearly dropped a tray of detonators last week and caused such a rumpus – she could have blown us all up by accident. I never say anything to Mam, else she would worry, but it's a job and we're helping keep Hitler at bay. My skin is a nice yellow now from the gunpowder and where my fringe sometimes comes out from under my turban it's turning ginger. Still, I'm lucky at least my skin hasn't reacted to the powders like some people's has.

I don't know if Rose has written, but we are all concerned about her. Ned got shot down coming back from a bombing raid in Germany and is now in the hands of the French Resistance. I think she worries that he'll get found by the Jerries and killed. Larry Battersby died after the railway yard got bombed. He wasn't such a bad fella, just not right for our Rose.

Connie and I have been to the pictures. Connie didn't see

much of the film, though. She was with an overattentive soldier,
unlike mine who was a true gent. I don't think we will be
seeing much of them again; they have now gone over to France.

We're going to go to another dance soon. There are soldiers
and airmen camped all around York. You shouldn't have left if
you need a man in your life. And, sorry, I know you will still
miss Josh. I'll write again soon. Let me know how you are doing.

All my love,
Molly
PS Mam sends her love and so does Connie xxx

Annie folded her letter up and put it in her trou-
ser pocket. The news from home was worrying. Ned
missing and Larry dead and Molly juggling munitions;
she should think herself lucky. It might be a bit on the
un-fragrant side, but she was safe and well fed. *Usually*,
she thought, as she gulped down a spoonful of porridge
and looked across at a now less worried Helen.

'Things all right at home, you two? Bernard says
there've been bombings in London and terrible
goings-on. It's a good job we live where we do, although
we aren't that far away from the airfields at Blackpool,
and they make them big bombers down at Warton, but
we're not supposed to know.' Lizzie whispered as if
somebody might be listening in.

'Yes, thank you, Mrs Farrington. My family has moved
out of London; they're living with my aunt in Dorset.'
Helen beamed .

'My sister's fiancé is missing in France, but they think
he's safe. He's a bomber pilot. And my other sister is

making munitions, but all is well, thank you,' Annie replied, pushing back her chair to take her dish to the sink with her porridge half eaten.

'Are you not eating it all? I've probably made too much. I'll put it in the pantry and you can have it warmed up in the morning. It's too good to go to the pigs.' Lizzie took the spoon out of the bowl and made for the pantry.

Annie looked at Helen, who quickly scraped hers into the pig pail and covered it with potato peelings. 'You're on your own there. I can't face this again,' Helen said, and then both girls laughed as Lizzie came back in.

'Now, isn't that nice to see and hear, that a letter from home was the right tonic for you? I'll tell that postie to come whenever he has a letter for you whether he likes it or not. He can be a lazy so-and-so when he wants to be, he takes naps in the hedges in summer, and it's a wonder he hasn't been sacked.' Lizzie stopped as there was a knock on the farmhouse door. 'Talk of the devil. But he's not usually this early.' She untied her mucky apron, put it on a chair and went to open the door, gasping when she saw who was on the step. 'Look what the winds have blown in, and so handsome in that uniform. You've not deserted already, have you?'

'How's my favourite aunty? No, it's a quick visit before I go and fight the Boche! I'm on a twenty-four-hour pass. I knew you'd be glad to see me.' The tall dark man that Annie recognized from the train walked in and picked up the stout Lizzie, twirling her around and kissing her on the cheek, which made her blush and giggle.

'Mike, behave yourself, we've company, although

they're just going out to help Bernard, aren't you, girls? He'll be waiting or skulking in the barn with a bad head if I know him.' Lizzie grinned.

'Ah, slops day, nothing ever changes. Now, I met this young lady coming to you on the train, but I don't think I got your name.' Mike looked quizzically at Annie and gave her the widest smile.

'I'm Annie. I remember you. It's nice to meet you again.' Annie lowered her eyes – he was good-looking and for the first time since Josh she felt her heart flutter.

'And this is?' Mike asked, looking at Helen.

'I'm Helen. Nice to meet you, Mike.' Helen looked with amusement at Annie and read the look between them – they might not know one another that well, but she could see the looks that they gave one another.

'You'd better get a move on, you two; those pigs will be wanting the slops you brought home yesterday. I should know. That used to be part of my job. Nowt like the smell of fresh pig muck in the morning!' Mike grinned. 'I'll still be here at dinnertime, don't you worry.'

'Well, he's a bit of a turn-up for the books: somebody different to talk to,' Helen said as they picked up their yard brushes and set off to clean out the pig pens and then feed the ones in their care.

'Yes, I met him when I came on the train; he was going to Preston to join his regiment. He seems all right, doesn't he?' Annie looked at a sow that had just given birth to seven piglets, all lining up to fight for their mother's milk. 'They're so cute when they're first born. Pity they turn into that,' she said and laughed.

'Don't you change the subject,' Helen teased as she strewed the clean straw for her pigs. 'I could tell by the way you looked at him that you might just have taken a liking to him.'

'He might have taken my eye, but I haven't forgotten Josh. Besides, he was a bit forward, don't you think?' Annie turned back to her work.

'Life's for living, especially at the moment,' Helen replied. 'We could be here one day and gone the next. If you get a chance of happiness, grab it.' She felt a slight twinge of envy over the good-looking lad who seemed to have taken a liking to Annie instead of her. She must give herself a home perm and some bleach. Her hair must look terrible, she thought, as they both got on with their work.

Later that day they all sat round the table for dinner.

'Isn't it good to see him, Bernard?' Lizzie said as she pushed fried egg sandwiches under everyone's noses. 'I've made you these, Mike, because I know they're your favourite and the hens are laying well at the moment. Waste not, want not.'

'You spoil me, Aunty Lizzie,' said Mike as he bit into the sandwich and wiped away the dripping egg yolk from his chin, winking at Annie. 'We don't get fresh eggs in our rations, just dried egg powder like most other folk. There are some good things about being out in the country. Folk in Preston have to queue for eggs and there's us eating them without thinking.'

'Aye, well, somebody forgot to take our surplus to

Clitheroe yesterday, else we could have had a few more coppers in the savings,' Lizzie said sharply, looking across at Bernard who was sat back in his chair and not saying a lot for himself. 'And he forgot to buy me some flour!'

'All right, I forgot the eggs and the flour! Will you give it a rest, woman!' Bernard leaned forward. 'Do you know where you are being sent, lad? Will you get to see Paris? I've always wanted to go there and they say the women are bonny over there.'

'Uh . . .' Lizzie muttered. 'Well, they wouldn't look at an old fool like you.'

Annie and Helen smirked – neither of the Farringtons was in the least attractive but, despite that, there was a strong bond between them.

'No, I've no idea. You don't get told anything in case it gets into enemy hands. We could be going to the moon for all I know,' Mike said. He looked at his watch. 'I'll have to leave shortly; my mate who joined up with me from Chatburn is picking me up at the bottom of the lane. We have to catch the two o'clock train back to Preston else we won't be back in time.'

Annie concentrated on finishing her sandwich as Helen looked across at her.

'Well, keep your head down, lad, and you let us know how you're going on when you can. These two will keep your shoes warm for your return. They might not be as strong but they're a good help. You'll be missing out on pig killing and tattie picking; I bet you're gutted by that.' Bernard smirked and looked at the lad he had just about brought up as his own when his father had died.

'That I am. I hope that you're paying these two well, because they deserve it. I know they do.' Mike looked across at the two girls and grinned. 'Make sure he pays you; he'll try and get away with not doing it if he thinks he can.' Then he winked at Bernard, hoping that he knew he was partly joking.

'You cheeky bugger, they'll get paid,' Bernard replied, then he stood up and patted Mike on the back. 'You take care. Keep that bloody big head down and come back to us.'

'Now then, Aunt Lizzie, don't take on so,' Mike said as he hugged a bawling Lizzie. 'We already had these tears last time I went. I'll be all right and I'll write when I get a chance.'

'I can't bear to think that you're going over there. The girls brought a newspaper back with them yesterday and I was reading what was going on. I'd have been better not knowing anything,' Lizzie sobbed. She held Mike tight before holding her nephew at full arm's length. 'Such a handsome lad, you come back to us, you hear.'

Mike winked as he pulled his cap on his head and looked at himself in the sideboard mirror, running his fingers through his newly clipped hair. 'I will, don't you worry. Now, girls, how about you walk me to the bottom of the lane and give my mate something to talk about? Not just one bonny Land Army girl but two!'

Lizzie shooed the girls away from the table. 'Yes, you two see him off, else I'll keep bawling and make a fool of myself.'

'That's it, one on one arm and the other on the other.

Let me go to war in style.' Mike grinned as they walked out of the farmhouse door and made it down the lane. 'It's been grand meeting you both. Do watch old Bernard, he'll not pay you if he thinks he can get away with it. He's a good soul but, as they say around these parts, he's a bit tight with his brass.'

'He gave us some spending money yesterday, but other than that not a penny since we came,' Annie said, noticing Mike smelled of Brylcreem – clean and fresh, unlike anything on the farm.

'He'll be right with you, he just needs telling, and then when he's coughed up you can go to the dances at Downham. It's not far away; twenty minutes on a pushbike. Every other weekend they hold them; they're usually packed and are a right good night.' Having reached the end of the lane, Mike unhooked his arms from both girls. 'My mate will be here soon and you're probably the last two English lasses that I'll see for a while. Do you mind if I kiss you both, just on the cheek? It will give me something to remember what I'm fighting for if I give up hope.'

Both girls looked at one another and shook their heads, smiling.

'No, go ahead. If it gives you a reason to fight, neither of us minds,' Helen said, stepping forward to let him kiss her on the cheek just as the sound of a van was heard coming up the road.

Mike smiled at Annie, held her close and kissed her too, lingering before stepping away from her and smiling.

'I leave you for ten minutes and you end up with two

women. Put them down and come on, else we'll be late,'
Mike's mate shouted.

Mike left both girls standing by the side of the lane.

'Take care!' Annie called and she wished she had said
more to him as they both watched the van make its way
down the road towards Clitheroe with the horn piping
loudly.

Mike looked back at the woman who had taken his eye
and would have taken his heart too if she'd had a chance.

The weekend and some time to themselves hadn't come
quick enough, and both girls enjoyed trying their hands
at riding their bikes.

Annie shook her head and watched Helen perfect-
ing her riding skills on the pushbike that they had both
been issued with but had never had time to use. 'Do you
think you'll be able to ride to the hall and back? You're
still not good at balancing. I can just see me fishing you
out of a ditch.'

Helen looked up and wobbled as she lost concentration while replying. 'Yes, course I will. I've come a long
way since an hour ago, and, besides, now that we've actually got paid, I want a good night out. I honestly thought
we were going to be working for nothing. A dance is just
what we want. There must be some good-looking single
farmers and where there's a dance there are bound to
be soldiers or airmen. I need a fella to dance with, just
as long as he doesn't smell of pig muck.' Helen sat up
straight and cycled around the farmyard, showing that
she was growing in confidence.

'All right, we'll go then. At least we have a dynamo on our bikes so we can make our way back in the dark. Bombers aren't going to see us around here, or at least I hope not.'

Helen sighed. 'I need a bath first; I'm sure I smell, even though I do my best to keep clean. Do you think Mr and Mrs F would mind if we filled the boiler and had a bath? I've noticed there's a tin one hanging on a peg next to the back door.' She got off her bike and joined Annie sitting on the garden wall.

'She won't know if we get a move on. She and Bernard have gone for supper with their neighbours. Come on, you get the bath and I'll fill the wash boiler. It doesn't take long to warm through, so we'll share it. I'm used to having a bath every week at home, but since I've been here all I've been able to do is have a strip wash. Besides, I don't fancy Bernard sneaking in and watching, which I bet he would if given the chance.'

'Yes, and then we'll go to Downham. I've seen it on the signposts. How big a place is it, do you think, and what should we wear?'

Helen was full of excitement – a night away from Pendle Farm and a soak in a bath was more than she had ever hoped for. It was her first Saturday night out for over six weeks and absolutely any old dance would do, she thought, as a short while later she reached for the galvanized tin bath from off the wall and struggled to put it in front of the fire.

'Another five minutes and the water in the boiler should be hot enough for one of us,' Annie said. Sure enough, she was soon starting to empty the warm water from the boiler while Helen started to undress. Even though there was nobody else in the house they both felt a bit vulnerable as a naked Helen let out a long sigh as she slipped into the water and then covered herself in soap.

'Oh, that's good, for once I feel clean.' She sighed and smiled.

'Hurry up, I need to get in while the water's still warm,' Annie said, standing with a towel round her as she waited for Helen to finish her bath.

'Climb in with me. The water's still warm enough for us both. It's big enough,' Helen said, and she moved to one side to make room for Annie.

'Go on then, I will.' Annie climbed in and closed her eyes. The warmth of the water was a luxury and as she squeezed in she relished the warm water and the heat of the banked-up coal fire.

Then they both stared in horror as they heard the back-door latch lift.

There was a shocked silence and then: 'Bloody hell, I'll go out more often if this is what I come home to! Sorry, ladies, I've just come back for a bottle of my homebrew; next-door has run out of ale.' Bernard lifted his hand to half hide his face as he walked to the pantry and back, sneaking a quick look on his return. 'You two have a good night. Don't let me stop you,' he said, and then closed the door behind him.

Both Helen and Annie looked at one another and then burst out laughing.

'Well, that serves us right for being sneaky about it,' Helen said, laughing. 'Did you see his face? Lizzie would have killed him. Come on, let's get dressed and get to this dance before he returns for another bottle.'

'I feel so embarrassed,' Annie said as she got dressed. She felt a little underdressed as she pulled on a red-velvet dress – the only one she had brought with her – while Helen slipped into a slinky lime-green number and added her lipstick.

'Forget it. He'll not dare say anything to Lizzie. Now let's get to this dance.'

The ride along the country lane to Downham was a haphazard one, Helen nearly losing her balance a time or two and ending up in the grass-filled banks and the hedges that were starting to look autumnal.

God, I hope it's worth this effort, thought Annie as they freewheeled down the hill and into the small ancient village, making their way over a bridge covering a clear stream before seeing the village hall next to the Assheton Arms.

'Well, there's a pub,' Helen said. 'We can at least have a pint if nothing else.'

'I don't drink! Never have done. I just don't fancy it,' Annie replied, as she dismounted her bike and pushed it towards the hall. 'And you're lethal on that bike without a drink in you anyway. Something's going on in the hall. Listen. I can hear laughing.'

'Go on then, get the door open and let's see what is happening in there, although I can't hear any music.'

Helen made a frustrated pretend kick at her bicycle as she dismounted; she'd had enough of trying to keep her balance and was dreading the ride home in the dark as she leaned it against the side of the hall. 'Perhaps we're early.'

Annie cautiously lifted the iron sneck of the hall door and walked in, only to be pounced on by a very posh woman dressed in tweeds and with a string of pearls round her neck.

'How lovely that you could join us. Land girls, how wonderful! Now you take a table and I'll bring you your cards, dice and pencils. We will be serving ginger beer and hopefully a biscuit.'

'We've come for the dance,' Annie said, and heard Helen sigh behind her as she looked at the sedate room of villagers all looking at them.

'Oh, I'm sorry, dear, the dance is next week. This Saturday we either play whist or a good rollicking game of beetle drive! Please join us. We can guarantee you a good time and you're here now.' The woman smiled and pulled out a chair next to a small table covered by a checked tablecloth and prettied by a vase of small flowers.

Helen put her head on one side and smiled, but underneath the smile Annie knew what she was really thinking. A beetle drive was for the elderly, not for two young women looking for love.

'Oh, go on, we've nothing else to do,' Helen said with a grin and she pulled a chair out from the table as Annie sat down and looked at the scoring card. 'And to think I could be walking down Soho with a soldier on my arm,' she whispered to her friend, 'and instead, I'll be shaking a dice for an arm of a beetle.'

'That's it, dears. It's threepence to join in and all funds go towards the village hall. We have some lovely prizes; we've even got a tin of Spam,' the woman in charge said and held her hand out for the money.

Helen just shook her head and smiled. Spam was the last thing either of them wanted. The night was going to be one of true excitement and romance, she thought, as she looked at the youngest man there who was at least sixty. Oh well, it was a night out, and she and Annie smiled and tried to look interested in their night of beetle and ginger beer.

15

The munitions production line was in full swing, with most of the women singing along to their favourite song so loudly that it covered the sound of the manufacturing, even though their singing was muffled by their face masks:

'Out in Arizona where the bad men are,
And the only friend to guide you is an evening star,
The roughest and toughest man by far is Ragtime Cowboy Joe.
He got his name from singing to the cows and sheep. . .'

Connie sang at the top of her voice as Pinky Tomlin sang his hit song over the tannoy and everybody else joined in except Molly, who wished they would all shut up and concentrate. Sometimes she thought she was the only one who cared whether they remained on this earth or got blown to high heavens with a slip of a hand and a dropped detonator.

Connie looked across at Molly and grinned. 'Lighten up, Mol. Live for the day; none of us might be here tomorrow.'

'I worry that's very likely given none of you are concentrating,' Molly grumbled. 'I watch the flaggers that take the filled boxes down to the magazine bunkers with such care, unlike some of us.' She carried on with her job as Connie looked at her, understanding how she felt but not as concerned.

Suddenly the sound of the air siren being wound up could be heard on the top of the Rowntree's building and the music on the tannoy came to an abrupt halt.

'All personnel, please make your way to the nearest shelter quickly, without panic. Do not rush or shove – keep your cool,' a nervous voice announced, which led to everybody immediately stopping their work and making for the nearest bomb shelter without even changing their clothes or giving the half-made munitions a second thought. They all walked briskly and fearfully to the large shelter underneath the Rose Garden.

'Bloody hell, Molly, look what you've done!' Connie said. 'The Jerries have heard you and they're going to make sure we go up with a bang!'

They hurried with the rest of their colleagues downstairs to the concrete and steel bunker under what used to be beautiful gardens. There was panic on the faces of the workers. It was times like these when reality came back to them and they remembered that the fine dust was really TNT and that adding the components of the detonators made their job lethal and put them at risk of having bombs aimed directly at them.

The silence was deafening as nearly five hundred workers crowded and sat together in the dim light of the shelter. The drone of German bombers could be heard directly overhead and the sound of guns along the banks of the Ouse protecting York boomed.

'Please let us all be safe and take care of my mam and Rose,' Molly whispered, praying for the first time since she was young.

They were sitting ducks and they knew it as they strained to listen for the sound of bombs falling, hoping above hope that the Germans hadn't realized that the chocolate factory was now dealing with ammunition. A few people were crying and some like Molly were praying as plane after plane went over their heads. The sound of ack-ack fire from British fighters could be heard and after a nail-biting few minutes, gradually the sound of combat above the shelter disappeared.

'Well, we live to fight another day.' Betty was the first to speak. 'The bastards didn't get us today.' Everyone could have collapsed into a heap as the all-clear siren sounded and the supervisor opened the bunker doors to release the smell of fear and the workers back to their positions.

Even the brazen Betty had shown fear and whispered a prayer. They all knew if a bomb had made a direct hit they would be goners, but now any fear had to be put to the back of their minds and they had to make sure there was plenty of ammunition to fight the Jerries at their own game.

'It's just in these times, when the planes are over our heads, that I realize what danger we're in, Mol. Otherwise, I try and forget and sing along to anything that's played,' Connie said. She looked at her closest friend – she was just the same as Molly but she tried not to show it. 'Come on, let's get back to it. There's no holding us two back.'

Everybody wondered where the bombers had raided and showed real concern for the people who would have suffered.

'I couldn't live in these big cities down south. London is being bombed every day, along with Coventry, Birmingham and even Liverpool. You wouldn't know if you were going to be alive from one day to the next,' Betty grinned. Then she winked at Connie. 'There's some parachute silk in my locker and those nylons that I promised you. Did you make anything with the last lot I sold you? And more importantly have you got my money?'

'I have. Now I've just to chat up my seamstress.' Connie glanced at Molly. 'Not that we have anywhere to go even if we have a fancy dress to wear.' And with that she pulled her face mask on along with her turban.

'I haven't even looked at the first lot, but I'll have a better look at the patterns and make a start at the weekend. There are only so many hours in the day. Twelve hours of work takes it out of me,' Molly moaned.

'Oh, poor you, we're all in the same boat, you know. Don't suppose you could make me something if I got you some more material? I could do with impressing a certain person, keeping him sweet if you know what I mean,' Betty said with a wink, and then she turned and looked at her lover, the guard on the door. 'Talk of the devil, you shouldn't be in here; you might see something you've never seen before,' she said and laughed.

'I've not come to look at you this time. It's her I want. Connie, there's a copper here, and he wants to see her. You've not said anything about anything, have you? I told you to keep your mouth closed,' he said gruffly, as Connie's face went ashen.

'I've said nothing, my love, so it's nothing to do with me. What have you been up to then? Have you been a bad lass?' Betty said to Connie.

'I've done nothing. All I do is work and sleep,' Connie replied and she started taking her protective uniform off and worrying about what a policeman wanted her for.

'Well, he's waiting, but he won't tell me why, so you'd better get a move on,' the guard grunted. He turned his back as Connie moved from the dirty to the clean side of the changing room and looked back at Molly as she changed back into her civilian clothes.

'I've done nothing, Mol; I don't know what he wants me for,' she said. Connie quickly buttoned her cardigan and followed the guard to the reception area.

'Well, perhaps your friend Connie has a secret side to her. Just as long as she doesn't drop me and my fella in it,' Betty said, glaring at Molly.

'She'd never do that,' Molly replied, but she worried what Connie had been up to that had made a policeman come for her to work. Had she gone back to her old ways or, even worse, when she had had to steal to keep her body and soul together? That was back in the days when she was growing up with a mother and stepfather that didn't care about her or her young brother.

'Miss Connie Whitehead?' the policeman asked, looking sombre as Connie walked towards him with all the eyes upon her.

'Yes, that's me. What do you want me for?' Connie asked, trying to think why he would be after her; surely he didn't know about the parachute silk, else the guard next to her would be the one being arrested.

'It's your mother. We were hoping that you still worked here else I'd not have been able to find you. Although this is as far away from making chocolate as you can get.' The officer stopped and looked around him. 'Like I said, it's your mother. Leeds got bombed heavily last night. Unfortunately, and I'm sorry to be the one to tell you this, but one of the casualties was your mother. She's alive but only just; she's been asking for you and I've been sent to come and get you. All she was able to tell us was that you worked here at Rowntree's. I'm sorry, lass.' The officer put his hand on her shoulder and watched Connie's face crumple.

'I haven't spoken to her for years now. Was Bill Tyler with her or was she on her own?' Connie asked and wiped away a tear.

'There was a man found dead next to her; he's un-identified at the moment. The main thing is that we get you to your mother. She's asking for you and her son Billy. Is that right and where is he at?' the officer asked and looked at the guard as if to tell him to go back to his post.

'My brother got adopted two years ago; my mother won't know that it was for his safety. I took him to a local orphanage and they had him adopted to an American family. Bill Tyler, who she lived with, was a cruel heart-less man; that's why I moved away from home and made sure Billy was safe in an orphanage. I had to for his safety!' Connie sobbed.

'Well, you'll have to be right with your mother now. They were living down by the canal docks and the Jerries bombed it hard last night. Now do what you have to and join me. I'm to take you to Leeds General if you're willing,' the officer said quietly.

'I don't think I want to go,' Connie said. 'I don't think I can face her.'

'You'll regret it all your life if you don't; she's your mother and you only get one. No matter what has happened in the past, put it behind you and make your peace before it's too late.' The officer spoke kindly – he'd seen enough heartache of late and hoped that Connie could give her mother some peace before her passing.

Connie dropped her head and wondered what she should do. She would love to see her mother and amend the past but it would break her heart either way. In truth, she was protecting herself from a dressing-down from her mother and if Bill Tyler was still alive she didn't want to see him.

'She may be dying, lass. Give her some peace,' the officer said, putting his arm round her.

'All right, I'll come,' Connie replied, feeling her stomach churn. Her mother was seriously injured – and she was the only family that she had and she had to be there for her.

A few hours later Connie followed the doctor along the rambling corridors of Leeds General Infirmary. The wards were full of injured people, bandaged and crying after the previous day's bombing, and Connie couldn't help but think of the damage that the bombs they were making could potentially do to innocent civilians in Germany – war had no scruples. She felt sick as the doctor in his white coat came to a standstill outside a small room and spoke to her in a quiet voice.

'Your mother has had the priest; there's not a lot more we can do for her. I'll warn you, it will upset you to look at her; sixty per cent of her body is covered in burns. She is lucky to still be here. She's only hanging on to what life she has got to see you, so say your piece.' The doctor opened the door and watched Connie as she put her hand to her mouth and saw her mother disfigured and fighting for her life in the hospital bed.

'Mam, I'm here, it's Connie.' Connie stepped inside and looked at the woman she had once loved, and still loved, now lying in the bed with a protective cage covering her body and her once blonde hair singed to her skull. 'Mam, I'm here now. I'm sorry. It's all right, and I'm here,' Connie whispered, and she summoned her strength to hold the one hand of her mother's that had no burns upon it.

'Connie, my lass, I'm glad that you've come. Is Billy with you? I'm glad that you kept him safe,' Sheila Whitehead whispered, and she turned her head to look at her long-lost daughter through dying eyes.

'Billy's not with me, Mam, but he's safe. You just take care of yourself, Mam. Don't worry about either of us; we're both fine.' Connie spoke quietly. She wasn't going to give her mother more pain in her dying moments.

'Promise me that you'll always be there for your

brother, Connie, and that you'll not think badly of me when I'm gone. Bill was a bad man, but I needed someone to help me live after your father died.' Sheila could only whisper and she tried to grip Connie's hand. 'Promise me that you'll be there for one another. Promise, please promise.'

'I will, Mam, I will. I promise,' Connie said and felt tears trickling down her cheeks. Her heart ached more than it had ever ached before. She was lying to her dying mother and there was nothing she could do. She had the address for her brother Billy's home in Montana somewhere but she had not looked at it for over a year now. She knew she would never be able to go to where he lived and check that he was all right.

'Thank you, my Connie. I love you. I can go in peace now. God bless,' Sheila said, and she let go of Connie's hand with a sigh.

'I love you, Mam. I hope you know that,' Connie sobbed and kissed her mother. She looked down at her as her life slipped away and noticed peace come over her face.

The nurse standing next to the bedside came and put her arm round Connie. 'It's best if you come with me; your mother's fight is at an end now. She's found her peace,' she said gently and she took Connie's arm and moved her away from the bedside.

Connie sat down on a chair outside room, her head in her hands, and cried like she had never cried before. She had lost her father a long time ago, when she was very young, too young to remember him, but now she had lost her mother for a second time but this time irreversibly and it cut like a knife. Even though she had not been the best, she had in her own way tried to provide and be there for her. If Bill Tyler had not come into their lives, they would have been fine. She couldn't have told her about Billy, it would have broken her mother's heart, but one day Connie would see him; and reunite. She didn't know how, but she would.

16

It had been two weeks since Connie's mother's death and two weeks of heartache at the Freeman family house.

'What a to-do, the poor woman. At least she got a bit of dignity with a proper funeral, albeit with only the five of us there,' Winnie said as she unpinned her best black hat and sat down in her chair. 'She can't have had an easy life bringing young'uns up without a man beside her; you can't blame her for shacking up with that Bill Tyler. Although I think I'd have been a bit choosier. Thank heavens our Rose was of an age that she was out working when my old man passed away, else we might have been in the same boat.'

'Thank you for helping out with the costs. I could never have afforded it on my own,' Connie said and hugged Winnie. She had been so grateful when her adopted family had suggested that they help to give her mother a decent send-off.

'Nay, it wasn't just me. Rose and Molly chipped in, and even our Annie sent something in the post. Besides, you're one of us now, you've lived with us so long. It was the least we could do. So don't you worry. Has that kettle brewed, our Molly? I am so parched. I think with fear more than anything – I thought our train would be shot at or bombed all the way back from Leeds. And when

193

I saw that big crater from the bomb that killed Larry Battersby it brought it all home. There's some heartbreak in the world at the moment.'

Rose sat down beside her. 'There's not a lot we can do about it, Mam. We just have to put up with it and hope that everyone sees sense eventually.'

'Have you heard anything about Ned? You must be worried to death,' Connie asked Rose as they all sat down together.

Rose sighed. 'No, but Peter keeps calling and making sure that I'm all right and tells me that he'll update me as soon as he hears anything. All I know is that he's still in hiding. I just wish he was back home with me.'

'He'll be back as soon as he can. Back with you safe and sound,' Molly whispered, and she put her arm round her oldest sister, hoping she was right. 'At least our Annie seems to be getting on with things, although it sounds a bit of a backwater where the farm is. I still can't imagine Annie cleaning out pigs and picking potatoes.'

'I know, who would have thought?' Winnie said.

She looked at the three girls. They were all having to alter their lives in line with the war; some of them were having it easier than others. She hadn't said anything to either Connie or Molly, but each time she sent the laundered shirts back to the soldiers she enclosed a little gift, either a piece of wrapped-up cake or ten fags, just something to let them know somebody was thinking of them. It was her contribution to their fighting of a war that nobody wanted or needed. Everyone was doing their bit to keep the country going, even Rose and the manufacturing of Rowntree's chocolates. At least they boosted morale when they were sent to the troops and were a treat if the ration coupon covered them. Her family were doing their best and she hoped that Connie's mother would be the only casualty within her family group.

Molly sat on the rugged front-room floor, pins firmly held in between her lips as she worked on the pattern of a frock that had taken her eye. She was going to make her own first and then Connie's. Hers would be the trial, she thought, as she pinned the paper pattern to the slippy silk, which she had chosen to dye light blue. It was going to be absolutely beautiful, she told herself, as she picked up the scissors and dared to take the first cut. Knitting was more her thing, but needs must when clothes were on ration. A new dress would be a treat for any dances that they might get to attend in the run-up to Christmas. A cardigan would have to be worn with it, she thought, because the material was so thin, but nobody would know what it was made of if she sewed it well.

'I hope that you're going to make it a bit shorter than what we're wearing now. Shorter lengths are more in fashion now,' Connie said, slumping into the worn armchair next to the unlit fire.

Molly lifted the first piece of pattern and laid it on the back of the settee. 'This is mine; I don't want it too short. I'll make yours shorter. It's terrible for fraying, so I'm giving the pattern a little bit of give, especially where the darts are. I'm not looking forward to sewing it; I hope my gran's sewing machine is up to it.'

'Do you want me to crochet a collar for you?' suggested Connie. 'I have some white silky cotton upstairs and it won't take me long. I'll make it so that you can button it on or leave it off. We can share it then; you wear it on your dress and I'll wear it the following time. I'll have done my bit then.' Connie looked pleased as she watched Molly sticking her tongue out and concentrating as she finished cutting the pattern out.

'That would be an idea. We're going to look like two princesses by the time we've finished,' Molly said, as she looked up at Connie. 'Trouble is, there aren't many princes about. Plenty of soldiers that come and go, but no princes.'

Connie sighed. 'We don't even have time to see them. But we live in hope. I thought you'd got yourself a man, but then he went to fight and you've never heard from him since. Did you ever write to him like he asked you to?'

'No, I keep thinking about it, but people seem to go to fight and never come back, so what's the point?' Molly shrugged and didn't realize that her mother, standing in the doorway, had heard the conversation.

'Molly Freeman, you write to that lad and give him something to focus on. All the lads that are fighting deserve kind words from home.' Winnie shook her head. 'What was he like, Connie? Was he handsome?'

'Well, let's put it this way, Mrs Freeman, if he said he was a movie star, I'd have believed him. She needs to write to him.' Connie was still peeved that she had got the short straw with fumbling Dan. Her eyes had straight away been drawn to Matt, but he'd not given her a second glance.

Molly blushed as she listened to her mother and Connie talk about Matt. 'Will you two shut up? I'm trying to concentrate.'

'Well, just write to him,' both Connie and her mother said together.

'I will, I will, when I get time,' Molly replied and got on with the job in hand.

17

Rose stepped out in her sharp suit, the one she had bought just before rationing had come in; it was the suit she wore every time she was called to a boardroom meeting. Her heart always raced when she walked up the stairs to the meeting room. She could understand now why Ned felt he had to join the RAF rather than sit in a stuffy room with a lot of wealthy elderly men. He had been the exception, accepting that women were just as intelligent as any man, even though they both knew women were still classed as homemakers and wives primarily and then workers. That was why she had been summoned; they needed an update on how the married women they had employed were coping. She knocked on the door and waited with bated breath to be called in.

'Do come in, Miss Freeman, and please take a seat,' Seebohm Rowntree said. 'We won't detain you long; we know that you'll want to get back down to production.' He ushered her to sit in a chair at the end of the table.

'Thank you.' Rose felt her hands go clammy and she wished she had a glass of water in front of her as all heads turned her way. She was more at home with the workers and she hated every minute that she spent with the elite and the owners of Rowntree's.

'I'm sorry to ask you to join us here this afternoon,

but we needed an overview on how the married women are coping in their roles now we are allowing them to work full-time and have the option of their children being cared for in the nursery. Do you think it is working or do you think that we should go back to just employing single women?' Seebohm looked at Rose expectantly.

'They all seem to be coping very well; of course sometimes mothers are torn when leaving their children in the nursery care in the morning, but once settled into work, they're fine. Production is keeping at good levels and our distribution of Jungle Chocolate is above what we envisaged,' Rose said with confidence, in support of the working mothers. She needed to look as if she were in charge of all the facts.

'Tuh, married women working here and children being looked after by the firm, the women should be at home keeping house with their children on their knee,' one of the older directors said and shook his head.

'These are difficult times, Oscar,' Seebohm commented. 'We need their labour and they need to see that they are helping the war effort in some way. Our policy of not keeping women on once married is long since gone. Now, on the Black Magic production line, I need to tell you that we have some extra workers coming; we have arranged with the government to take some Polish and Indian workers, and we are to erect some more Nissen huts on Wigginton Road for these workers specifically. I will need everyone to show them the courtesy and respect that they deserve and for them to be taught the skills they need. Some of the Polish will also be working at the munitions plant; they have had it hard in their country with these blasted Nazis. Now, I'm going to leave their integration to you, Miss Freeman. Any problems, you must let me know. The first group is to be with us at the start of November, just ready for the Christmas rush – not that there will be much of one this year.' Seebohm looked at his fellow directors and pulled a grim face as they all looked glum.

Rose nodded. 'I can do that. We will, of course, make them welcome. Will they all be able to speak English or will they have to learn on the job?'

'I honestly don't know, Miss Freeman; we will have to see when they arrive.' Seebohm looked at Rose. 'I'm afraid there will be no extra pay for this, Miss Freeman. These are hard times for us all.'

Rose dropped her head and stood up from her seat. 'I know, sir. They are indeed.'

'By the way, Miss Freeman, is there any news of Ned? Our thoughts are with him and you. And, I will be honest, we could do with him back.'

'No, sir, he's still somewhere in France. Safe with the Resistance, I sincerely hope. I do so wish for him to be returning home shortly.'

'I'm sure you do, Miss Freeman, I'm sure you do,' Seebohm said sympathetically, and then he moved on to the next item on the agenda as Rose left the room.

'You look tired, Rose,' Ivy said, studying the girl who was looking after her so well and balancing her work life while fretting about her son Ned.

'I'm all right. I just seem to have a lot on my plate at the moment and I can't stop fretting about Ned. I mean, we have no idea where he is and if he's still well or even alive.' Rose looked at her mother-in-law-to-be. She knew that she too was worrying.

'I have every faith in him returning, Rose; he's a fighter is my Ned. If he wants something, he will go all out and get it. And there's nothing more sure than that he will want to come home to you and me. It will all turn out right, my lass. Now hold your tears, because, listen, it sounds as if Peter is pulling up outside – that's his car's engine if I'm not mistaken.' Ivy sighed. 'He might have some news and let's hope that it's good. You've got to give Peter credit; he's looking after us both with Ned being away.'

Rose looked out of the window. 'Oh, it is him.' She sniffed and blew her nose and wiped away her tears. 'I can't let him see me like this; he risks his life every time he flies, just like Ned, and there's me crying. I'll sort myself out, then go and let him in.' Rose stood up, pushed her handkerchief up her sleeve and turned her tears into a smile. Peter was always a welcome visitor; he brought her and Ivy hope no matter if he had news of Ned or not.

'Peter grinned as he opened the garden gate and walked up the path to greet his best friend's intended. 'Hey, Rose. You look as lovely as ever; it's good to see you.'

'You too. You know you're always welcome,' Rose replied, opening the front door wide as Peter brushed past her stopping quickly to kiss her on the cheek.

'Now, here's something to make you and Ivy smile. I've brought coffee and a packet of biscuits that I snaffled out of the NAAFI. We have some Yanks staying with us and they don't seem to be going without anything back home.' Peter passed a paper bag containing his contraband to Rose. 'Ned will be all right, you know – no news is good news.'

'I know, but that doesn't stop me from worrying.' Rose sighed. 'Thank you, this is a real treat. I'll put the kettle on; we haven't had coffee for months. Look, Ivy, we're being spoiled with coffee and biscuits.'

Ivy smiled at the dashing young man who now called regularly to keep them in touch with the base, but of late she wondered if there was another reason too. 'Aye, that's grand, Peter, but I wish you had good news of my lad instead.'

'I've not heard anything about him, but we won't until he's back home and safe, else it puts his life at risk if any correspondence gets leaked. Sorry, Mrs Evans. I wish I had some good news, especially as Rose looks so down at the moment.'

'She's tired as well. She's been telling me she's going to be in charge of some Polish and Indian workers at Rowntree's, so that will be added pressure.' Ivy pulled her blanket round her and made herself comfortable as Peter looked across at her.

'We have some Polish airmen; they stick to their own language when they're flying but they're good men. They just want to get their own back on the Germans. Ned would like them,' Peter replied thoughtfully.

'No doubt he would. He was a good judge of character, just like his old mother.' Ivy watched Peter as he pulled out the small table as Rose brought in a tray with coffee and biscuits on it.

'This is a real treat, Peter; it's so kind of you.' Rose smiled as she passed round the coffee and biscuits. 'Just the thing to cheer me up.'

'I'm glad, and one day I hope to bring you both the news that you're waiting for.' Peter sipped his coffee and watched Rose; she was beautiful and he had always envied Ned ever since he had first seen her.

'So do I. I think about him every day and pray that he's safe.'

'Like I told Ivy, no news is good news. I really think that he will still be safe, else we would have heard by now. I can't stay much longer. We have a briefing at eight, so I'll take my leave and let you enjoy your coffee.' Peter stood up, leaving his coffee half drunk.

'I'll walk you out.' Rose followed their visitor to the door.

'You look after yourself, Peter, and behave yourself,' Ivy shouted after them.

'I will, Mrs Evans, or at least I'll try to,' Peter replied, and he placed his cap back on as he walked out of the front door with Rose following him to the garden gate.

'I've brought you something else. Hopefully you like them.' Peter smiled as he reached into his jacket to pull out a packet of stockings that he had bartered with an American airman for. 'I couldn't give them to you in front of Ned's mother.'

'Oh, Peter, you shouldn't have,' Rose said. 'These are like gold dust, and they're just my shade.' She took the packet from him as they stood at the gate. 'That is ever so kind of you.'

'Yes, I should. Anything I can do to cheer you up is a bonus to me,' Peter replied, enjoying the smile on Rose's face. He couldn't help the feelings he had for her that he knew he shouldn't have.

Rose blushed. 'How can I ever thank you? I'll wear them next time I have a boardroom meeting; they'll look a lot better than the gravy-stained legs I usually have.'

'Well, I rather hoped that you might like to wear them to a dance that we're holding over at Elvington. We are, as I say, inundated with Yanks staying with us and the powers that be have decided to hold a dance to improve morale and to make our American cousins welcome. I'll be there for you to dance with; you'd not be on your own. I promise I'd behave myself. After all, I'm Ned's best friend.' Peter took Rose's hand and looked at her expectantly.

'Oh, Peter, I shouldn't. I don't think it would be right with Ned still missing,' Rose said quietly and dropped her head. 'He'll come back and I will be here waiting for him. Would you like to take the nylons back and give them to another girl?'

Peter let go of Rose's hand as she made it clear that he had overstepped his mark. 'I'm sorry. I just thought that a night out might be good for you. Please, you keep the nylons; they're given in friendship, nothing else.'

'Thank you. You're a good friend, Peter, and I'm

grateful that you're here for both of us. Ned will want to thank you on his return and, as I say, he will return; he has to. Until I know different, I feel I should stay home and keep true to him. I'm sure you understand.' Rose felt tears welling up in her eyes; she would always be Ned's, whether he was dead or alive.

'Of course. I was being foolish to think that you could enjoy yourself at a dance at the base with Ned missing. Please forgive me, but the nylons are still yours. Now, if you'll excuse me, I'd better report back to the airfield and that meeting.' Peter tried to smile as he opened his car door. He had hoped that Rose would join him at the dance, but he should have known better.

'Will we see you next week, Peter? I do hope so,' Rose said as he turned on the car's ignition.

'I'll see. It depends on what the Germans have in store for us. You take care, Rose, and, of course, if there's any news, I'll let you know.' Peter waved and put his foot down. He needed to sort out his inappropriate feelings for his friend's girl.

Rose walked back up the garden path and noticed the lace curtains at the living-room window twitch. Ivy had been watching them both. Well, she needn't worry; Peter was Ned's friend and they both had morals.

Molly stopped her work as she listened to the announcement over the tannoy. 'Listen, Connie, just what we needed to hear!'

'*A dance is to be held at Elvington Airfield to welcome some visiting Americans. If you fancy dancing the night away, transport is available to the airfield. Pick-up is this Saturday at seven thirty outside the Minster. Return transport will be at one a.m. Learn the latest dances from America and come and have a good time and its free to all who attend.'*

All the young women and even some of the married ones showed their excitement and willingness in making the visiting Americans welcome. The Yanks brought things that the British could only dream of.

'Well, guess who's going to be going to that? And it's a Saturday so we won't be working. You've got to get our frocks finished, Molly, and I've got to finish making the collar, no matter how tired I am tonight.' Connie grinned and looked at Betty who was also smiling and singing along to the song that followed the announcement. 'Are you going, Betty?' Connie asked.

'Too right, but don't tell that bulldog over there,' she said, looking across at the guard that was her usual date. 'What the eyes don't see, the heart doesn't grieve about.' Betty winked; she wasn't going to miss out on a free night out at the expense of the Yanks. It wasn't every night the airfield opened its gate and you didn't have to pay for a thing.

18

'Come on, ladies, give us your hands and we'll pull you up.' The most handsome airman that Molly had ever seen held his hand out for Connie and Molly to grab before hoisting them up into the back of the army truck that was already nearly packed with excited women all dressed in their best and smelling of a mixture of perfumes and hairspray.

'Hang on to these ropes and then you won't fall out, ladies. My friend who's driving is bad at corners and he doesn't like driving in the near dark. Hold on tight now. I'll just pull this back flap down and we'll soon be there,' the tall good-looking American said. The truck was filled to the brim and the engine started much to the excitement of the crush of young women.

'If he's anything to go by, we are going to have a good night, girls,' Betty said, as she pushed her way next to Molly and Rose. 'Did you hear that accent? It makes me go weak at the knees.'

Molly looked at Connie and shook her head, hanging on for dear life as the truck sped down the narrow road to the airfield a few miles out from York in the clear space of the outlying fields.

'Yes, I love their uniforms, and they sound so different. It's going to be quite a night. I know it is.' Connie squealed as they went over a bump and all the passengers in the lorry laughed – it was the most excitement any of them had encountered for months. The chatter was loud and excited as they climbed down from the back of the lorry a short while later.

'Oh, Mol, these dresses are all right, but they don't half crease easy,' Connie said after being held tight round the waist and lifted out of the lorry by one of the American servicemen. 'Do you think we look all right?'

'We're just as well dressed as anybody, and we have stockings on, which a lot of the girls haven't. Just look at this place, all these huts and hangars, and just look at the tower up there looking out over the airfield.' Molly was more in awe of what was around her than how she looked as she followed the stream of girls to a large hangar guarded by a man with 'MP' on his hat and armbands. 'I've never been here before, even though Ned is based here; it's always been off-limits to civilians.'

'That's it, ladies, keep walking. The field is off-limits to visitors. You can stay as long as you want in the hangar, providing no light leaks out, but our Military Police will have you in the clink as soon as you can say "as sure eggs is eggs" if you venture anywhere else.' The airman grinned and winked as he saw his harem of young women into their hall of dreams. 'We Americans know how to have a good time. There's plenty to drink, eat and the music, well, we've brought our own band with us, so I hope you ladies like to jive.' The soldier had brought them to the huge doors that were to be kept open until darkness came when they'd have to close to stop the light from within attracting aircraft.

'Jive, what's jive?' Molly asked Connie. She caught her breath as she walked into the hangar. At the far side was a makeshift stage with many seats and music stands on it, but the walls and windows were covered with balloons and the American flag alongside the Union Jack. The centre of the hall was empty but down either side were long tables with more drink and food on them than any of the girls had ever seen.

'It's a right fast dance, Molly; have you not seen it being done? Lord Almighty, what a party. Just look at it and look at the men . . .' Connie gasped. 'There's our lovely boys in blue here, the Polish and then there's the Americans . . . It's like being given the first choice in the best box of chocolates that Rowntree's ever made.'

'Too true, Connie; it's like going to heaven,' Betty said, pushing her way past both girls and making a beeline for the band where she started talking to one of the trumpeters.

Molly sighed. 'We aren't with her, Connie. She's just man mad. Her poor husband. She can't be true to him and she never even seems to try to be.'

'Can you blame her? He might never come back and we might not be alive tomorrow; we should grab happiness while we can. I aim to, and you should find yourself a fella. The one you waved off has never written to you yet. He'll have said that to women wherever he's been, so don't keep your heart for him.' Connie spoke firmly and walked over to take a bottle of beer from a blond airman who was handing them out. He had the whitest teeth and the widest smile that Connie had ever seen.

Molly looked around her. Connie was right; she'd not heard from her good-looking Matt since he'd been gone, even though she had put pen to paper quite a few times. Everyone was having a good time and she should too, she thought, when she felt a hand on her arm and heard a familiar voice.

'Hello, Molly, have you decided to join the party? I don't suppose Rose came with you, did she?' It was Peter, who smiled at the younger sister of the woman that he was fighting secret feelings for.

'Oh no, she wouldn't come here unless Ned was here, and besides she'll be looking after Ned's mother. I've come here with Connie, but she's a bit occupied at the moment.' Molly glanced across at Connie, who seemed to have managed to capture the attention of a young serviceman that had caught her eye.

'Yes, she does look like she's enjoying herself,' Peter replied. 'I didn't think Rose would be here, but I did ask her. I thought it might do her good. Cheer her spirits!'

Molly seemed distracted; she was looking around as the band started to play and the airmen and the local girls started to pair up.

Peter sipped at his drink. 'Grr. . . they even bring their own music with them. Glenn Miller – if I've heard it once, I've heard it ninety times since the Yanks got here. Us men who've always been here are having our noses pushed out. You girls are star-struck with them and their ways. Yet this lot has nothing to do with the war yet, and never will by what they have been saying. It's all right them dancing the night away but they aren't fighting for their country.'

'I'm not bothered about them at all,' said Molly. 'But I can't believe all this food, music and drink. It's as if there is no war on.'

'Good job they're just visiting, although we could do with Eisenhower's help. They would have been better coming to back us up rather than showing us their technology, partying and then going home. Bloody show-offs,' Peter growled, watching the men that England could dearly do with having fight by their side.

Molly smiled as a young man approached them.

'Excuse me, sir, but may I ask this young lady to dance? That is if she is free?' the young man asked, looking at Peter and then Molly.

'You ask away, lad. I'm just a friend. Molly, the night is yours . . .' Peter said and he gestured for her to join the lad on the dance floor.

''I, er . . . I don't know this song, but I'm willing to try and dance to it,' Molly replied, listening to the tune and noticing Peter looking dejected before she took the hand of the American airman.

Peter knew that the women were infatuated with the Yanks with their slick ways and their sharp uniform and different accents. The one good thing that they had brought with them was a good bottle or two of whisky, though even that they cheapened by calling it Bourbon. He would go back to his bunk and enjoy a drink on his own without the sound of American music and star-struck women who were not interested in the English pilots while the Yanks were in town.

'So what's your name?' the young man asked Molly.

'I'm Molly, Molly Freeman. I work at Rowntree's chocolate factory in York,' Molly replied, as she tried to concentrate on where her feet went and think about where the young man had his hands on her body. 'Are you a pilot?'

'Lord, no, ma'am, I'm just ground crew. Although one day I aim to fly, yes, ma'am. I'm not going to be on the ground forever. I'm Mark, Mark Regan from Pennsylvania; my family have an automobile firm out there. My pa said I was an idiot for joining the air service, but I couldn't have worked alongside my pa; we would have ended up killing one another.'

'Oh, when you say automobile firm, do you mean a garage?' Molly asked as she tried to concentrate.

'Shucks, no. My pa makes cars – he has his own factory, and we can make up to twenty cars a day most days. But it isn't for me. Besides, my older brother is the better businessman.' Mark looked at Molly. 'I know this is quite personal, but why are you and some of the other girls a yellowish colour?'

'I hoped you wouldn't notice. I must have used nearly all my powder compact on my face tonight. I know I said I worked in a chocolate factory, but at the moment it's been taken over by the ministry. I fill bombs . . .' Molly whispered, immediately regretting her confession. 'But we are not supposed to say, so shh!'

'No way! So all of you who have the same colour

are doing that?! Jeez, what a job! You risk your lives making bombs to drop on those that are trying to kill you Brits. You are one brave lady, and I'm glad and proud that you're on my arm. Of course you'll need us Yanks to stop these Jerries. You just don't know it yet,' Mark said, and he smiled as they caught their breath between dances.

'If you think so, but our lads are just as good; we'll win with you or without you,' Molly replied, sticking up for the British. The cockiness of the visiting Americans made her feel sorry for the lads who risked their lives every day and had to put up with that attitude.

'Well, there is one thing; you can't throw parties like this without our help. Now grab my hand and let me show you this dance; everyone's doing it in the States. It's called the Lindy Hop. Watch those two over there for a minute. That's my mate Jack – he can really dance!'

Molly watched an airman and a woman dressed in a short skirt and knitted cardigan go to the centre of the room, as the band played a heavy beat with trumpets blaring. The young man took hold of his partner's hand and pushed and pulled her back and forth, twirling her as they danced to the beat. 'See, doll, it's easy. Come on, I'll show you.'

Molly pulled on Mark's hand. 'No, I couldn't honestly. I couldn't!' she cried as he dragged her next to the dancing couple, others not far behind.

'Yes, you can. You'll enjoy yourself. Just do what you feel. Just feel the beat; it's as easy as that.' Mark pulled on Molly's arm. 'Go on, go for it, gal, have yourself a good time –that's what life's all about.' He grinned as Molly smiled and laughed and felt her new skirt fly up around her, her confidence growing as everyone else joined in. Her new American friend was showing how life could be lived and she was enjoying every minute. 'That's it, feel the beat and grab my hand now – backwards and forwards,' Mark said and he grinned as the two of them danced for all they were worth.

'Well, Molly Freeman, I didn't know you could dance like that.' Connie looked at her best friend as they met one another in the toilets to discuss their evening.

'I didn't either. I'm shattered, but isn't it fun?' Molly bent double and tried to catch her breath and to cool down her cheeks. They felt aglow with the heat of the dance floor. 'I've never, ever danced like that, isn't it good?'

'It is. I must admit I'm having a brilliant time. Isn't it funny our boys are just standing and watching while the Yanks are showing us a good time? Have you tried their bottles of beer, or lager as they call it? And the bowl of punch is unbelievable, but I must not have any more – it's making me light-headed.' Connie giggled and then powdered her nose.

Molly looked at herself in the mirror and wished she was better looking. 'I've had some of that punch, but my mam will play heck with me if I come back drunk. What's your fella called? You made a beeline for the blond in the band, but now you're dancing with another bloke?'

'He's called Chuck, and you'll never guess where he's from? I'm sure the gods have fated him to me.' Connie leaned back on the wooden door of the toilet and grinned.

Molly grinned back at her. 'I truly have no idea where Chuck comes from. Heaven perhaps by the look on your face?'

Connie patted her hair in place and reapplied her lipstick. 'Better than that, he's from Montana. Can you believe it? Montana, Molly, the same place as Billy. I couldn't believe it! I've asked him all sorts about where he's from; it sounds like cowboy county, and I just can't believe it! But what about your fella? He can dance if nothing else.'

'He's called Mark, he's from Pennsylvania and his father manufactures cars. Not a garage – he actually makes cars! He's got a brother and he's ground crew for the airmen that are with him. Other than that I can't tell you much because all we've done is dance; he won't sit still or talk.' Molly sighed but she didn't feel the excitement Connie had. Mark was all right but it wasn't like when Matt had first spoken to her. She wished he would write to her; she had done so to him through the address he had given her but she hadn't heard a thing back since they had said goodbye outside the Minster.

'Just all right, Molly? Chuck is better than all right. I hope I get to see him again. He's so big and strong and his accent is to die for. Come on, we can natter more when we're back home, but I'm not going to waste a minute here.'

She pulled on Molly's arm and dragged her back to the main dance, waving at the handsome Chuck, who was waiting for her on the other side of the dance floor.

'See you later, Mol.'

'Yes, I'll see you later,' Molly replied and looked around for Mark, who she had hoped would also be waiting for her. However, she saw him on the dance floor with another woman in his arms, who she recognized from the offices at Rowntree's. She shrugged. It was no big loss; he wasn't her sort anyway. She had been quite glad he hadn't talked a lot to be honest; he wasn't that handsome and his voice was high-pitched and she found the Yankee drawl irritating.

She made her way to some chairs at the far end of the dance floor and sat down in them, slipping one of her shoes off. It had been rubbing all night and she could feel a blister forming as she ran her hand over her heel.

'Has our Yank friend stood you up? He likes his dance too much.'

Molly looked up and saw an English airman in uniform smiling down at her rubbing her feet.

Molly smiled and slipped her shoe back on her foot. 'Yes, it would seem so; I couldn't keep up with him anyway.'

'May I join you? I've brought drinks; I thought you might require refreshment after all that exercise. I'm Richard, Richard Robinson, and I have two left feet and I find this music and the visiting Yanks irritating to say the least. So I'm afraid I won't be asking you to dance.'

'That's all right; I think I've had enough dancing for

tonight. Please do join me and another drink is most welcome. I'm Molly. I live in York.' Molly took a small sip and looked at the slightly older man next to her who was obviously a bit worse for drink.

'Hello, Molly. I take it that you work in the munitions factory, which, of course, is top secret, so we won't talk about it.' Richard smiled and took a drink.

'Yes, I do. Everybody knows us, don't they, because of our skin colour.' Molly sighed.

'Our brave little canaries. It's a badge to be proud of. Without you we wouldn't be able to fight a war, so don't you be ashamed of it.' Richard sat back. 'Just look at all this drink, food, music. Cigarettes, anything you want, the Yanks have brought with them while our poor lads are laying their lives on the line.' He sighed and shook his head.

'They do seem to have come with everything that we don't have,' Molly said, suddenly spotting Betty sneaking out of the building holding the hand of her latest conquest.

'It'll be a different story when they really start to get involved. That is, if they ever do. The war's only just starting. I've had a long day and to be honest I'm in no mood for this frivolity, but we have to be seen to welcome our American cousins, who we may need sooner than they realize.' Richard took a sip of his drink.

'You sound as if you have had a bad day. Do you want to talk about it if you can?' Molly said carefully.

'No, I shouldn't, and besides you're here for a good time, not to sit with a mope like me.' Richard tipped his glass up and downed the rest of the drink. 'I needed that. Do you mind if I get another? Are you joining me?' Richard stood up and signalled for her to drink up.

Molly shook her head; she knew she had better take care, else she would find herself legless. She wasn't used to too much drink. She watched as Richard helped himself to another glass of punch and then came back to sit next to her.

'The problem is, my dear; I'm not suited for my job. I shouldn't tell you this, but I help find and reunite our pilots when they're shot down in foreign fields.' Richard now had a slight slur to his voice. 'This lot enjoying themselves like they are doing is just rubbing salt into my wounds.' He took a long sip. 'The things I hear are horrific and shocking and today, well, today, I heard terrible news about two of our best that were in hiding in France. Shot they were by the bastard Nazis in cold blood.' Richard held his head in his hands.

Molly held her breath; could he be talking about Ned? Had something happened to Rose's Ned? 'Are they local men? Do you know their names?' she asked, trying to hide the concern in her voice.

'Now you're asking too much and I've told you too much. I shouldn't drink! Loose lips and all that . . . Ignore my ramblings before we both get into bother. I'll go and leave you in peace to enjoy the company of these young men while you can,' Richard slurred as he stood up and swayed with his glass in his hand. 'I thank you for your company, my fair maiden, and goodnight.'

Molly watched helplessly as Richard walked unsteadily

away from her, but made a split-second decision and rushed across to him, catching his arm. 'I have to ask. Is one of the airmen Ned, Ned Evans? Please, you've got to tell me!'

Richard put his finger to his lips. 'Shhhhh! I can't say.' Then he wandered into the crowd, leaving Molly feeling in need of home.

'What a night! I don't think I've ever enjoyed myself as much in my life.' Connie giggled and hung on to Molly as they climbed back into the lorry to go home. 'I think I could have died in Chuck's arms. He's so handsome and so, so American . . .'

'I'm glad that you've had a good night,' Molly said and tried to smile. All the women in the lorry were laughing and singing but her heart felt broken. Should she say anything to her mother and Rose or should she keep what Richard had said to herself? It could be any airman that he had lost; it might easily not be Ned.

'It was blinking brilliant. Ooooh . . . hurry up, Betty, the lorry is going . . .' Connie shouted as Betty with her high heels in her hand ran barefoot to catch the lorry and got hoisted up at the last minute by her airman.

Betty caught her breath. 'What a night, girls! Had to finish my date in a hurry. I don't know about you, but American relationships were definitely firmly sealed tonight!'

'I hope we'll be asked back if they stay any longer,' Connie said, and she sighed as they passed through the checkout.

'So do I. I can't live without my ciggies and nylons,' Betty said. She thought briefly about her husband whom she had not heard from in three months. If he came back to her, fair enough, but just in case she was going to cover all options.

19

Winnie had waited up to make sure her girls came back safely, but she knew instantly that something was wrong with her youngest. 'Come on, Molly, what's wrong? Something's been bothering you since you came back from the dance at the airfield. You've not been yourself. You didn't get up to anything you should be ashamed of, did you? Because it's best if you tell me now.'

Winnie was sitting quietly with Molly, her bedtime drink in her hand. 'There's Connie full of it, singing every cowboy song that she's ever heard, and then there's you as quiet as a mouse and looking miserable. What went on? Don't think you can tell me any rubbish. I know you, Molly Freeman. There's something the matter!'

'I had a different night to Connie. I didn't enjoy myself.' Molly sighed. 'I danced with one of the Yanks, who thought he was God's gift and wasn't bothered about anything but dancing. Mam, there was just absolutely anything you could wish for at that dance because America isn't at war yet, and I just don't think it's fair. All our cities are being bombed and they come here and party.'

Winnie hugged her coffee and wondered if she should say what she was really thinking.

'It's not their war, love, at the moment. And long may it stay that way, else it would be more heartache than ever. Their time will come. Is that what's really bothering you or is there more? I know you're an adult now, Molly, but I still worry about you and I know there's something the matter.'

'I don't want to say, Mam,' Molly said. 'It will cause too much upset and, besides, it may have nothing to do with us anyway.' She felt her stomach churn; she wanted to say something, but she didn't want to cause any bother.

'If it's worrying you, then it's worrying me already, so tell me and then perhaps I can help,' Winnie said, trying not to sound too harsh.

'Well, after I'd danced with this lad, an older British officer came and sat with me and he was a bit worse for drink. In fact, he was quite drunk. That's when I started thinking about how unfair it was for our lads at the airfield.'

'He didn't do anything to you, did he? He didn't . . .' Winnie folded her arms and looked cross.

'No, Mam. Even though he was drunk he was the perfect gentleman. But he did tell me that he dealt with missing pilots and the Resistance that gets them out of France. The reason he was so drunk was that he'd heard two pilots had been found and killed by the Germans. That's why he wasn't happy with the party. I just thought . . .' Molly hung her head.

'You thought that it might be Ned? Well, Rose has had no news and if the airbase had heard, they would have let her know, so don't even think of it. Ned will be fine,' Winnie said firmly. 'He'll return home and, when he does, there will be the biggest wedding that you have ever seen. You'll have to get your sewing machine out again then. New dresses will be needed all round.' Winnie hugged her daughter close. 'You always worry about everybody, Molly; you just think of yourself for once. There are so many things we can't change in this war, but we will come out the other end of it, believe me.'

'I just hope it isn't Ned, Mam. Rose would be heart-broken,' Molly sobbed.

'Well, it won't be. Now you get yourself to bed. It's work again in the morning. Connie's been in bed for a good hour, but then again she looked worn out. It must have been all that dancing and flirting.'

'Yes, she met a fella from Montana and got on well with him,' Molly replied and made her way to the stairs.

'Yes, I must have heard him being mentioned a thousand times this weekend, Chuck! What kind of a name is that?' Now get yourself to bed and stop worrying — no news is good news — and I'll see you in the morning.'

'Night, Mam, thank you. I love you,' Molly said quietly, and left her mam backing up the fire with slack for the night.

Winnie put the scuttle full of coal down by the hearth and sat in her chair. This was the time she loved to be by herself; the day was over and her girls were asleep in their beds. She thought about what Molly had said and closed her eyes. She'd lied through her teeth; she didn't know if Rose would have been told yet, and she too was concerned by this news. She just hadn't wanted Molly fretting unnecessarily over something that couldn't be undone anyway. That was her job: to worry about her family. Molly was working every day in munitions along with Connie, both at the risk of being blown up at any time. Rose looking after Ivy, along with the pressure of a job that she was struggling with and thinking about Ned. As for Annie, she only got a letter as and when Annie saw fit to write home and it was always about pigs and farming. Who'd have thought her Annie was as happy, literally, as a pig in muck, farming? Winnie closed her eyes. Lord knows what her old man would have made of it all, but sometimes she really missed him and could do with him back by her side. She got up from her seat and wound the grandfather clock that had watched over several generations of the Freeman family with its steady constant tick, no matter what the world threw at them. But now the day had beaten her and she needed her bed, she thought, and she yawned and started up the stairs.

'Ey up, Winnie, you've got a letter here from France for your Molly,' the postman said as he stood watching her scrubbing the front step with a donkey stone in her hand. 'I don't know why you women still bother with that, not now in these times. Some of the streets around here are flattened and there's you scrubbing the door-step.' He held the letter in his hand and leaned against the red-brick wall of the terraced house.

'I'm doing it because I've pride in my home, Walter, and no matter what that bloody Hitler throws at this family we'll always have a clean threshold to cross over. He'll not get my standards to slip, no matter what he does.'

'You women, I can never understand you,' Walter said, as he handed Winnie the letter. 'Hope it's good news. I seem to bring more bad than good nowadays,' he muttered and then moved off.

Winnie looked at the letter. She had a good idea who it was from, and she was glad that the young soldier had taken the time to write to Molly. At least he was alive or was at the time of posting the letter; it would cheer her up, she thought, as she swilled the bleached water down the street and brushed her part of the world spotlessly clean. She placed her wet brush upside down next to the front door to dry. The phrase 'putting the brush' out came to her, meaning that she was available for gentleman callers, and she didn't want anyone to think that of her no matter how old she was, but she ignored the thought and carried the bucket through to the backyard. Then she went back to the kitchen to put the letter on the mantelpiece for Molly to open when she arrived back from her shift.

Winnie was startled out of her thoughts on hearing a knock on her open front door and a very well-educated voice asking, 'I say, hello, is there anybody there?'

'Erm . . . yes. I'm here. Can I help?' Winnie wiped her hands on her crossover apron and went to the door. There in front of her stood a young man in military uniform with a swagger stick under his arm.

'I'm terribly sorry to bother you, but I'm looking for a Winnie Freeman. I believe that she lives here, and I've just come to pay my respects and thank her for her kindness,' the young officer said, looking at the elderly housewife who stood in front of him.

'Are you sure that you want Winnie Freeman and not Molly or even Connie?' Winnie asked and looked at the young man who she'd never seen before, thinking he was perhaps somebody the girls had met at the RAF base.

'Oh yes. I believe Winnie works for Rowntree's and has been kind enough to do my washing and send me small gifts of baking. It has kept me feeling positive while I've been in training camp. I just wanted to meet her and suggest that we keep in touch now we're about to move out. Have I got the wrong address perhaps?' The soldier smiled.

Winnie smiled back at him. 'Ah, there's been a misunderstanding. My daughters work at Rowntree's, but it's me that does your washing and has been sending small gifts.' She saw the soldier realize that the woman he'd come to meet was neither young nor available. She looked at the badges and stripes on his uniform. 'Now who are you, the corporal or the sergeant? I'm afraid I don't know my army stripes.'

'Ahh! I'm Corporal Michael Grady of the First Division Yorkshire Fusiliers. So it's you that I must thank for your kindness. Which I do, I am most grateful for the thought put into each delivery,' the soldier said, not entirely able to hide his disappointment.

'I'm a bit too old in the tooth for you, more like a mother than a prospective girlfriend. Forgive me but I can see the disappointment on your face. However, I do make a good cup of tea, and although I've just been scrubbing the step there's always something good to eat in one of my cake tins.' Winnie smiled. 'In fact, I think there is the smallest piece of Madeira cake left, just as if it's waiting for you before you leave us.

'I'm sorry, was I that obvious?' Michael said and blushed.

'It's all right, lad. I'm not offended. Now, I'm parched. Let's have that drink of tea and you can tell me a bit about yourself, and I'll show you a picture of my daughters and I'm sure any of them would be proud to have you write to them.'

'Are you sure? You look busy.' Michael didn't want to look ungrateful.

'Yes, now come in and have a cup of tea. I'll share my ration, I tend to use the tea leaves until I can get the last drop out of them and you must have the last slice of cake. You'll not be getting any, I suppose, where you'll be going.' Winnie sighed. 'I don't know, what a waste – all this fighting over nothing. All our young men with their lives on the line because of a crazy man. Is it France you are going to or can't you say?' Winnie asked as she put the kettle on to boil and strained the breakfast tea leaves to get yet another brew out of them.

'I can't say, but let's just say it's warmer climes,' Michael replied, watching as the smallest sliver of cake was put on a plate in front of him. 'This is so kind, Mrs Freeman. I feel guilty eating it when food is scarce.'

'Don't you feel guilty for one minute, my lad. Just your keep your head low and make sure you get back to your family, that's all I ask of you. Oh, and that you enjoy every crumb. I've enjoyed doing your washing; it was my way of contributing to the war effort. I'm only sorry that I'll have come as a bit of a disappointment to you.' Winnie laughed and reached for the photograph of her three girls. 'These are my girls, all doing their bit to keep the enemy from the door. I couldn't be prouder.'

'They're all very beautiful, Mrs Freeman. I would have been more than happy to have met any one of them and I wish to thank you again for all that you have done for me. It's good to be shown a little kindness in this hard world.' Michael sipped the tea and looked at his watch. 'Time to head back to base, I fear, but it's been a pleasure to meet you.'

'And you. Now you take care of yourself and I'll tell my girls that you called. They'll be sorry that they missed you.' Winnie followed the young soldier to the door and then quickly called him back to her. 'Here, this is for luck, because I know your mother would do it if she was here.' Winnie balanced on her toes and kissed the surprised young soldier on his cheek. 'You make sure you look after yourself and you come home.'

'I will, thank you, Mrs Freeman,' he replied, nodding at Winnie's next-door neighbour as she watched him leave.

'Aren't you a bit too old for putting the brush out, Winnie Freeman? What will your girls have to say?' her neighbour joked as she watched the young man go striding up the street.

'I've been doing his washing through Rowntree's; he thought I was a young lass, the least I could do was kiss him. Poor devil,' Winnie said and rested for a moment on the door frame.

'That's what you tell me. Lucky I believe you, but

there's many a good tune played on an old fiddle and I wouldn't mind a tune or two with him,' said her neighbour with a grin on her face.

'Oh, don't you think we are far too old for that sort of thing? But we can both dream and remember when we weren't,' said Winnie as they both returned to their housework with smiles on their faces.

'I swear I'm packing munitions in my sleep, I feel so tired,' Molly sighed as she opened the front door of the home that they were always grateful to return to after a long day at work.

'I know, but I'm not forgoing another dance or the pictures just to catch up on sleep. A girl has to have some fun. I so hope that Chuck writes to me; he promised he would exchange addresses, you know?' Connie slipped off her shoes as soon as her feet hit the hall carpet and leaned against the wall as she took her coat off. 'I keep thinking of him and what Montana must be like, and hoping I did the right thing by leaving Billy in the orphanage to be adopted out there in the Wild West.' Connie sighed and dreamed of handsome cowboys on horses and her younger brother running wild and free on the prairie that Chuck had told her about.

'I think the days of cowboys and Indians have gone. He's probably living in a normal house with a father who is a doctor or dentist or banker and has never seen a horse or a prairie,' Molly said, hanging her coat up. She shivered. 'It's getting colder. I hope Mam's got a good fire going.'

'You're wrong. Chuck says it's all prairie, mountains and blue skies, and, yes, there are still cowboys and Indians, so you can smirk all you like, Molly Freeman. I believe him even if you don't,' Connie retorted as they both entered the kitchen and made for the warmth of the fire. Autumn was on its way out and the girls were beginning to feel the cold.

'You both need to put your vests back on and even your liberty bodices if they still fit. We can't rely on coal being delivered like it used to be. The delivery man signed up and there's only one man in the yard,' Winnie said as she took in both girls warming themselves at the fire.

'Mam, we're grown women. We're not going to wear those awful liberty bodices,' Molly growled. 'I hated mine, with the rubber buttons down the front and the tape binding. It was just another thing I had to learn to fasten.'

'But they kept you warm – that is when you had it on. Nine times out of ten I used to find yours hidden under your pillow you hated it that much. You always were a stubborn one.'

'I was not. That's our Annie; she's the one that does as she likes and says it as it is, and she always has been,' Molly snapped.

'I wish she'd write home more,' Winnie replied and then remembered Molly's letter. 'Oh, and that reminds me, there's a letter come for you today.'

Connie gasped excitedly. 'Oh, for me! It'll be Chuck! He said he would write once he was home.'

'Sorry, Connie, it's for Molly, and it's from France by the looks of it. You've got to give your Chuck a bit more time yet. Lord, he won't be halfway back to America, let alone have time to write and send a letter to you,' Winnie said sternly, noting the disappointment on Connie's face.

'He can suit himself. He might have taken my eye, but it doesn't matter if he doesn't write. It's his loss,' Connie said sharply.

Molly felt her heart skip a beat. 'For me? Has Matt written? I didn't think he would – I just thought he'd go over to war and forget about me.'

'Well, it looks like he's kept his word, so he must be a good'un. He's obviously thought of you, else it wouldn't be there.'

Connie watched as Molly put the letter into her skirt pocket; she knew she would be reading it in the privacy of her bedroom and felt a pang of jealousy. She had taken everything that Chuck had said with a pinch of salt and did secretly doubt whether he would write to her or even remember her. In truth, she knew that the Yanks were all mouth and trousers, as Betty had said earlier at work. She probably wouldn't hear from him ever again.

'Are you not going to read it? I wouldn't be able to wait,' Connie enquired as they pulled their seats up to a meagre meal of corned beef and mashed potatoes.

'No, I'll wait. I didn't think he would write to me so I'm going to hang on every word.' Molly remembered her dark-haired handsome soldier and blushed as she looked down at the small portion of food and thought about the kiss he had given her when he had

233

said goodbye. 'I'm just glad to hear from him and know that he's safe and alive.'

Winnie smiled at her daughter. Unlike Connie, Molly would keep her feet on the ground and be there for her man when she was needed. 'I got a surprise visitor this morning,' she said. 'Corporal Michael Grady. He came to thank us for doing his washing. I think he was a bit disappointed when there was just me at home.'

'Oh, I wish I'd been at home to meet him. Why did he come here?' Connie asked.

'I've been sending what I can for a treat back with the washing and a note thanking him for his courage. I thought he might like to know we were there for him. He was a very well-spoken young man. Unfortunately he was being sent into action, though he couldn't say where to.'

Winnie finished her supper and sat back and looked at the two girls. 'These lads are laying their lives down for our freedom, girls; you must respect them and wish them the best even if they don't write to you. Because God knows what they'll have to go through for us.' She sighed. 'Your father thought that there would never be another war like the last, but this one I fear is going to be even worse. Let's just hope we all keep safe. Now, who's washing up, or is it me as usual?'

At this Molly pushed her chair back, unable to wait another minute to read her letter from the handsome Matt.

20

'Remember, girls, October and November are the months for slaughtering on this farm. All the porkers are off to the slaughterhouse and the *special ones* will be seen to next weekend. The farrowing sows and piglets stay to make sure we have pigs to slaughter next year. Once the tatties are lifted we can let them into those fields. They like nothing better than to root about and get shit up, looking for the odd potato that we've missed.' Bernard Farrington leaned over the pen gate and thought about the brass he was going to make in the coming week or two; it was now that all his hard work paid off.

'I know they're bred for food but I've become quite close to some of these pigs. They all have their own ways once you get used to them,' Annie said to Helen's disgust.

'How can you become close to a pig? Don't be so soft,' Helen replied. She was grateful that for a short while their life was not going to be filled with the smell of pig muck.

'It's true. That'un over there likes its back being scratched just in a certain place, and Rommel over there doesn't like cabbage leaves in his slops,' Annie said.

Bernard laughed. 'Rommel? That's an insult to the pig! But, yes, you're right; they're just like us if truth be told. We'll make a farmer of you yet, lass. But it's a big mistake getting too close to them because they're all going to end up on somebody's dinner plate and make me a bob or two.'

'I often think about them when I'm eating my egg and bacon and feel guilty, and then I remember how hungry I am and try to forget. As long as I don't know which pig I'm eating I'll be all right,' Annie said, and looked away from her wards that would soon be no more.

Bernard puffed on his pipe and smiled. 'Well, we'll be keeping one of the *special ones* for the house. I've never seen fatter pigs, with all those scraps we get for them. The government's ration of pig feed is all right, but it's people's and restaurants' leftovers that have fattened them up.'

Helen sighed. 'I can't think about it. I truly did not have a clue where my bacon came from when I was in London and sometimes I wish I didn't know.'

'You should know where your food comes from, else you could be eating any old rubbish. These pigs have been reared with love and care. Everyone is connected to the earth if they did but know it.' Bernard pulled on his pipe and smiled; his land girls weren't as strong as his nephew but they gave him many an hour of amusement with their struggles to become farmers, though at the same time some worries as they got used to his ways. 'Anyway, let's get ourselves in for our mid-morning brew; the postman's just been and no doubt there'll be either bills or bad news waiting for me. It's always one or the other.'

Annie and Helen followed Bernard into the house, both walking inside with their mucky boots still on, but remembering to give them a quick clean with the yard brush before entering – they had grown used to the ways of the Farringtons and the smell. Lizzie Farrington bottomed the kitchen every Saturday morning, swilling and scrubbing the stone-flagged floor with bleach, but the rest of the week it was given just a quick sweep accompanied by a few choice words to whoever brought the most muck in on their boots. Cleanliness was not high on Lizzie's list. However, at the present, she was a little bit more particular, as she knew folk would be arriving for their cuts and she didn't want to be gossiped about in Clitheroe.

'I hope you've brushed those boots; you never know who'll pull up at our door at the moment and I've to have everything spotless this week when all the pigs go to market and the pig killer comes. He likes all his knives good and clean. That reminds me, Father, we need the water boiler from out in the outhouse filling; he goes through buckets of boiling water when he's scouring the bristles off the pigs.' Lizzie was in a stern mood, she didn't like visitors and she didn't like the extra work that came at pig-killing time.

'There's a letter come from Mike. He says he's on the Belgian border and then the rest is crossed out so I can't read it. He must have said something he shouldn't and those that are in charge have blocked it out.' Lizzie sighed. 'It isn't as if we're friends with Hitler. I can't see any sense of all this censoring to the likes of us.'

'But the letters might fall into the wrong hands, so they have to be censored. He must be all right then, that's good to know, ' Bernard said, and sat back, relaxed, in his chair as Lizzie poured them all a cup of tea and put some buttered oatcakes in front of them.

'He's sent you this and all; it was put inside our letter.' Lizzie turned and passed Annie an envelope with her name on it. 'I don't know what's in it, but I guess lavender by the smell.'

Annie looked at the small envelope with her name written on it and blushed. 'For me? It can't be for me.'

'Aye, well, it is, lass; it's got your name on it,' Lizzie said, and she stood over her as she opened the letter.

Helen glanced over too.

'It is lavender: three sprigs tied with a blue ribbon.' Annie pulled the partly crushed stalks out and smelled it and then reached into the envelope for the small card that was within and read the wording: *A sweet smell to remember me by until next time we meet. Mike xx*

'Now, isn't that just like him? He's taken a liking to you, my girl. I'll have to give you the address so you can send a letter to him. Perhaps we have the makings of a romance. Who would have thought that of our Mike; he's a dark one.' Lizzie chuckled as she went about her business.

'Aren't you the lucky one?' Helen said and winked at Annie from the other side of the table. She hadn't been attracted to the dashing Mike, but she found herself quite envious of the sweet-smelling gift.

'I'm very lucky; I'll keep it under my pillow and it'll

help me sleep,' Annie replied, quickly putting it back in the envelope and placing it safely on the kitchen dresser. 'He must have picked it in Belgium or France. It's come all that way just to me.'

'The lad must be smitten with you; he always did have a good eye for a bonny lass,' Bernard said as he put his cup down heavily. 'But never mind his soft words. Come on, you two, back to work; we've pigs to sort and plough blades to sharpen and none of it will get done by itself. Time waits for no man.'

'And don't forget to bring my boiler in from the out-house, else there'll be no pig killing!' Lizzie yelled as all three walked out of the farmhouse and back to their work.

The following morning everyone was up early. The fattened pigs had to be loaded into the butcher's wagon and that was a job and a half as Annie and Helen found out.

'You make them go where you want them to go with this board and a stick. Hold it at one side so that it doesn't know where it's going and pat it gently with the stick until it makes its way up the ramp and into Alf's wagon.' Bernard showed the girls and then stood back. 'Don't rush them and don't let them slip else they'll bruise and then that leg of ham or pork will not be fit to eat.'

The day had come when Helen and Annie picked their pigs and took them out of their pens and quietly guided them to the wagon of death and watched as Alf the butcher looked at each one as it entered the wagon and then closed the tailgate to keep them in.

'I hate doing this. We're sending them to their death,' Annie said and tried not to look at her favourite, Rommel, as she guided the grunting, complaining pig into the wagon.

'Aye, but you're keeping a lot of Lancashire and Yorkshire folk fed. Just think of that, lass. They'll be grateful to you when they're tucking into their Sunday roast of pork or a rasher of bacon.'

Alf grinned when she shook her head. 'I don't think I'll eat bacon ever again without feeling guilty,' Annie said. She looked at Helen who was following her with one of the thinner porkers and even she had a tear in her eye.

'I don't like being part of this. I'm one of the last faces that they'll see and I've betrayed them,' Helen said and wiped her nose on her sleeve.

'They're only pigs; they haven't any feelings,' Alf said, securing the tailgate of his wagon.

'Nay, I'll argue against that, Alf. Pigs are very clever animals; they let you know when they're content with their lot and you do get attached to them,' Bernard replied, and for a moment Annie thought he was going to cry too.

Alf grinned. 'You've been too long with them, Bernard; you are going soft in your old age. You'll not be saying that when my cheque is in your bank.'

'Aye, and you'll no doubt benefit from a few dodgy sales with no questions asked. If you can't make money

240

when there's a war on, when can you?' Bernard winked at the red-cheeked rotund butcher.

'I know nowt of what you're talking about. Straight as the day is long, that's me. Honest Alf, the butcher.' Then Alf slapped Bernard on his back and climbed into the front of his wagon, which had seen better days, and filled the farmyard with smoke as it backfired and made its way down the farm track.

'Well, that's them gone for another year. We'll have a good tidy-up, sweep the pens clear and then get ready for tomorrow. If you think today's been bad, you'll not like tomorrow.'

Bernard put his head down and picked up a yard brush. Even he didn't like to see Jim Mackreth coming up the road with his bag of butchering knives to kill and prepare the house pig, and this year doing two more for those in Clitheroe that had clubbed together for him to rear and deliver them bacon, chops, liver and whatever else could be made out of the pigs. Not a thing would be wasted; the only thing not being used would be the squeal that it made as its throat was cut and the blood drained from its body to be made into black pudding.

The following day was even worse for the girls.

'I can't stand it. Please make it stop!' Helen cried as she stood outside the pigsties that held the animals to be slaughtered. Bernard had at least known to warn them that it was not a nice sight as he and Jim Mackreth walked in with two long pieces of wood and rope and tackle to hoist the pigs upon to be butchered.

'It's terrible. I hate it. The poor things. I swear I'm never going to eat another mouthful of bacon ever,' Annie replied with her hands over her ears, and then silence fell, apart from the men and Lizzie talking quietly.

Then Lizzie came out from the pig hull, where the poor creature hung, with a bucket of the pig's blood that she was stirring constantly. Its throat had been slit and the animal drained of blood. She looked at Helen whose face was as white as a ghost.

'Here, Annie, you've the stronger stomach. Take this stick and keep stirring. Don't stop, else it will clot and be no good for anything. Come on, Annie, this makes black pudding, but it's got to be stirred else it congeals.

Annie took the stick and the bucket of dark red blood and did as she was asked. It looked disgusting and smelled of iron and soon spattered her hands. Never before had she been asked to do such a thing and her stomach churned as she stirred until the blood had cooled down.

Both girls looked through the open pig hull's door and saw the butchered pig hanging up by its back legs as Jim Mackreth slit its belly and took out its innards.

It was barbaric and Helen had to look away as the smell reached her nostrils. She felt her stomach heave.

'Don't you be bloody sick. Go and get a bucket of boiling water. The bristles need shaving off next and that can only be done with boiling water to soften them.' Then Bernard moved to the next pig hull for the next slaughter to begin.

Helen couldn't go fast enough to the house for the boiling water; she had got the easier job and she knew it. How Annie could stir the blood she didn't know. There would be no way she would be eating any black pudding now she knew how it was made. It wasn't a southern delicacy and now she knew why. As she filled a bucket full of boiling water and started back to the scene of the slaughter, she passed Annie and Lizzie coming back to the house with two buckets of blood. Hopefully the carnage was over, Helen thought, as she put down the bucket of water and hightailed it away from where Jim Mackreth was carving up the pigs. She would not be eating anything for a day or two she decided as she entered the farmhouse kitchen and found Lizzie and Annie greasing large roasting tins, ready for making black pudding in the already fired oven.

'Bernard will be bringing some pig fat down; it needs cutting into manageable pieces. Can you do that or are you still feeling sick?' Lizzie asked, noting the look of horror on Helen's face.

Helen shook her head. She was feeling sick at the thought of it.

'Well, you chop the sage up then and mix it with that cooked pearl barley while I sort out the other things that need doing. Annie will chop the fat up when it comes and then into the oven it goes when mixed together. We're going to be run off our feet these next few days. Folk will start knocking on the door wanting their cut. They can have most things but not the hams and bacon; they need curing for a month or so, so Bernard will see to them.' Lizzie was in a flap. She knew exactly what was going to happen: people would come and ask for their part of the kill and Bernard would let her handle all of them, even though she was also making the puddings, sausages and faggots. It was always the same. 'Damn Bernard and his money-making schemes,' she said out loud, swearing under her breath.

Annie and Helen looked at one another and knew to get their heads down and just get on with their jobs and not ask questions. It had been the day from hell and both had hated every second; they had never expected an experience like that and they were not likely to forget it quickly. Farming pigs and seeing what became of them had changed the way they thought of farming and animals; it would be a while before they'd be enjoying their fried breakfast in the morning.

Over the next few days folk had come and gone, picking up their parcels wrapped in newspaper and carrying them away under their arms, all smiling as they walked away. Saving all their scraps and the payment to Bernard Farrington had been worth every penny. 'Proper meat and bacon and ham to look forward to' were the words uttered by all the callers and Lizzie had shone with pride when they had complimented her on her puddings and faggots.

Much to the two girls' disgust the black pudding had smelled delicious when it was cooking and any thought of the stirring of the blood was soon forgotten when Lizzie had fried it and presented it with a fried egg and

244

some of her heavy stodgy bread. They both knew that they would need every calorie they could get for the coming weeks of back-breaking work that was vital for keeping the country fed.

Here's the man that ploughs the fields,
Here's the girl who lifts up the yield.
Here's the man who deals with the clamp,
So that millions of jaws can chew and champ.
That's the story and here's the star.
Potato Pete! Eat up, eat up.
Ta-ta! Ta-ta!

'All it does is rain, I'm soaked and my hands are frozen,' Annie said as she put her foot down hard on the spade and unearthed another root of potatoes and put them into the large basket to be carried to the horse and cart when it was full. 'I'd rather be mucking out the pigs, I think, than this.' She threw what was left of the dying plant to the centre of the furrow and stood up and stretched her back. Her hair was sodden with rain as she looked at the full length of the field that had to be harvested and felt a pang of despair. The mist hung around Pendle and the trees had now nearly all lost their leaves. Winter was on its way.

Helen sighed as she picked what potatoes she could find from the heavy earth and added them to her basket. 'I just keep thinking of this weekend. Come what may we're going to the dance at Downham, and let's hope that we have got it right this time and it's not another beetle drive.'

'I'm not that bothered really. I bet it's only old folk that go there anyway. Plus, I'm so tired. I'd just like a lie in bed come Sunday now we don't have as much work to do with the pigs.'

'Well, that's another thing. Do you think Bernard will want us both once the potatoes have been harvested? I bet not!' Helen stood up and looked around her at the grey day and sighed again. 'I think I'm going to get transferred somewhere nearer home; it's so dull up here and it's not going to get any better.'

'You'd leave me here on my own?! You can't do that – I'd be lost without you!' Annie exclaimed, spotting Bernard coming towards them from the far end of the field.

'You'd be fine, gal. They favour you anyway and you've got their nephew Mike sweet on you. You've fitted in like a pig in muck here if you'll pardon the expression,' Helen muttered under her breath as Bernard walked towards them.

'Now then, lasses, how are we doing? I thought I'd better come and help now I've done all the jobs at home. Not a right good day for it, but it has to be done.' Bernard took a spade and bucket from the back of the cart and strode over to an untouched row of potatoes.

'It's a wet one, Mr Farrington, that's for sure, but at least we keep warm with all this digging,' Annie replied. She looked up at Helen as she mouthed *creep* at her and grinned.

Bernard looked up at the cloudy skies and suddenly shouted, 'Lasses, listen! Get down, get down under the cart – there's an aeroplane and it's coming this way. We never have hardly anything fly over here. It must be a Jerry.'

'It'll be nothing; it's only a plane,' Helen said and kept on digging, but Annie ran over to her as she saw the outline of a Heinkel bomber flying below the cloud, the prominent signs of Germany on its wings. Annie pulled Helen to the side of the cart as the bomber flew low over them and Bernard crawled round to join them.

'Bloody hell, bloody Germans, but they're not going to make it over Pendle if they're not careful,' he said, watching as the plane tried to gain height. Then, out of the billowing clouds and hot on its tail, came a Hawker Hurricane, the pilot firing his guns, lighting up the air with orange flames as he chased the bomber across the Lancashire skies.

'Go on, lad, get the bugger! He must have bombed somewhere and be limping his way home by the looks of it.' Bernard swore and stood up and shook his fist at both planes as they disappeared into the clouds, then all three listened for the sound of the Hurricane shooting the enemy out of the sky, but heard nothing. 'I bet he's only just made it over Pendle. I've never seen an aeroplane that low. Did you see the swastika on the wings? We could have been killed if he hadn't been being chased.' Bernard sounded as excited as a young lad as he wiped his brow with his cap and picked up his shovel. 'Bloody

Germans,' he muttered and then went back to his digging before looking at Helen and Annie. 'Go on then, get back at it.'

That evening in the quiet of their bedroom Annie looked at the picture of Joshua with love and sighed. 'I'll never forget you, Josh, but it was not to be,' she whispered as she placed it in her bedside drawer. She glanced at the photograph of her mother and all her sisters smiling at her and reminding her of home. She had been so busy that she'd not had time to miss them, but now with work lessening and with every root of potatoes dug up she had started thinking of home and wondering if she would be there for Christmas. She enjoyed her work on Pendle Farm; despite the muck and the smell it was good to work on the land. She enjoyed knowing her hard work was feeding people and that she was doing some good. She also looked at the sprigs of lavender Mike had sent her that she had placed by her bedside and the card that Lizzie had given her with his contact address. She ran her fingers over the lavender and smiled, thinking about the young soldier whose job she was doing. She would write to him and she would write home too; it was time to catch up with those she loved or could perhaps grow to love in the future, she thought, as she reached for pen and paper from the open drawer and sat on the dressing-table stool looking out at the dark evening. The stars were shining over Pendle as she wrote her first words to Mike and she found that they came a lot easier than she had anticipated.

Helen appeared and slumped down on her bed, making all the springs within it squeak. 'Well, I've done it, Annie. I've told Mr and Mrs F that I want to move on and go back down south. It's where I belong. It's too rugged up here for me, my accent sticks out like a sore thumb and I'm not cut out for this sort of farming. Hop picking or apple picking, that's more me. We always go hop picking in Kent every year, but it's nothing like this. I was stupid just to go where I was offered. I should have been placed nearer home; there are more people needed down south so I know they'll grant me a transfer'

Annie licked and sealed her envelope to her mother and placed it next to the one for Mike on the dressing table and looked at her friend whom she was really going to miss. 'Oh, Helen, I was hoping you were going to stay. How did they both take it?'

'Huh! I think they were glad to hear it really. All the pigs have gone and in a few days all the potatoes will be up; there's no need for the two of us. Bernard is going to take me into Clitheroe tomorrow and then I'll catch the train down to my aunt's. Then I'll apply for a new place-ment nearer home.' Helen started to open her drawers and to take the few clothes that she had out of them.

'That quick? I thought you'd at least stay until the month's end, and then it's getting near Christmas and we will all be going home for a week then at least.' Annie felt bereft at the thought of her friend leaving her.

'Like I said, I think Mr F was glad that I said I wanted to go. I could just see he was. He asked if you were think-ing along the same lines and he looked relieved when I said, as far as I was aware, you were staying. See, he does favour you!'

'Don't be daft. They treat us both the same. Who am I going to do my moaning to now?' Annie went across to sit down next to Helen and put her arms round her. 'Will you be all right? You know there's dogfighting in the skies nearly every day down south; it's possible that you'll be going back to a more dangerous place than here.'

'I'll be just fine. I'm more at home down there and anyway, by the looks of it, a romance is going to be building. Letters to Private Michael Farrington, eh? So you haven't been able to resist.' Helen smiled. 'I hope that he keeps out of danger and that you keep on writing to one another. Plus, you write to me. Do you hear?'

'Of course I will; we have a bond not many others have. A bond in pig muck and tatties, as Mr F calls them.' Annie hugged Helen and they both shed tears together.

'When this war is over we'll meet up. We'll both have a husband on our arms and perhaps even children around our feet,' Helen said, wiping away her tears.

Annie dried her eyes. 'Perhaps a husband, but not children, not for a while anyway. As long as we keep safe that's all I wish for, but I aren't half going to miss you, Helen.'

'And me you. Now stop blubbing and don't forget to post your letter in the morning. You'll have a good catch with Mike; he's quite handsome and I'm jealous.'

Helen smiled as she looked around the bedroom that had been her home for the last three months. She had done well to stay that long; it was a long way from the streets of London and the shops and nightlife that she'd been used to. Annie had settled into farm life better than she had and she was glad for her, she thought, as she dragged her battered leather suitcase from beneath her bed and started to pack for her homeward journey.

22

'Is that Betty being sick again?' Connie said to Molly as she returned from the toilets.

Molly shrugged her shoulders. 'Sick as a dog. Has been every morning this week. She'll lose her job if she's not careful. She needs to have some time off and go to bed for a day or two until she mends.' Molly carried on fill-ing the munitions as if she had been doing it all her life.

'I think it's bed that's got her feeling sick, or too much of it with a certain guard,' Connie replied. 'Have you noticed he's jiggered off and we have a new fella on duty this week? He's a lot nicer and all.' Molly looked puzzled. 'She's . . .' Connie motioned with her hands, making a large bump on her stomach, and grinned as finally the penny dropped with Molly.

Molly looked shocked and blushed. 'Oh, Lord, no! What will her husband say when he comes back from the war? She can't explain a new face at the table away so easily.'

'She's the only one here that won't want her man to return from the front. The question is, will it be the guard's or is it the Yank's that she was late to catch the truck back because of? You could tell she'd been up to no good.'

Betty came back looking pasty-faced and decidedly quiet compared to usual.

'Are you all right, Betty? Is it something you've eaten?' Molly asked, pretending to know nothing.

'It must be, but it'll be sorted in the next day or two. I'll be right by the weekend.' Betty wiped her chin and went back to her station, putting her protective gloves on and concentrating on her work; she didn't want to talk to anybody and hoped nobody knew about the situation she was in. It was better if she kept quiet.

Connie looked at Molly and winked; nobody else might have noticed but they had, no matter how loudly Betty sang 'Ragtime Cowboy Joe'.

'Lord above, Molly, how many letters do you write to this fella of yours? The army is going to need a tank to deliver his mail,' Winnie said as she looked at an envelope Molly had asked her to post as she and Connie rushed out of the house to get to work.

'I don't write that many, Mam. I'll pay you for the stamp tonight when I come home. Thanks!' she shouted as she and Connie slammed the door behind them and made their way down Belgrave Street in the complete darkness of the November morning.

'You do write a lot to Matt. What on earth do you find to write about?' Connie asked as they turned they made their way towards Warwick Street and joined the queue of people waiting at the munitions gates to be let in as the night shift left.

'This and that. I even tell him what I've had to eat, what clothes I'm wearing, anything I can think of, because he says it keeps his mind focused on coming home. He says it's terrible wherever he's at. His letters are that censored I never know where that is, but it all sounds awful and he fears for his life every day. I worry about him. Sometimes I wish we'd never met in case I lose him and then he writes to me and I remember how it felt when he said goodbye and kissed me.' Molly smiled and felt all warm inside. Although they'd only shared a small amount of time together, their feelings were growing for each other with every letter.

'Does he ever mention that horrible friend of his Danny?' Connie asked, pulling a face.

'No, I don't think they were that close; he'd just got a lift into York with him,' Molly replied as they made their way into the factory and changed into their usual turban and overalls. 'Where's Betty? She usually queues up with us, but she's nowhere to be seen.'

'She's probably being sick at home; she'll be upset if she is. The last thing she wants is for her pay to be docked.' Both girls looked at one another as the new guard patted them down in his usual daily search; he was a lot gentler and more polite than the previous one.

'Well, she's not going to be able to hide her condition for much longer, no matter what she does. Lord help her when her other half returns home,' Connie said, and then she prepared herself for another day of singing along to the tannoy and packing munitions, which seemed nothing unusual now, as all the women got back into the swing of their work with only Betty missing from her station.

*

Back at home, realizing there was nothing for supper, Winnie put her hat and coat on and made her way out of the house and up the street – she was going to have to go and queue with the rest of the housewives outside Allen's the butcher's on Haxby Road and see what she could get with her meagre ration book. With a bit of luck Bill or young William would give her a bit extra. He was always bountiful with his promises, but putting them into action was another thing, she thought as she stood in line with many housewives that she either knew or recognized.

'I swear this old devil holds back some meat for those he favours,' one of the women standing with her hands folded and headscarf tied tightly round her head complained. 'Her there always gets a bit more than she should,' she said and she nodded to a woman with blonde permed hair. 'She probably pays him in kind.'

'Well, there's a lot of that going on, Sandra. I had a terrible time this morning. The two children of my next-door neighbour Betty knocked on my door. You should have heard the crying and carrying on from them. It took a while to calm them down enough to find out what had happened to their poor mother. The ambulance came and then the police, and all hell broke loose. Heart-breaking it was to see those two children being taken away in tears.' Sandra's companion folded her arms tight under her bosom as Winnie tried to listen into the conversation.

'Why, what had been going on, Minnie? Betty, is she the one who works in the munitions?' Winnie was now doing more than listening in to the conversation with this mention of Betty and munitions.

'They carried her out on a stretcher; I found her dead when I rushed back with her children. Lying in a pool of blood – it looked very much as if she'd, you know . . . tried to get rid of a baby and it had gone wrong.' The woman pulled a face. 'I always knew she was a bit of a tart; there's her husband away fighting and she was having the time of her life. And those poor children, they've been left all alone .'

'Oh my Lord, how could she take that risk? Those poor children. What will become of them?' Sandra asked, shaking her head and looking at Winnie. 'It all goes on nowadays; everyone lives for the moment and never thinks of the consequences.'

'I think my daughter knows her from Rowntree's, assuming it's the same woman. I'll have to tell her the news if she hasn't heard.' Winnie shook her head too and moved along as the women got served one by one.

'Yes, well, I think she's been going with the guard there, so they say,' Sandra said and turned to her friend. 'I bet all sorts goes on at that place, and the Rowntrees are supposed to be such God-fearing people.'

'One woman who was probably lonely and bringing up children alone shouldn't be the centre of your gossip. Rowntree's cares for all its workers whether they're making munitions or chocolates,' Winnie said sharply. 'And we shouldn't talk ill of the dead. The poor woman must have been desperate.' She stepped up to the counter, thankful that it was her turn to be served. She found herself nodding at Bill Allen's offer of pig's liver for tea, even though she knew Connie was not keen.

'Well, she got the end she probably deserved, raising her skirts for anyone,' Sandra said and looked in disdain at Winnie.

'No good comes of gossip,' Winnie retorted sharply as she put her precious pieces of liver in her shopping basket and passed Bill her ration book and thanked him. As she started to walk away she heard Bill Allen address the gossiping Sandra.

'How about a few slices of tongue? Seems it would be apt this morning.'

A sound of disgust came from Sandra along with: 'There's no need for your sarcasm, Bill Allen, else I won't be giving you my custom.'

'Suit yourself, Sandra, I was just asking,' Bill said, before calling Winnie back to him. 'Here, Winnie, three sausages for you and the girls! They are doing a grand job making munitions and keeping our lads armed. I'd meant to give you them the other day when you asked and I took your tokens if you remember.' Bill winked and put the three precious sausages into Winnie's basket. 'We'd be lost without the Rowntree lasses – no matter what they get up to.'

Sandra looked daggers at both Winnie and Bill. 'I'll be taking my custom elsewhere in the future,' she said haughtily and walked off with her friend behind her. 'It's obvious to me that favours go a long way on this premises.'

Winnie smiled at Bill. 'Thanks for those.'

'No problem, Winnie. Anyway, she can't say anything about anybody; her old man came back from the Great War to find her in bed with his brother. I remember it as clear as day. No good comes of gossiping and she should know it well.' Bill grinned.

Thanks a lot, Bill. My girls will really enjoy them.' Winnie smiled but she still felt sadness at the death of Betty. She wouldn't be the first or last woman to lose her life after trying to get rid of an unwanted baby.

'Oh, Mam, these sausages are absolutely lovely. I don't know how you managed to get them, but we are so grateful,' Molly said that evening as she savoured every mouthful with fried bread and powdered scrambled egg.

'Well, it's through bad news, I'm afraid, and Bill Allen sticking up for decency. I take it your friend Betty wasn't at work today?' Winnie looked at her two girls while they ate their late tea and braced herself to tell them the news and of her run-in with Sandra.

'No, but what has that got to do with sausage?' Connie asked. She pushed her empty plate back and listened to what Winnie was struggling to tell them both.

'Oh no, not Betty, she was the life and soul of our team; she was always singing and acting the fool.' Molly wiped away a tear while Winnie told them the terrible details of her death. 'She must have been desperate. She could have had the baby adopted or even brought it up, although I didn't even know that she had two children already. She never mentioned them.'

'A baby would be the last thing she wanted, but what's going to happen to her children? I've never heard her mention her parents,' Connie said quietly, thinking about her brother and hoping that he was being looked after and loved.

'The authorities will look after them until somebody comes forward to claim them or their father returns from the war. There's enough death without the Bettys of the world losing their lives to backstreet abortionists; it's him or her who should be dead not Betty,' Winnie said quietly. 'If either of you girls gets into the same situation, don't think you'll be standing on your own. I'll be there to support you. But the best thing to avoid that is, as I say, keep your legs together, no matter how much sweet talking you get.'

Connie and Molly both blushed – though a lecture about morals from Winnie was not new to them. Every time they went out they were told 'to behave themselves'.

'Anyway, on a brighter note, we got a long overdue letter from Annie today. Plus, you, Miss Whitehead, have a very well-travelled letter all the way from America; you must have left an impression on that young airman, Gus, Tex or whatever his name was?'

Winnie passed Annie's letter to Molly and enjoyed the smile on Connie's face as she took in the American stamp in the right-hand corner of her letter.

'He's called Chuck and I can't believe he's written. I'd given up on ever hearing from him,' Connie said and beamed. 'I'll read it later.'

Molly looked up from quickly reading the few lines that Annie had sent. 'Well, she sounds happy. Pigs and tatties, who would have thought it of our Annie? She says she might get home for Christmas. It will be good to have all of us back together again. Is there no letter from Matt today?'

'Molly, for heaven's sake, he's fighting for his country not writing letters to you every day,' Winnie replied, surprised to notice a tear falling from Connie's eyes.

'Poor Betty,' Connie said. 'She was a good soul; she just loved life too much. We'll have to tell those at work tomorrow if they haven't already heard.'

'Yes, and we'll have a whip-round for some flowers or something for her children. I wonder when the funeral will be and I wonder whose baby she was carrying?' Molly quietly said.

'Well, I think it's pretty obvious, seeing as the bulldog guard has left his post. I never want to wear those stockings she got from him again or that dress that you made out of parachute silk; it will remind me of her every time I look at them.' Connie sighed. She was going to miss Cowboy Joe Betty, but her heart was racing as she went up the stairs to read her letter from her own cowboy, Chuck from Montana.

23

Molly walked idly through the streets to where Rose lived. Although they worked in the same place, Molly hardly ever saw her sister. Rowntree's operated on two levels, one for the government and one for their own products, and the two hardly crossed paths. It was Sunday morning and various church bells were ringing out in the dank November air as she thought about her sister and if she still had hopes of Ned returning home. It would soon be Christmas and it would hurt if she had no Ned by her side, but it would be the same for many a family throughout the country, with most men fighting abroad in one country or another. Molly had not told anyone apart from her mother about the officer at the airbase who had been upset over two airmen being shot dead by the Germans. It was for the best, like her mother said, she thought.

She passed through the garden gate that led to her sister's home. The well-attended garden had the last remaining roses of the year looking sorry for themselves against the heavy dark skies. Frost would finally put their fight to an end, thought Molly, as she waved at her sister at the window and opened the door without even knocking.

'Hello,' Molly called, as she entered the hallway and

closed the door behind her. 'I thought as I hadn't seen you for so long that I'd call round and have a catch-up.'

Rose came out of the front room and smiled at her. 'It's good to see you. I never have any time to see you, although I do pop in and see Mam occasionally, but you're usually at work. I thank heavens that I don't work the hours that you girls do in munitions.' She hugged Molly and kissed her before urging her to join Ivy and her.

Molly sighed. 'I know. I haven't time for anything nowadays and I never see you at lunchtime like we used to. I wish those days were back again.' She looked at Ivy. 'Hello, Mrs Evans, how are you keeping?'

'A lot better than some. At least I'm on the right side of the ground, which is more than can be said for some. Rose has been telling me about the lass that you work with. What an awful do. The poor woman must have been desperate.' Ivy wrung her hands and looked at Molly as she sat down across from her.

'Yes, she must have been, and yet she was the one that was always full of life at work. We're all going to miss her, especially her singing.' Molly tried to smile.

'Poor, poor woman. Anyway, never mind, nothing is going to bring her back now, it's her family that will have to live with it.' Ivy looked up at Rose sadly.

Rose sat on the arm of the settee. 'Well, her sister is going to take the children in. From what I understand she lives in Birmingham; their father is fighting in Belgium. I shouldn't be telling you this. Although she's worried that he'll wash his hands of them and his wife's burial arrangements when he hears what happened – things have not been good between him and his wife for years apparently.'

Ivy sighed. 'Aye, there's some uncaring folk in the world. No wonder she looked for solace somewhere else. Now, how about we have a brew of tea, Rose, if we have any? Things are getting tighter and tighter at this house, but yours will be the same is it, Molly? Your mother was saying so the other week when she came round. It's all work and no play for everyone at the moment.'

'I'll take you into York next weekend,' said Rose. 'We'll have a look in one or two of the shops and see what we can afford for Christmas. I haven't seen oranges and bananas or months now; they're so hard to get hold of with the blockades and Lord knows what we'll be having for Christmas dinner.' Rose looked down at her feet and tried to stop the tears. 'I'm dreading Christmas if it's without Ned. We should have been planning our wedding and now I don't even know if he's dead or alive.'

'Now then, don't take on. No news has got to be good news. We both know Ned never gives in; the French Resistance will be looking after him. They'll make sure he returns.' Ivy gave Molly a knowing stare and then patted Rose on her knee. 'Go on, pet, make us all a brew. Keep yourself busy and stop that head from thinking.'

'Do you want a hand, Rose?' Molly asked as her sister went into the kitchen.

'No, pet, you stay with me and keep me company,' Ivy quickly replied. 'Rose'll be back in a minute.' She reached forward to take Molly's hand and whisper low so that Rose couldn't hear her. 'Your mam told me what that officer at the airbase told you. Now you keep it to yourself. I've not heard anything from anybody. He'll be all right, pet, or else we'd have heard by now.' Ivy shook her head. 'Don't give your sister any more worries; she's enough on with what's going on at her work. We'll keep the faith and hope that he comes back to us safe and sound.'

Ivy smiled as Rose entered the room with the tea tray and deftly changed the subject. 'Are you going to tell Molly about the new workers that you've got helping make chocolates and the like? You've had a few problems with translations but otherwise you seem to be coping.'

'Oh, we're getting there. You must have noticed them anyway, the Indian and Polish workers that the government have sent to help out at Rowntree's, Mol? They're working in the chocolate department, but soon you'll have them working in munitions. It's only the language problem that gives me headaches, otherwise they seem lovely people and work just as hard as the rest of the workers. They all seem to have settled in the prefabs that were specially built for them, and they're polite and willing so that's all you can ask for.' Rose poured the tea and sat down opposite Molly and tried not to let her sister see how tired she was.

'I've seen new people coming and going and Mam said that you had new employees. They'll have to speak pretty good English to be safe in munitions, but then they'll soon get into the swing of the job, like the rest of us,' Molly said and smiled. 'I bet they are causing problems, especially in the card box-making department; it used to confuse me and I can speak good English.'

Rose sipped her tea. 'Just a few problems here and there.'

'That's not what you told me. You said the Polish never shut up chattering no matter how you tell them to be quiet,' Ivy said and sat back in her chair.

'It's just I don't know what they are saying, so I can't tell if they're giving the wrong instructions to one another until it's too late and the damage is done. We'll get there in the end,' Rose, diplomatic as ever, replied and then went quiet.

'Well, I think I'll go and have ten minutes on my bed and leave you two to talk. I didn't sleep that well last night. There was the drone of aeroplanes going over at about two in the morning and I couldn't get back off to sleep for thinking that we might have to go to the Anderson shelter. I hate that place,' Ivy growled as she struggled to get up with her stick and said goodbye to Molly. Rose had to give her a hand into the hallway and up the stairs before coming down and joining Molly.

'She's getting worse. She frets about Ned, I know she does, but she doesn't let on to me half the time.' Rose walked over to Molly and hugged her. 'It's so good to see you, Mol. Lately it's been all work and looking after Ivy, and I'm always worried about Ned. Is he alive or is he dead? Is he being fed and looked after or is he lying in a concentration camp uncared for by the Germans? Like Ivy I struggle with the nights: you wake up and think the worst, and then it's with you all day too.' Rose took her handkerchief out from up her sleeve and blew her nose. 'I'm sorry I didn't mean to cry; there's you handling explosives every day and being a trouper while I'm still in my old job and am just like any other woman with their fiancé or husband in the forces.'

'I know you'll be worried about Ned, Rose; you're bound to be. He'll come home, don't you worry. I just know he will. Does Peter still keep in touch? Does he not hear anything through the base?' Molly asked and felt her heart breaking for her sister.

Rose sniffed. 'No, he's not been calling so much, and I worry that he was getting a little too friendly, although I'm sure I've read it wrong. He knows I'm loyal to Ned and always will be.'

'Oh, Rose, what a carry-on, and you'll be busy at work with Christmas coming up. No wonder you look so tired.'

'That's the two of us, Molly. You look tired as well; twelve-hour shifts must be putting you through hell, never mind the responsibility of it all. The sooner this war ends, the better. At least it's not a matter of life or death if boxes of Black Magic and chocolate for the troops don't get out on time. Although if you listened to them in the boardroom, you'd think it was.' Rose wiped her nose and tried to smile.

'I wish I was back there making boxes, Rose; it was a lovely job, and I didn't realize it at the time. Even Connie's missing it.'

'Mam says she's infatuated with a visiting cowboy from the airbase. I hope he doesn't break her heart,' Rose said anxiously.

Molly smiled at her oldest sister. 'He wrote to her last week, so she's as happy as Larry, and so is Annie being a land girl in Lancashire. She says she hopes to be home at Christmas, so we'll all have to get together.'

'And you, my little sis, are you still writing to your soldier and is he safe?'

Molly blushed. 'Matt. I am. Mam says I write far too much, but he's so easy to write to and I can't stop thinking about him.'

'Then you keep writing, our Molly, and let's hope he keeps safe,' Rose said. She felt a wave of sorrow come over her – she missed her Ned so much.

'I will and don't you give up on Ned; he will return,' Molly said and hugged her sister.

The following day the workers on the munitions line stopped everything at ten o'clock. It was the day of Betty's funeral and the tannoy that blasted out the latest songs was turned off for five minutes as they all stood and remembered her.

After they'd paid their respects and got back in their cubicles to carry on with their jobs, Connie said, 'I'm going to miss Betty so much; she was brash and said it as it was, but she was all right. The poor woman wouldn't have known what was going to happen to her when she did what she did and, of course, the authorities haven't the time or the inclination to find out who did the butchering on her.'

'Yes, it's not going to be the same. She was always wheeling and dealing or mouthing off about something. You're right: she was brash, but a good sort.' Molly took stock of her job and then picked back up where she had finished, measuring out the fine powder into the shell casing. 'I wonder who's going to replace her. There's also another person wanted three cubicles down. Pauline has been taken off making munitions; her skin can't take the irritants any more. I've seen they've been advertising for folk to work here, but they can't have found anybody yet.' With twelve shells filled Molly sent her tray to be taken down to the arsenal where the filled shells were held safely deep below ground.

'Well, don't look now, but it looks as if we have two new recruits; they're coming this way with the supervisor. I don't recognize them, do you?' Connie looked over at the two women who were dressed in the munitions uniform.

They watched as the supervisor placed them next to one another.

Connie listened in to the conversation between all three and then conveyed it to Molly. 'Polish, they're Polish and they can only just speak English. I hope the supervisor stays with them all day and shows them what to do. It's Anna and Frida by the sounds of it, but I'd better look as if I'm working seeing as the supervisor's next to me.'

Connie glanced at the new faces and smiled, but they were too busy concentrating on learning their new job to respond. There would be time to get to know them later, she thought, as she got on with her work.

'The two new women looked as if they soon got the hang of things; they might not speak the best English but they seemed all right. We can't speak Polish, so how

272

can we judge them?' Molly said as she pulled her bed-covers up round her and yawned.

'I hope the supervisor keeps an eye on them for a little longer; they would concentrate more instead of jabbering if they'd been split up. Anyway, let's see how they go, and I'll try and help if I can.' Connie punched her pillow into shape.

The long and short of it was that Connie missed Betty and had really wanted to go to her funeral, but work had to come first over her friend.

'Lord, have you listened to them? They've never stopped talking since we came into the changing rooms,' Connie said the next day as she pulled her turban tightly round her head and went from the outside zone to the clean zone and on to her work area.

'Yes, they know how to talk. And they're so loud. Or is it that we're just not used to their accents? They don't sound that friendly towards one another.'

Molly decided that she would talk to them. She stopped and turned and waited for Anna and Frida to catch them up, smiling. 'Hello, I'm Molly, and this is Connie; we work next to you,' Molly said, taking the time to talk slowly and clearly. 'You're from Poland?'

'*Tak*, we Polish. Sorry, not good with English,' Anna replied. She looked at Frida who said nothing. 'We not like working here but is better than home and we want help defeat the Germans.'

'It's a dangerous job that you are doing. Care is needed,' Molly said as she entered her cubicle.

'*Tak*, we know. We take care,' Anna replied and shrugged her shoulders before addressing Frida in Polish.

Connie sighed. 'Well, not very chatty, but at least we tried. I'm glad you told them it was dangerous because I watched them when they were on their own and I don't think they know that it's gunpowder they are handling. I'll keep an eye on them today because I know the supervisor is busy – it seems that there are more of our Polish allies working over in the other part of the factory and she is torn between the groups.'

'We'll both keep an eye on them and then they can't go wrong, although you're the nearest to them.' Molly looked down the production line, everyone was busy. The tannoy was wishing everybody a good morning but over the top of the greeting Anna and Frida's voices could be heard as they started their shift.

By mid-morning Anna and Frida's voices were raised even more. They started to shout at one another and when Connie looked across it was clear they were arguing. Anna was getting more and more annoyed by what Frida was saying and because of that she wasn't concentrating. She slammed one of the newly filled shells into its box.

'Oh, Lord, she's going to blow us all up. I'm going to say something,' Connie whispered to Molly. 'Come and back me up, will you?'

'Can't we get a supervisor?' Molly said, reluctant to get involved in an argument at the best of times.

'It's act now and live another day or let them blow us all up! Even the girls across the belt are looking at them.

They're obviously not friends! They argue too much, and we can't afford that on such a dangerous production line.' Connie opened her protective door and marched into Anna's cubicle, Molly following her.

Anna glared at them.

'Anna, be careful with this!' Connie held the powder for the shells up. Else we go BOOM! BANG! We all die!' She used hand gestures and looked at Frida as well as she said it. 'No arguing, concentrate!'

'*Nie*, not until timer is added when finished and gone from here,' Anna said. She looked angrily at Connie and Molly.

Molly put her hand on Anna's arm. 'No, it goes BOOM if knocked or banged, and you would go up with it and all of us. It does that without the timer if dropped. Take care and no arguing.' Molly's legs were shaking as she saw the supervisor rushing towards them.

'Have we a problem here, girls?'

'Yes we do. They don't seem to understand that it's explosives they're handling or they do but they think it needs a timer adding before it is dangerous. We've nearly been blown up here,' Connie replied as she squeezed out of Anna's cubicle. 'They're not friends either; perhaps you should put Mary between them and then they're separated and we can watch and help.'

Frida spat at Anna and glared at her. 'Friends, we are not friends! She take my man. I hate her!'

'That's what the problem is then,' Molly said, sighing.

'Leave it with me. I'll sort this. Now you two get back to work and I'll find a translator from the chocolate factory to talk to these two and explain better. Anna and Frida, come with me.' The supervisor waited for them both to follow her.

Connie and Molly looked at one another; even when they had first started and were somewhat ignorant about what they were doing, they had never come as close to causing a catastrophe. A few of their colleagues stopped work and patted them on the back and thanked them for intervening. It had been worrying them all and they were glad somebody had stepped in to sort the two girls out.

The following day, Frida caught Molly and Connie as they changed, with no Anna by her side. 'Thank you,' she said quietly. 'Not know it was dangerous. I was angry with Anna. She stole my man in Poland. We not friends just because we are in the same work and, er . . . house?'

Molly smiled. 'You made us all worry. We thought we were all going to die.'

'Sorry, I have temper . . . I think that is what you say.' Frida hung her head.

'No problem. Where is Anna this morning?' Connie asked Frida.

She blushed. 'She in chocolate factory and I happy!'

All Molly could think was that poor Rose might now be lumbered with the bad-tempered one – as if she hadn't enough on her plate. But who was going to replace Anna on their production line?

24

'That lad of ours never stops writing to you; he must have taken a fancy to you good and proper,' Lizzie Farrington said, as she watched Annie open the latest letter from her nephew. 'He never thinks to write to me any more. It's always you,' she said with a note of envy in her voice.

Annie opened the letter and smiled; Mike had written at least once a fortnight since she had started replying to him, mainly sharing stories about the Farrington family and the goings-on at Pendle Farm. They both seemed to share the same love, or sometimes hatred, of the things that went on there and the family. He also told her in snippets of what was happening in his life, so Annie looked forward to reading the latest update from the front.

But from across the room Lizzie immediately noticed Annie's cheeks draining as she read the latest letter; she looked shocked. 'What's wrong? You've stopped smiling. Is he all right? What's up?'

Annie gasped and felt a cold shiver come over her. 'Er . . . he's been shot. He's in a military hospital somewhere in France. He says not to worry, that it's not life-threatening. A sniper hit him when they were going through a French village; he's been hit in the ankle.'

Annie sat back and put the letter down and sighed. 'I hope he's all right.'

'Well, he's obviously not all right! Are they sending him home or is he staying there? He'll be no good to them if he can't walk.' Lizzie snatched the letter from under Annie's nose before she could stop her and read the contents of the personal letter.' It sounds nasty; he's lucky to have got away with his life. But he can't be that bad. He's wittering on about walking you down these lanes in spring, the soft lump. What does he mean by saying that he'll bring you more lavender to help you cope? Cope with what? Are you not sleeping? Is that why he sent you those sprigs?'

Annie hesitated. 'I don't know what he's on about there; happen he's on drugs and not thinking straight. He must be pretty badly hurt if he's in hospital. Do you think they'll send him home?' She'd become quite close with the Farringtons' nephew and the hope of perhaps seeing him again in the flesh lifted her spirits.

'Well, if he does come back, he can't go to his proper home as it is. It'll need airing and a right good clean if I know him. He's never looked after himself since his parents were killed over eight years ago in a train crash. That's why I've partly adopted him, he's worked for us ever since then. He might be a cheeky devil, but he's a good lad.' Lizzie folded her arms. 'If he's that badly injured that they send him home, he'll have to come and stay here. I'll have to write and tell him, and then he won't argue.' Lizzie sighed. 'I can't understand why he's talking so much about lavender; he's never been a gardener.

Happen there are fields of lavender around where he is, but I doubt it; it's winter after all.' Lizzie shook her head after rereading the letter. 'You have taken his eye, haven't you? As long as you don't go breaking his heart, lady! I'd never forgive you if you did. Not that I think you would. Different with the other one who went back home; she would – too flighty by far for our Mike.'

'Do you think they will send him home? It is near Christmas, will that help?' Annie asked and found herself hoping that he would come home, wounded or not, and that she would get to see him.

'I don't know. However, if he did come home for Christmas that would work out just grand as your room would be spare and aired. You'll be wanting to go home for Christmas after all.' Lizzie noted the mixed feelings on Annie's face at the thought of getting home, but missing her nephew. 'My Mike coming home, I hope he's not hurt too badly. I'll have to go and tell Bernard the news. He doesn't seem to want to come in for his drink this morning, too busy talking to the posh man from the War Ag about getting a tractor to plough the fields this spring. Why the sod wouldn't come in and have a brew, I don't know; you'd think that he'd never seen a farm kitchen before.'

Annie smiled to herself; *the posh man from the War Ag* had put his handkerchief to his nose as soon as he had stepped into the kitchen, where Lizzie had a pig's head gently simmering in the boiler in the corner of the kitchen. The smell was absolutely putrid to an uneducated nose, but the brawn that would be made from it would be so appetising once you'd forgotten the smell of it cooking. No wonder he was doing business out in the yard; it was much fresher out there, even though very cold.

Annie reread her letter again and smiled at the mention of lavender. How she hoped that Mike would return – although the injury was bad news it would be good to have him back in person, even if only for a short time. She only hoped that if he was coming back he would arrive before she left for home, she thought, as she wandered out into the yard.

Bernard stood against the now empty pig pens. He rubbed his hands and looked at Annie. 'It's bad news about our Mike, but at least it doesn't sound as if it's life-threatening and it'll get him out of harm's way while he's in the hospital. The old lass has set her head and thinks he'll be coming and staying with us. That'll suit the pair of you by the sounds of it.'

Annie blushed. 'I don't know what you mean, Mr Farrington,' she said quietly.

'Well, I've never known our Mike look at a lass like he looked at you, and the poor postman is wearing a whole new path to my door with the letters that pass between you.' Bernard grinned.

'We're just friends, Mr Farrington.'

'Aye, that's how it starts. Been there, and look where I ended up! Being hounded every day for my brass and being henpecked to death by the old wife. Just like the hens she's gone to collect eggs from. She mentioned that you'd want to go home for Christmas, but I hope that you'll be coming back after. You've been a dab hand with everything you've done.'

'I will if you'll have me. I never thought I'd enjoy it so much here,' Annie replied and looked around her. Even without Helen as company she was still enjoying her new way of life.

Aye, you can come back; there must be farming in your blood somewhere, you've fit in so well. Well, lass, there'll be no horse and plough for us this coming spring, the man from the War Ag says we can get our land ploughed by one of these new Fordson tractors. That is, if we make use of any of the bits of land that we don't already plant in. Bernard chuckled. 'You know me, I nearly bit his hand off; less work and more brass, I'd be daft not to agree. Now I've nowt for you to do this afternoon so what are you going to be doing apart from writing back to our Mike?' Bernard looked at the lass with added colour in her cheeks and a fresh complexion.

'I think I might have a walk up Pendle Hill. I've looked at it every day since I came here but never walked to the top.' Annie gazed at the dark menacing long hill with a disturbing history.

'You do that, lass, but mind the witches don't get you. They're still there, you know, albeit just in spirit, poor misunderstood old women.' Bernard took hold of the yard brush and started to clean his boots. 'I'd better tell Lizzie to clean the kitchen floor. I don't think the poor devil was impressed when he came in. She never will be a good housewife, but she's my old lass and that's all that matters.' Bernard winked as he made his way back into his kitchen in half-cleaned boots that still had the muck of the yard on them no matter how he cleaned them.

Annie puffed and panted her way up the side of Pendle Hill. It was steep and rugged, looking over the Ribble Valley like a huge sleeping lion. It dominated the valley with its dark history of wrongdoings and witches in the seventeenth century. The Farringtons' farm was named after it and lay just below it in a sheltered spot and it would have been standing when all the trials and inquisitions of the women had taken place in Lancaster Castle. Annie shuddered in the cold winter wind as she passed the dilapidated house where, according to Bernard, Demdike, famous for being one of the accused witches, had once lived with her family. It looked dark and dank as she rushed past it and she felt icy fingers go down her spine as she pushed history's murky past behind her.

It was good to be out on her own with no thought of work. Not that work was a worry for her; she was literally like a pig in muck, loving learning her new job and actually enjoying her new life with the Farringtons. Annie put her best foot forward and took a deep breath to reach the very top, walking over grassy moorland and following the well-worn tracks made by sheep as they grazed the hillside. Reaching the very top eventually she stood and looked around her – although the wind bit at her face she felt invigorated and full of life, even though the world was at war. She looked down one side of the hill into the sprawling countryside of Lancashire with its mill towns and industry and to the north she viewed the open countryside of Yorkshire. The peaks of Ingleborough and Whernside in the distant dales were just visible. She was on top of the world, she thought, as she wrapped her coat round her. York was beautiful and full of history but here she had found contentment in the most unlikely place. She thought of her mother and sisters back home; she missed them, but sometimes there wasn't time in the day to think of them. It was only of a night that she longed for the chatter between them all and the jokes, usually at other people's expense. Now, in the mucky setting of the farm, she had found contentment and friendship, especially when it came to the letters between her and Mike.

She smiled to herself. Lavender, bless him. Poor Mrs F, she hadn't realized what that was all about, that he was sending it to her to help with the smell of the house. She prayed that his wound would not cause him too much pain or be prolonged, and at the same time she hoped with all her heart that he would be sent home because of it. This time they would do more than just smile at one another across the kitchen table, she thought, as the wind blew even fiercer. As she looked to the north it looked like clouds were starting to gather and maybe even snow was threatening. Time to turn round and go home, back to the grubby home of the Farringtons – it might be mucky but it was filled with love, she thought, as she struggled over the grassy hillocks down the steep slopes of Pendle Hill to where her heart belonged.

25

'Bloody Christmas, bloody war, bloody chocolates,' Rose said as she stepped into the front room where Ivy was sat listening to the radio.

Ivy reached and turned her radio off and looked at her daughter-in-law-to-be and shook her head. 'It's not ladylike and it doesn't become you. I take it you've had a bad day? I know you're angry with the world, but cursing won't do you any good. Now come and sit down here next to me and tell me your worries.' Ivy patted the seat next to her on the settee.

'I'm sorry, Ivy. It's just everything is getting to me and I'm so tired.' Rose pulled her coat off and slumped down next to Ivy. 'And it's snowing!'

'That's what we get in December, and I can sympathize with you being tired – there isn't a night that I don't toss and turn and think about that lad of mine. Things are ten times worse in the darkness of the night.' Ivy held Rose's hand and patted it. 'The good thing is another week and you'll be free of work for a while. At least Rowntree's and the munitions factory are recognizing that we need to celebrate something, even though we might be fighting over who gets the wishbone at the Christmas table because meat is so scarce.'

'I hope we can do a little bit better than a wishbone.

My mam says we're invited there as long as we can bring a bit of something to help out. A bit like a Jacob's join, where everyone brings a little of something. I never thought we'd have to be doing that at Christmas; things are getting worse food-wise.' Rose shook her head. 'But that doesn't worry me the most. I just wish Ned was home. It's the not knowing. He's on my mind all the time and I don't want to sit round the Christmas table without him there.' Rose wiped her eyes and sighed.

'I just know in my bones that he's still with us. Don't ask me how but I do,' Ivy said soothingly. 'He'll be back; we just have to be patient.'

'Oh, Ivy, I hope you're right. I just feel so low sometimes and even Peter hasn't got the time to come like he did, so I don't hear anything from the base.'

'Well, you know why he's stopped coming. There's all hell let loose in those skies above us, and he'll be one of them keeping us safe. I read and hear it every day. The Battle of Britain, that's what we are in; those down south and in manufacturing towns are going through hell. The airmen are fighting for our very existence, so be thankful that Ned is hopefully safe in France. He's maybe better there than up in the skies.'

'I know. I'm just feeling sorry for myself. There are people ten times worse than us; it's just I miss him.' Rose sat up and looked around her. 'I'll stop moaning. How about we put some decorations up or is it too early? I bought some crêpe paper the other weekend. We can cut it into strips and fold it over into squares and make a streamer. It will give us both something to do, and keep us occupied after our tea. Besides, like I said, it's snowing so it must be nearly Christmas.'

'That's more like the Rose I know. Yes, we will, and you can get some holly from the market this weekend and put it on the windowsills. We'll not let Jerry spoil our Christmas. Keep your pecker up. You've got to, pet, and just hope for the best.'

'Are you coming with me to market? I promised you a shopping day. Do you think you could manage the walk into town or is it too far?' Rose looked at Ivy. Ivy had got worse at walking over the last few months. In fact, it was she had given up on life if the truth be told.

'No, I'll not bother, love. These old legs would only let me down and there's nothing that I want. When you get to my age you don't need a lot and I gave up on Christmas presents a while ago. There are no young children in the family to give to.'

'I thought a walk round the Minster and to hear the carollers might lift both our spirits, and they always sell hot chestnuts and hot toddies in the square. Surely they'll still be able to do that? It isn't Christmas without that.'

'No, you are all right, lass. You go and come back and tell me all about it. Enjoy some time to yourself; you deserve it,' said Ivy, remembering the times when she used to do just the same and loved looking in the many shop windows along the Shambles. That seemed an age ago, she thought, as she watched Rose go into the kitchen to prepare what she could find for their main meal. Oh so long ago, when times were so much better.

She closed her eyes and prayed that Ned would return to them both safe and well.

Rose was wrapped up the following weekend in her winter coat and a hand-knitted hat that Molly had given her for Christmas the previous year. Molly made everybody something each year, but this year she wouldn't have time she, thought, as she pulled the hat over her ears.

It was bitterly cold with a good covering of snow on the ground as she walked through the gateway of Bootham Bar and towards the tall majestic Minster. It looked like a scene from a Christmas card as she spotted the Salvation Army singing right in front of the Minster. The haunting words of 'Silent Night' floated in the air and she stood and listened with tears coming to her eyes. Of all the carols, 'Silent Night' was the one that she loved the most and she couldn't help but feel a pang of pain as she thought of all the servicemen on both sides of the war who would have sung the same words in their own language. If only music could make the world a safer place, she thought, as she passed the chestnut seller with his brazier full of roasting chestnuts, like he had been there hundreds of years. She would buy some and take them back for her and Ivy to share, she thought, as she walked out towards the crowded narrow street of the Shambles. She stopped outside a small bookshop and looked in the window, spotting a cookery book of ration recipes and wondered whether her mother would appreciate it for Christmas. She was just about to go inside when she heard a voice she recognized and felt a hand on her arm.

She turned round quickly and looked at the man who was Ned's true friend. 'Peter, I didn't expect to see you here.' She gasped as she saw his face. 'I'm sorry, I'm being rude, but you're hurt.'

'Oh, this is just a flesh wound. A piece of shrapnel got a bit too close for my liking when we were flying over Frankfurt. It's really nothing to worry about.' Peter put his hand to the scar that still bore stitches on his cheek. 'The main thing is, we all came back alive – a bit battered but we made it home.' Peter gazed at Rose. 'How are you? You look thinner and pale.'

'I'm all right. Everyone is thinner, aren't they? We have no option but to be slim as things are.' Rose looked down and then gazed back at Peter. 'I don't suppose you've heard anything about Ned, have you? Nobody tells us anything.' She found herself clinging to the sleeve of Peter's coat as she asked and felt her stomach churn as he looked at her gravely.

'No, I'm afraid not. There is a rumour going around the base that the Resistance in France are planning something before Christmas, but that could be anything; we often hear rumours of this and that, and they mean nothing to us at Elvington. I keep hearing "Shelburne Line" being mentioned, something to do with a route out by the Resistance, but I don't want to give you false hope, Rose,' Peter said quietly.

'Any news would be welcome, just anything,' Rose pleaded.

'I know. If I hear anything, I'll let you know, I promise. Look, I'll have to go; we're on a two-hour leave and I have to be back before midday. If I don't see you before, try and have a good Christmas.' Peter bent down and kissed Rose softly on her cheek. 'Take care, Rose.'

Rose watched as Peter walked away. Could Ned perhaps be on his way back home or was the talk nothing at all to do with him? She closed her eyes and listened to a brass band playing 'Away in a Manger' and hoped above all that Christmas would bring her exactly what she wanted: Ned back in her arms. But just a glimmer of hope had come into her life and she entered the bookshop and bought her mother the recipe book that she knew would probably be glanced through, bits digested and then discarded for her own ideas.

'Thank heavens we finish for Christmas soon.' Molly yawned and dragged her feet as she and Connie walked home through dark cold streets.

'I've never been as tired in my life. I think all I'll do when we finish is sleep. Sleep and eat if your mother has managed to snaffle food away. That is all I'm going to do,' Connie repeated. She put her arm through Molly's. 'I might go to the dance on Boxing Day at the airfield, but I don't know. It isn't as if Chuck will be there.'

'I notice he's still writing to you, and you to him. You do know that you might never, ever see him again? He's thousands of miles away. I wouldn't waste my time on him,' Molly said. 'Go and get yourself a nice lad from this country.'

'Listen to you! Who's writing to a soldier not even in this country and knitting him balaclavas in the middle of the night; no wonder you're so tired.'

'That's different,' Molly replied. 'At least he's English and will hopefully come home sometime, and I had to send him a Christmas present; it's only right.' They turned the corner to their home. 'Oh well, here we are back home again, back to your mam wondering how she's going to feed us all this Christmas. I won't be bothered if we're only given warmed-up potatoes, as long as I get some time off from that munitions factory. Honestly, she should stop worrying.' Connie turned the front door handle and both of them quickly entered the house and yelled hello to Winnie.

Winnie was stressed as she placed her latest concoction of corned beef and potatoes fried in a patty in front of them both as they sat down at the table.

'Oh, Lord, you two, what a day! I got a letter from Annie; she's coming back to stay with us on Monday. That doesn't give me much time to air her bedroom and get extra food in. I thought I was so organized, but I'm not at all. I just don't know how I'm going to cope. And I was daft enough to ask Ivy and our Rose to join us. I only hope that they manage to bring something with them for dinner.'

'Mam, calm down. It won't matter what's on the table, as long as we're all here together. Won't it be nice to see Annie? It seems ages since we saw her. I wonder if she's changed.' Molly tucked into the patty and put her thumb up. 'This is good, Mam. It's a good job we have a few tins of corned beef in the pantry.' She winked at Connie. Lately it had been corned beef hash and corned beef fritters, occasionally interspersed with a tin of tongue in sandwiches. Their entire fresh meat ration was being kept for Christmas and nobody dared complain to the matriarch of the household.

Winnie smiled. 'It's amazing what you can do if you put your mind to it. I found a right good recipe for carrot fudge; I thought I'd make some for Christmas, just in case Rose doesn't bring us any chocolates. I can't see Rowntree's giving anything away this year.'

Connie looked across at Molly and smirked. Carrot fudge did not sound that appealing.

'Really, Mam, stop worrying; there'll be chocolates. Rose will bring some misfits if nothing else. Christmas will come and go; it's one day of the year when family is more precious than any food or trimmings. I just wish Ned was with us; we'll all be feeling for Rose and Ivy.'

Winnie sighed. 'That we will. There's nothing I can do about that.' If only there was a way – she'd do anything for her girls to be happy.

It was Annie's last day on the farm before returning home and her bags were packed as she made herself ready to leave the Farrington family.

'Now, have you got everything and can you manage to carry it all?' Lizzie Farrington asked Annie as she stood in the doorway of Pendle Farm.

'Yes, thank you, Mrs Farrington. You've been too kind. My mam will write and thank you.' Annie held on to her small suitcase and the bag that was filled almost to bursting with meat, eggs and butter that Lizzie had insisted she take home with her.

'Well, I know that you city folk can't get anything decent to eat and we have plenty. Now, when you come back, you call me Lizzie – Lizzie and Bernard that'll do for us.' Lizzie stepped forward and hugged Annie. 'You will come back to us, won't you? Bernard says you're a good worker and you're a good lass.'

'I hope to, Mrs Farrington. I don't know how it's happened, but I love my new life here,' Annie replied, fumbling with her heavy load.

'Get sat up next to Bernard and he'll take you to the station. He'll have the same trip tomorrow to pick up Mike. It's a pity you're going to miss him, but I can't say I'm not grateful because he can have your bedroom once I've changed the sheets. Now, go on, enjoy your Christmas with your family.' Lizzie watched as Annie climbed up next to her husband and the cart set off down the farm track to Clitheroe. She was going to miss the land girl who had proved her worth to them. However, Mike was coming home and she couldn't wait to dote on him and welcome him back if only for a short while until his injury healed.

'So you're leaving us and my old lass has loaded you down with stuff. She's done right; it'll make your Christmas with a bit of luck,' Bernard said as he encouraged the horse into a trot despite the covering of snow that had fallen lightly in the valley bottom and deeper on the surrounding hills.

'She has, and my family will be so grateful. If I know my mother, she'll be worried sick about how to feed us all. She always likes to put on a spread at Christmas.' Annie hesitated. 'I wish I'd have been able to stay just another day until Mike had come home. Can you remind Lizzie that there's a pair of handkerchiefs and a Christmas card for him on my bedroom table along with a present for both of you two.'

'Eh, lass, you shouldn't have bothered with anything for us two. But Mike will be suited. I'll enjoy teasing him about it when he arrives home. It's a pity you're going to miss him. He must not be fit for fighting, else he wouldn't be coming home, but it will be good to see him.' Bernard smiled, he was going to make his nephew's life hell with his jokes about falling for a land girl and not even being there to court her.

Annie stood on the platform of the small station at Clitheroe a short while later, her ticket and luggage in hand as Bernard waited next to her.

'The signal's up; the train's nearly here. It usually comes as that one across the way pulls out from Preston.' He nodded to the train that had just pulled in on the upward line and the sound of carriage doors clattered, letting passengers out to cross under the railway line and be on their way home. 'Here it is. Give us your bags, lass, and I'll lift them in for you,' Bernard said, as the train drew up to the platform. Once her bags were in beside her Annie went to the door and pulled on the strap of the window and leaned out to say goodbye to Bernard as the train built up steam.

'You take care, lass. Safe journey,' Bernard said and waved her off, but then he turned suddenly as he heard a voice he recognized.

'Annie, Annie! Happy Christmas! I'll still be here, I hope, when you come back. I'm sorry I've missed you!' Mike yelled as he limped on crutches towards the leaving train.

Annie leaned dangerously out of the window and waved and waved frantically, calling, 'Happy Christmas to you and all, Mike. I'll write.' She kept waving until she could hardly see Bernard and Mike standing together in the steam of the train. She felt her cheeks burning with colour – if only the train had been ten minutes later, they could have said hello properly.

When she finally sat down she felt all warm inside despite the cold day; she had seen Mike before going home, no matter how briefly, and he didn't look too badly injured. Although she loved her family and home she couldn't wait to return to Pendle Farm, especially if Mike was going to be still there.

'Just look at you! Are you sure you're the Annie who left us this summer?' Winnie hugged her daughter and looked at her. Her skin had a healthy glow and she had grown her dark hair long and the few pounds that she had put on made her look even more attractive. Winnie smiled and took her suitcase as they walked back along the streets to their home.

'I suit farm life, Mam; I've enjoyed myself, although it's hard work. How are you? You look tired.' Annie gasped as she noticed the bomb damage around the station and felt sad when she saw the end of a terraced row of houses in rubble after being targeted. 'We're lucky where I'm at; we don't have any of this. It must be frightening. No wonder you're not sleeping.'

'We're getting off lucky,' Winnie replied as they hurried back home. 'It's the likes of London, Liverpool and the other big cities that are taking the brunt. We're left alone most of the time, but you can't help but go to bed and wonder if you're going to be alive in the morning. That's probably why I look tired. Plus, I worry about you all, even though there's nothing I can do for you.'

'Well, you don't have to worry about me. I'm the happiest I've ever been. The Farringtons have looked after me well and I love the work, but you'd not approve of Lizzie's housekeeping; it's not the best.'

Annie grinned as her mother turned the key in the lock and she knew as soon as she walked in that the lavender polish had been used liberally in honour of her return and Christmas.

'What on earth is in that bag you're carrying? It must weigh a ton by the looks of it,' Winnie asked, as they took their coats off and waited for the kettle to boil.

'Lizzie's sent you it; she thought it would help with Christmas. She can't do with anybody going hungry, even though she's not the best of cooks.' Annie pushed the bag across to her mother and watched as she unfolded the newspaper that each piece of meat was wrapped in and caught her breath.

'Oh, Annie, just look what they have sent you home with! And have they always got this? How the other half live!' Winnie gazed at the huge joint of pork, the sausage, bacon and dairy produce that had been sent to help her out. 'And there was me worrying about how we were going to manage. I'll get it put in the pantry now, although I'll cook the pork tomorrow; you can't be too careful with pork. I know it'll be a day early, but I don't want everybody ill over Christmas.'

Annie sipped her tea and looked around the spotless kitchen that she had missed so much. It was a million miles away from the kitchen at Pendle Farm yet she loved both. 'Are we all going to be here for Christmas Day, Mam? It will be nice if we are.'

'Yes, we are. That is, except for Ned; we've no idea where he is, whether he's still alive or if he'll ever come back to us. Rose is in such a way with herself and I daren't say much to her. So go gentle with her, Annie?'

'Of course,' she said, looking concerned. 'And Molly and Connie? I take it Connie's still with us?' Annie asked, partly hoping that Connie might have left her family home; she still thought of her as a cuckoo in the nest.

'Both as yellow as canaries, but don't say anything to them. It's from making the munitions. But they don't seem to mind. Molly says it's her badge of honour, that it shows she's doing her bit for the war effort. Connie's saving up to move out, I think, although she's gone quiet of late since she's started writing to this American called Chuck that she met over at the airbase.'

'Molly, I know, is writing to a soldier out in France or Belgium. She writes and tells me occasionally. She sounds smitten!' Annie said with a yawn.

'She does, and you, have you got a man in your life?' Her mother asked and smiled.

'I might have. I'm not saying more than that, because I don't know myself really.' Annie thought of Mike waving on the station and knew that she had, but she wasn't going to tell her mother.

'Secretive as ever, Annie Freeman. You don't change. Now, you look tired, go and have a lie-down in your bedroom. It's all aired and there are clean sheets on the bed. Molly and Connie won't be back until eight. You'll hear them because they're always noisy when they return, and they will be especially so with it being the last day of work for a week.

I can't believe it's Christmas Eve tomorrow. I haven't even bothered putting a Christmas tree up. It doesn't seem right with Ned still missing.' Winnie sighed.

'I think I will, Mam, if you don't mind. I was up early this morning and travelling makes me tired.' Annie got up and kissed Winnie on the brow. It was good to be home; she had missed the smell of her mother's baking and her cleanliness and her love.

Annie woke to the sound of Connie and Molly's voices down in the kitchen. They were laughing and joking about something and she heard her mother chastising them both. She yawned and looked around her at the familiar furniture and the patchwork quilt that she had helped stitch with her grandmother. It was good to be home and away from the smell of the pigs and farm. She yawned again and sat up on the edge of her bed and decided to join her family downstairs. She lumbered to her feet and made her way down to them and the warmth and smell of what her mother was cooking for supper.

'Come and sort these two out, Annie. Just look what they have done! And there was me not going to bother this year,' Winnie said, as she pulled her pan of ham hock and pea soup to one side, urging Annie to join her.

'Annie, you're back!' Molly shouted and walked over to hug her sister. 'We couldn't let you come home to a house without a Christmas tree, so Connie and I went past the market and brought one home. It's a bit scraggy, but it's a tree.'

'It looks just lovely, or it will do in the morning when we've decorated it. It's good to see you both,' Annie replied, smiling at Connie as she welcomed her home.

'We've bought a tree, but you've done even better, looking at that pork. I can't wait to have a slice of that.' Connie licked her lips. 'I'm glad to have you back at Christmas; we've missed you.'

'Yes, missed her moans and grumpiness.' Molly grinned. 'It's not been the same without you.'

'I've missed you too. Now, I'd change your face powder if I were you, it's a little too, er . . . yellow.' Annie grinned at them both and wondered if she'd been too rude.

'Cheeky bugger,' Molly said and walloped her sister. 'We could say the same about you with those rosy cheeks. It is good to have you back. I've missed the sarcasm. I have a feeling it's going to be a good Christmas.' She hugged Annie again. 'You could really do with a bath, Annie; you smell of farm.'

'I don't.'

'Oh yes you do,' all three said, laughing. 'Or you do to us. Hay and muck!' Molly said and grinned.

'I'll make you a bath and wash your clothes after supper,' Winnie said soothingly, but for now you can all catch up over your soup and tomorrow we will get ready for Christmas now we're all more in the mood.'

Winnie felt warm inside; her family were all going to be together for Christmas and that's all a mother could wish for.

'Now this is Christmas. A tree up in the front room, the fire lit and the radio playing Christmas carols.' Molly looked round at her mother sitting knitting and Connie and Annie playing whist at the table. 'It's been a lovely evening with us all here together, and tomorrow Rose will be coming with Ivy. It's just a pity that Ned can't be with us.'

'I wish Chuck could be here, but at least he's sent me a card and he's safe at the moment. Although he says some in America say they should be more involved in our war,' Connie said as she played her next card.

'If they have any sense, they'll keep out of it; there's enough young men losing their lives,' Winnie said, counting her stitches as she finished off the arm of her sweater for Ned when he eventually came home – if ever.

Molly sighed and looked up at the angel on the top of the tree. 'Don't say that, Mam. You know I worry about

Matt. I think about him every day. I hope he's got my balaclava; at least that will keep him warm.'

'Sorry, love. I didn't mean to hurt your feelings. He'll be safe, don't you worry. Surely none of them will want to fight on Christmas Day, not if there's a Christian bone among them. Dad always used to remember when both sides stopped fighting on Christmas Day in the last war, and they sang hymns together and even had a game of football between the dugout trenches of each other's lines. No matter what side they're on, Christmas should be respected and remembered for what it stands for.'

'Let's hope so, Mam, just for one day.' Molly hoped with all her heart that Matt and all soldiers would have one day of peace. Along with feeling gratitude that Annie now smelled of soap and not the farmyard, she listened to the radio and thought of her Matt and wished he was with her.

'Merry Christmas!' Rose shouted down the hallway as she wheeled Ivy in her wheelchair down the narrow passage trying not to scratch the paintwork.

'Leave this contraption here, Rose. I can walk the rest,' Ivy moaned. 'I hate being seen in it. I wouldn't use it at all if my legs weren't so bad.'

Molly came and took Ivy's hand and guided her into the front room and sat her in the most upright chair, turning to give Rose a look of sympathy for putting up with Ivy's moans. 'We're in here until dinner is ready. Come and sit with us and open your presents. Sherry, Mrs Evans? My mam has got one on the go in the kitchen. She's just peeling the carrots. Perhaps you'd like to try the carrot fudge that she's made?'

Ivy took one look at the gelatinous orange squares and shook her head. 'No, a sherry, dear, please. I don't think that's quite me.'

Rose grinned. 'We've brought chocolates anyway: a box of Black Magic and a bag of misshapes, plus some KitKats. If I can't bring home some chocolate at Christmas, then who can? There are also your Christmas presents here.' She looked across at Annie. 'It's good to see you, Annie. You look so well.'

'Thanks, Rose. How are you?' Annie noticed the

drawn, pale face of her sister and knew the answer without her replying.

'Oh, you know, battling on like you do. Now, is Mam in the kitchen? At the risk of getting my head bitten off, I'll go and help her.'

'Yes, we thought we'd keep clear. You're braver than us. Everything has to be just right, although Annie brought some lovely pork home with her and that's already cooked, so I don't know why she's flapping. It's only an ordinary roast dinner; with suet dumplings for pudding seeing as she couldn't get any dried fruit.'

Ivy shook her head. 'Christmas dinner has to be just right. I know why she's worried. You go and help her Rose; there'll be something you can do.' Ivy took a sip from her glass and felt contentment as the warmth of the sherry trickled down her throat.

'Anything I can do, Mam?' Rose asked as she walked into the kitchen, noticing the usually scrubbed pine kitchen table was covered with the best linen tablecloth and laid with an assortment of cutlery for seven people. 'There's a place too many, Mam; there's only six of us!'

'Oh, Lord, my head is in such a tizzy – I thought there were seven of us. It'll have to be for the white rabbit; it's bad luck if I slide it away.' Winnie stirred the gravy and poured it into an enamel jug, ready for everyone to help themselves to.

'You've always said that ever since we were little. I don't know where you get it from, but I'll leave it for now.' Rose spotted the roast. 'That pork smells and looks wonderful – how good of the folk to send it to us with Annie. She seems and sounds happy. I'm glad one of us is.'

'I know how you're feeling and I wish Ned was here with us too,' Winnie said. 'I've put him a present under the tree. I managed to finish knitting him a jumper last night. Now whether it will fit him, who knows? The best thing we can give and send him is our love and hope that he will be with us here next Christmas.' She tested the carrots for softness.

'I saw Peter when I was shopping the other day; he's been injured by some shrapnel and has a scar across his face. He looked to be in a sorrowful state. He was telling me that there's a new plan in the offing to rescue shot-down airmen, so perhaps my Ned will be one of the first they help.' Rose sat down on a chair and played with a knife and fork.

'As long as it's just his looks that have been damaged. Poor lad. Let's hope that he's right about the plan and that Ned is with us sooner than later. Now go and tell them that dinner is ready and for all of them to come and grab a seat.'

Winnie strained the carrots and placed them in a serving dish along with some well-cooked Brussel sprouts that filled the kitchen with their sulphurous aroma.

'Dinner is served, everyone! Come quick and then Mam can calm down and enjoy the rest of her day. The washing-up is on us three as usual.' Rose looked around and admired the Christmas tree with its tinsel and glass baubles as she helped Ivy up from her seat. 'Are you all right, Ivy? You can sit at the end of the table and then you don't have to walk too far?'

Ivy laughed. 'I'm all right now I've had a drop of your mother's sherry; it cures any aches and pains. And I'm looking forward to this proper piece of pork.'

'Yes, it looks good; Annie's done well bringing that home. Now you sit down here and I'll sit next to you.' Rose led Ivy to the table, sat her down and turned to help Winnie hand out the loaded plates.

Winnie put a full plate down in front of Ivy and smiled. 'Are you all right, Ivy? I've not had the chance to talk to you with getting dinner ready. That will fill a corner.' And then she scowled as she heard a knock at the front door. 'Who's that just as we're sitting down to our Christmas dinner? Just typical, isn't it? Rose, tell them to come back later.' Winnie carried on dishing out Molly's and Connie's plates.

Rose made her way towards the front door, ready to give the caller his orders with a stern face. She opened the door without any thought and her heart missed a beat as she gazed in wonder at the man on the step. It wasn't – It couldn't be!

'Happy Christmas, Rose. Lord knows I've missed you so much.'

Ned looked thinner and unshaven as he stepped across the threshold, picked Rose up and held her in his arms.

'Happy Christmas, my love. I'm home and it is so wonderful to see you.'

Rose gasped. 'Ned, Ned, you're home! Oh, how I've

306

longed for this moment,' Rose whispered, and she kissed him and held him tight. 'I can't believe it. You're the best Christmas present I could have ever wished for.'

'What's all the noise about? Who is it, Rose? Tell them to bugger off – your dinner is going cold,' Winnie shouted as the two kissed passionately.

Rose held Ned's hand and dragged him into the kitchen to a table of astounded faces. 'No, Mam, I'm not going to do that. Set another dinner for the white rabbit because our Christmas is now complete. It's Ned – he's home!'

'Oh, my lad, I thought I'd lost you!' Ivy cried and held her arms out to be hugged.

'You can't get rid of me that easily. It is so good to see you all.' Ned smiled and felt tears well up in his own eyes as everyone came and hugged him and kissed him.

'This is the best Christmas ever and nobody could wish for more.' The family was complete, Rose thought as they all looked at one another.

'Happy Christmas, everybody,' they all said together with tears running down their cheeks as they hugged each other tight and were thankful for the safe return of Ned and a perfect Christmas table.

If you loved *The Chocolate Box Girls at War*
then discover where it first began in
The Chocolate Box Girls,
the first book in the Rowntree's series.

I

York, 1935

'Molly Freeman, this may be your last day in school but I am still your teacher.' Mrs Stanley yelled loud enough for all the pupils at Haxby Road School to hear, let alone the day-dreaming Molly.

Molly quickly brought herself back to the world of the schoolroom as she heard Mrs Stanley shout at her to concentrate on the job at hand, just as a blackboard rubber whizzed past her ear and landed on the varnished wooden floorboards of her classroom, leaving a cloud of white chalk dust floating in the summer's air like a host of tiny fairies.

'Sorry, Mrs Stanley, I was just looking out of the window, it is such a nice day and I've only another hour before I leave school for good anyway,' Molly said quietly, hoping that her teacher of the last year would understand.

'There is another hour for you to learn and put some common sense into your head, Molly Freeman. You will need every ounce of knowledge when you join the real world because, believe me, you will look back and realise just how happy your days here at school were.' Mrs Stanley looked over the top of her glasses and glared at the girl she had tried to prepare for the rest of her life, just like she had prepared countless pupils before her. However, in Molly Freeman's case, she pitied her future bosses; she was by no means the brightest button in the box and if her siblings had not already been working for York's main employer, Rowntree's, she would have struggled to get herself an interview even.

'I'm sorry, I'll try to concentrate.' Molly put her head down and looked at her arithmetic book, but could not see the need for any of the elaborate fractions and equations that she was supposed to be able to work out. What would she need these for? She was going to make chocolate like the rest of the family and would have no need for such knowledge. Her mam had always said, 'Do your best and that's all you can do,' and that's what she had always done, regardless of what Mrs Stanley said to her. She glanced over at William Allen as she put her head down and tried to concentrate on her sums, but he stuck his tongue out at Mrs Stanley and then grinned cheekily at Molly as she sniggered.

'You might think that I cannot see you, Molly Freeman and William Allen, but believe me I do have eyes in the back of my head. Any more disrespect from either of you and it will be a caning that you will be receiving on your last day in school.' Mrs Stanley turned and stared at both of them as she finished writing on the blackboard.

'Sorry, Mrs Stanley,' William and Molly said together, not daring to look at one another.

'Just get on with it, and then you can leave with your heads held high,' Mrs Stanley said and sat down in her chair. This was one of many classes that she had seen through the last year of schooling. Most of them were following in their parents' footsteps in family businesses, some were leaving to work in the local shops and some of them, like Molly, were hopefully going to work at the sprawling chocolate and pastille firm that had spread over the outskirts of York. The unshowy, philanthropic Rowntree family were to be praised for bringing much-needed work to the ancient city; not only had they helped people afford their own homes and take pride in themselves, but with their strong Quaker values they had put York onto the map. They had also made her own life easier, especially when it came to the likes of Molly, who she knew would be nurtured by them once at work. Elizabeth Stanley put her head down and started to check the papers that she would have to take home with her that evening, but for now, at least, the classroom was quiet and that was just how she liked it.

Molly concentrated on her arithmetic, but her mind was focused on going home and leaving the school that she had attended since the age of five. It wouldn't matter what she put in her book, she thought, nobody would be bothered once she had walked out of the doors. So, instead of figuring out the set sums, she sketched pictures of her classmates in the margin, cartoon-like and funny, just like she thought of them. Finally, just before the bell rang for the end of the lesson and the end of the summer term, she sketched Mrs Stanley as a long, tall skinny woman with extended arms and huge glasses and whiskers – every pupil laughed about the whiskers on the end of her chin, which she obviously didn't know were there. She sat back and grinned and added a caption, 'Mary Hairy Stanley, the worst teacher ever!' Then she closed the book and watched as the minute hand finally reached half past three and a child in a lower year rang the home time bell.

That was that, then: school was done for good and at long last she could hope to make some money to help the family. She stood up and pushed her school chair under the oak desk which so many past pupils had scratched their names into when bored with their lessons, and placed her book under the desk lid. School was over and now it was out into the wide world, whether she was ready or not.

'Well, that's it and it's about bloody time – my father has been wanting me to help him in the shop for weeks now. I can learn far more working with him than I can in this place,' William Allen said as he walked out of the school with Molly, not giving it a backward glance.

Unlike Molly, who lingered at the doorway and wondered if Mrs Stanley's words were right about school days being the best. She had struggled at school sometimes, but she had always known that it was for her benefit that she attended. Unlike William who was often absent, only to be found working in his father's butcher's shop on Haxby Road – for he had a future working in the family business. She, however, did not have secure employment yet and even though her siblings already worked for Rowntree's, and she was to attend an interview on Monday, she was dreading entering the sprawling works of the chocolate factory. She had heard her two sisters gossiping and talking about their work life and coming home each evening smelling of the chocolates that they made and packaged, and it sounded a completely different world to the safety of the school. They both came home exhausted and full of moans most days, having to think for themselves but at the same time sharing the comradeship of working together and gossiping around the kitchen table.

'I'll see you then, Molly, I'll probably be serving you or your mam in the shop next time you see me,' William said, pushing his hands into the pockets of his tight-fitting trousers. He was a big lad, well fed at home, unlike most of the rest of her class, whose families struggled to feed them.

'Yes, I'll see you, William. You take care,' Molly said, watching as he walked down the road towards home as a pang of panic overcame her: she was about to enter into the world of work and she was scared.

'Is that you, our Mol? Well, that will be that then.' Winnie Freeman had just finished making a pie crust and was wiping flour from her hands onto her cross-over apron. She looked up towards the kitchen doorway as she heard the front door slam on the small terraced house that she and her three daughters lived in.

'Yes, Mam, I'm home. Is there anything to eat, I'm starving,' Molly said as she entered the kitchen and slumped into one of the rickety wooden chairs set around the kitchen table.

'You can make yourself a sugar sandwich, but only one, mind. I only got that loaf of bread this morning and already it's half gone because your two sisters insisted on taking their own dinners to work with them. You would all eat me out of house and home if I let you.' Winnie sighed as she ran a knife around the edge of the enamel pie tin, tidying up the crust before placing it into the oven of the Yorkshire Range. 'I don't know why either of them can't have their dinners in the dining block with the rest of the workers instead of taking what they can get from under my nose.' Winnie watched as Molly sliced a doorstep from the loaf and buttered it liberally before sprinkling a good spoonful of sugar on it and biting into it. 'Don't make another, you have meat and potato pie for your supper. Although there's not much meat in it . . . I'm sure that Thomas Allen's scales are wrong; I don't seem to have got much for my money.'

'William is starting work for him full-time now, he says,' Molly said, licking the sugar crystals away from the side of her mouth.

'He might as well have been this last month or two; he never seems to be at school, from what I hear. The truancy officer is always knocking on the door, according to Lizzie Mason, but they'll not get any sense from that family, no matter how many times he knocks on their door.'

'Well, he's no need of school, he's known all along that he is going to work for his father,' Molly said, looking at the loaf and hoping that her mother would allow her another slice.

'No, you don't, miss, you'll thank me in another year or two when the boys are showing interest in you. Nobody wants to be walking out with the plump one; a slim waist and a petite figure are what's wanted. Especially if you are to attract somebody with a bit of money in the bank,' Winnie said, smacking Molly's hand as she reached for the carving knife. 'And as for William working in his father's shop, he still needs to be able to weigh things correctly and to charge properly. Although perhaps that's what is wrong with his father, perhaps he makes it up as he goes along,' she continued, as she started to peel four potatoes to boil in a pan to accompany the pie.

Molly retracted her hand sharply and watched her mother as she filled a pan with cold water for the potatoes.

'Mam, I don't want to go to work for Rowntree's, I've been thinking I'd rather go and work in a shop or happen to learn to type and be in an office,' Molly burst out, looking worried as she saw her mother's face cloud over. Nobody ever questioned her mother's decisions, she was the matriarch of the family, and she had held her family together since the death of her husband from a particularly bad bout of influenza nearly ten years ago. Her word was set in stone.

'Don't be daft, our Molly! You, work in an office? You can barely spell; you even say to yourself that the words don't make any sense to you, no matter how much you look at them. You should be thankful that Rose got you the interview on Monday; she's put her neck on the line for you. It was either Rowntree's or Terry's on the other side of town and you wouldn't want to trail there every morning. Besides, you haven't even been taken on yet, but you should be all right, as long as you don't say you struggle with reading.' Winnie looked at her youngest – she knew she had problems, but at the same time she was not daft, she just couldn't make sense of letters like she should.

'I won't, Mam, but they may ask me to take a test, our Annie says they will, so they'll soon find out. That's what I'm worried about.' Molly sighed. Annie had tried to get into an office job, and she was a lot brighter than Molly, but she had frightened Molly with her talk of the test that she had been put through. Even though Molly knew that she would not be given a second look at an office job, she was worried about any tests that she would have to do for even the most menial of jobs.

'They are a good, understanding firm, they'll find you a place. They know your sisters are good workers and you've come from the same stable, so they'll take you on,' Winnie said as she added salt to the handful of potatoes and hoped that she would be proved right.

But Molly hoped that her mother was wrong for once; the smell of chocolate filled the house and the surrounding streets all the time and she had wanted to break the trend in the Freeman household.

'Hey up, the other eggs have chipped,' Winnie said, meaning her other two daughters had arrived home from their shift, as she heard them entering the house chattering excitedly. 'They'll just have to wait for their teas for a minute, I must be running late.'

Rose, the tallest and oldest of the sisters, entered the kitchen first, pulling off the white turban that protected her blonde hair that was immaculately held in place by hairgrips. Her make-up was like that of a movie star too. Rose loved to look just right and she had taken the eye of many a fella as she walked the two streets to and from the factory. She had also impressed the management and been told that she was going to be put in charge as a Grade A overlooker once the new product that they were developing was in place. This was good news for Rose as she was walking out with Larry Battersby and everyone knew that wedding bells would soon be ringing – every penny would be needed for them both to set up home together.

'Now then, our Mol, how was the last day at school then? Are you ready to join us Chocolate Girls come Monday?' Rose said cheerfully, leaning against the pot sink as her other sister Annie lit a longed-for cigarette and sat down across from Molly with her legs crossed and her turban still covering her head of tight dark curls.

'I don't know. Annie, do you think I'll be all right? I'm beginning to worry about working there,' Molly said, looking at her other sister who, unlike Rose, didn't care about how she looked, or what folk thought of her; she was the tomboy out of the trio.

'Of course you'll be all right; we'll be there to look after you. Just try not to be put into the Card Box Mill, the stink of glue really gets on your chest,' Annie said, taking a long drag on a Craven A cigarette, which made her cough.

'Not as much as those things do, our Annie, I wish you would stop smoking, it is most un-ladylike,' Rose complained and then turned to look at Molly kindly. 'You'll be fine, love, wherever they decide to put you. The Rowntree family might be strict but they are fair and care about their staff, they have to, or else they wouldn't be honouring their religion. Quakers are known for their caring ways.' Rose put her arms around her youngest sister briefly to reassure her.

'Listen to her! No wonder she is getting a promotion, creeping and sticking up for the management. They are like any other business; if you don't make them money then they will get rid of you. Just like they sacked Brenda Crosby the other week,' Annie said, shaking her head as she remembered that one of her friends had been given instant dismissal without listening to a word in her defence.

'That's because she had been helping herself to the chocolate bars and selling them on to her friends. What else were they supposed to do?' Rose said, glaring at Annie.

'She swore to me that she didn't, that that old bag Agnes Moore, her overlooker, just held a grudge against her. I believe her as well,' Annie said, flicking her butt end into the fireplace and hoping that her sister would not argue back.

'You need better friends, our Annie, everyone knew what she was doing and it was just a matter of time before she was caught. She's lucky that she didn't get the police knocking on her door.'

'Girls, please, no arguing, just for once let us have our supper in peace,' Winnie said and smiled at Molly. 'You will be just grand, love. Just do your best, keep yourself tidy and mind your own business, that is all that they will want. Now, Annie, put the kettle on and change that look on your face, it's as black as the chimney back and it will stay that way if the wind changes.'

'Well . . .' Annie moaned.

'Well, nothing, kettle filled, please, and stop your whinging. We will have a game of rummy after supper, that will pass the night,' Winnie said as she prodded the potatoes with a fork to check if they were ready.

'Count me out, Mam, I'm meeting Larry, we are going to the pictures. There's *Shall We Dance* on at the Odeon and I love Fred Astaire and Larry loves Ginger Rogers.'

'Fred Astaire, Ginger Rogers, listen to you, what's wrong with Laurel and Hardy, now they give you a good laugh,' Annie said as she filled the kettle and placed it on the range.

'Annie, you would argue with your own shadow if you could. Now all of you, let's have some peace and enjoy our supper together in a civilised manner.' Winnie sighed, her girls had all had the same upbringing but none of them were alike in their ways and it often led to many an argument. However, all her girls had spirit and knew right from wrong so she couldn't have done too badly, even though sometimes it had been hard bringing up three girls on her own for the best part of ten years. With Molly finally going out to work and Rose heading for marriage, life should finally become a little less hard.

2

Monday morning had come around all too soon for Molly's liking. She lay in bed listening to her two sisters who shared a bedroom getting ready for work and could hear her mother in the back yard filling the boiler in the outhouse for the Monday wash. She pulled her bedcovers over her head, blocking out the sunshine that was coming through the skylight window of her attic bedroom. She felt sick as she thought about what she had to do that day: it would be the start of her new life as a Rowntree's employee if things went well, and if they didn't she had no idea what to do. There wasn't much employment in York except the chocolate and confectionery factories of Rowntree's, Terry's and Craven's, and out of the three, Rowntree's was the nearest, being only a couple of streets away from where she lived. So it went without saying that she should hope to get taken on there.

'Molly, move your shanks, its seven fifteen and your interview is at nine,' her mother shouted from the bottom of the stairs, and then her bedroom window shook as her sisters slammed the front door in their hurry to get to work and to clock in on time, running down the street arguing with one another as ever.

'I'm coming,' Molly replied and felt a wave of nausea

overcome her yet again as she climbed out of bed and looked at herself in the wardrobe mirror. She analysed every inch of herself as she pulled her nightdress over her head, did up her skirt and buttoned the ditsy patterned blouse that her mother had ironed especially for her interview. She studied her reflection as she pulled her knickers and socks on and realised that she was still a schoolgirl in looks, unlike her sisters, who were grown women and beautiful. She had bobbed, short, mousy-coloured hair that she held back with a hair clip, and freckles over her nose. She was gangly and not yet fully grown where it mattered, unlike Rose, who had the best figure anyone could ask for. Nevertheless, it was what God had blessed her with. There was no way she could change it now, she thought, as she washed her face in the bowl that stood on the washing stand and hoped that she looked the part.

She ran down the stairs and outside to the back yard to spend a penny on the wooden-seated lavvy next to the outhouse. Steam was coming out of the outhouse where her mother was preparing the weekly wash and she could hear her putting the tin lid on the huge pot that she washed the whites in and smell the carbolic soap and Dolly Blue that her mother used religiously every washday. She sat on the lavvy seat and wished she could disappear and not have to face the day, but her mother was not going to let her, and sure enough here she was knocking on the lavvy door.

'Tea's on the table and there's some porridge in the pot. We can't have you fainting at your interview. I'm about to scrub the front doorstep, so move yourself,' Winnie called as Molly reached for a sheet of last week's cut-up newspaper to wipe herself clean.

Monday was her mother's busiest day; it was washday, step-scrubbing day and it was the day the rag 'n' bone man came. Shouting his usual call of 'Rag 'n' bone!' and exchanging a new supply of Dolly Blue bags, or donkey stones that her mother scrubbed the front doorstep with until it was almost white, for leftover bones. The bones went to be sold to the glue factory, and any outgrown clothes or rags traded were to be sold on as shoddy to the nearby mills. The rows of terraced houses might not be the wealthiest ones in York but there was pride within the women who lived there, and if a standard was not kept then it would be worse for the woman who let the row down. Windows were cleaned, steps scrubbed and the nets kept pristine just to prove that you were a good housewife.

Molly looked at the porridge that had been left for her in the pot. It had skinned over and congealed and she didn't fancy it, even though she was hungry and her stomach was churning, so she poured a cup of tea and looked at the clock. Another half hour and she would have to be out of the house and walking the few streets to the Rowntree's works. She looked at the washing-up that had been left behind and decided to do that to distract herself and help her mother. Pouring hot water from the kettle into the sink she washed everybody's breakfast pots and left the porridge pan to soak. Another ten minutes and she would go, she thought, it was always better to be early than late, so her mother had told her.

'Oh, Molly, look at your skirt, it's soaked from you washing up, and you can't go to an interview with that big wet patch on you,' Winnie exclaimed, looking across at her daughter as she made her way back through the kitchen. 'Go and get changed, you'll have to go in your other skirt, the one you had on yesterday, although it's not as good or as pretty, but at least it's not covered with washing-up water. But hurry up, it is nearly eight thirty and your interview is at nine.' Winnie sighed, noticing the panic on her daughter's face as she ran up the uncarpeted wooden stairs as fast as she could. Poor Molly, she was the kindest out of her three daughters, but nothing ever went right for her, no matter how she tried.

'That's better, not as posh as the one you were supposed to go in but at least it is clean,' Winnie said as Molly pelted back down the stairs and stood in front of her. 'Hands, nails, are they clean? They always look at your hands,' Winnie told her and held her hands out for Molly to place them in hers for inspection. 'Yes, you'll do, now remember your manners and no matter what they ask of you, you do it. You need this job and it's good of our Rose to get you this interview. Now, get gone and don't dally.' Winnie wondered whether to give her youngest a hug for good luck, but hugs were few and far between on her busiest day of the week and Molly would only cling to her and cry by the look on her face.

'Mam, I don't know if I want to go,' Molly said, looking

pitiful as her mother walked her up the oil-clothed hall-way to the front door.

'You go, and you come back and tell me that you start working at Rowntree's tomorrow. We need the money; you need the money now that you've left school. You are not a little girl any more, Molly, now go.' Winnie virtually pushed her out of the front door and over her newly cleaned step and watched as she walked down the street, giving a final backward glance at her as she turned the corner. 'Please let them take her on, I know that she will be looked after at Rowntree's,' Winnie whispered under her breath, before going to find the bones that she had kept for the rag 'n' bone man who she could hear yelling at the end of Rose Street.

With each step, Molly felt more butterflies in her stom-ach and more fear as she neared the sprawling complex of the Rowntree's factory. It was a huge complex, cover-ing most of the north side of York, with its own railway sidings and a small station called Rowntree's Halt and its own wharf on the Foss Lock. Along with the huge fac-tories that filled the air with the smell of chocolate, there were tennis courts, a library, a swimming pool, dining rooms, a cinema and even garden allotments to keep their employees happy and fit. There was everything an employee wanted and needed as long as they were will-ing to work hard and be proud of the job they did.

Rose and Annie had told her everything about the place and she had often met them outside the blue fence and gates that surrounded the factory after work, but as she reached one of the main gates, she could easily have fled, the terror inside was so bad. She looked up at a large clock positioned just inside the fence, reminding the employees to hurry if they did not want their pay for the day docked. Ten minutes to go, she was in good time, she thought as she passed the red-stoned arts and crafts building that was the library, and the flower beds which contained a memorial to the founder Joseph Rowntree, as she made her way to the sprawling dining block where Rose had told her the interviews were taking place. She tried to compose herself and smiled as one of the workers passed by her with a smile and a reassuring word.

'They don't bite, you'll be fine, love,' said the woman with the same white turban on her head that her sisters wore.

Molly smiled back and breathed in. 'I will be all right; I will get this job and make my mam proud of me,' she whispered to herself as she pushed the heavy oak doors open.

'Here for the job, are you?' an efficient-looking young woman asked her, showing little interest beyond that.

Molly nodded.

'Wait over there then, somebody will be with you shortly,' the woman said, pointing to a wooden desk where another young girl was sitting.

Molly tried to say thank you but only a squeak came out and the secretary looked at her as if she was an inconvenience to her day.

'She's a flarchy one, as my mam would say, couldn't work all day in those heels,' the lass sat next to her said

328

and grinned. 'You here for the job and all? I didn't want to come but my mam said I had to and besides there is a train that brings me straight here, which is not something you can knock when you live out at the end of the world in Selby.' The lass grinned again. 'Besides, I need some money, I don't want to live at home for ever, it's hell there at the moment. My mam lives with this fella and my baby brother Billy is always bawling. I need to get out before it drives me crackers.' She pulled a face behind the secretary's back as she turned and gave her a black look. 'I only live two roads down, it'll be easy for me to come back and forward to work,' Molly replied, trying not to look at the lass whom her mother would have called a bit common.

'Well, that's all right for you then, I don't suppose you've got a spare room at yours, I could leave home then and have no travelling.' She looked at Molly with a twinkle in her eye.

'No, I live with my mam and my sisters; I sleep in the attic bedroom as it is,' Molly said quietly.

'Bedroom to yourself, eh! Luxury, I share with two of my sisters when they are at home, I dread when they come home from tattie picking. Mucky back-breaking job, you wouldn't get me doing that,' the lass said. 'Anyway, what's your name, I never heard you give it when you came in?'

'It's Molly, Molly Freeman. Should I have given my name when I came in, she never asked for it?' Molly looked worried and thought of walking over to the secretary who was now sitting behind her formidable oak desk.

'Nah, there's only me and you waiting, they'll know who we are. I'm Connie, Connie Whitehead. Whitehead by name and whitehead by nature. My mam says she doesn't know why I'm so blonde when all the rest of us are quite dark. I think I must have been the milkman's.' Connie laughed and then went silent as the secretary put her finger to her lips.

'I'm just a little nervous, I babble too much when I'm nervous,' Connie whispered and then went silent as she could hear footsteps coming down the winding stairs towards them both. Looking up they saw a young girl not much older than themselves but dressed for office work, and with an air of superiority about her.

'Interview? Are you two here for the interview? If you are then follow me,' she said, turning back up the stairs expecting both girls to follow, walking with confidence and not even bothering to wait for their answers.

Connie shrugged her shoulders and stood up, followed by Molly, and they both followed the untalkative girl to the top of the stairs where she motioned for them to take a seat on a long leather bench next to glass cabinets filled with commemorative chocolate boxes for special occasions like Easter and Christmas. Both girls gazed at them and knew to be quiet.

Molly felt her stomach churn as a door along the corridor opened and a woman dressed in a smart plain suit stepped out and looked at them over the top of her spectacles. Her hair was tied back in a neat bun and her facial expression did not change as she looked at both the girls.

'I'm Mrs Spencer, now come this way with me, we need you to fill in a form or two and take some tests to see which part of Rowntree's you will fit into the best.'

Mrs Spencer led both girls to individual desks not too dissimilar from school ones and gave them a form to fill in giving details of themselves.

Molly looked at hers and felt a panic come over her; could she fill it in correctly and without making a mess and blotting the ink? She picked up the ink pen and started to complete her personal details. She was aware of how quickly Connie had completed hers and looked up at Mrs Spencer as she finally finished her form, a look of worry on her face.

'Now we want both of you girls to take some tests to see what part of Rowntree's you would excel in,' Mrs Spencer said, and noticed both girls look at one another with worry on their faces.

'It's nothing to be anxious about and won't take long, and then we will need you to visit the doctor and dentist.'

Molly felt sick; she had never been to a dentist, and what if she couldn't manage the tests? Her sisters were always making fun of her for sometimes not being as sharp as them. She said nothing as Connie was sent through one door and she through another across the way where two women were waiting to assess her skills.

'Hello, Molly, don't worry, it's not like an exam,' said the younger of the women, and it was then that Molly noticed a man in the corner taking notes, which made her even more worried.

'Here you will find different shapes to go into these

holes in the board, but not all the shapes will have a matching hole. It is up to you to decide what goes where and how fast you can do it. Do you understand?'

Molly nodded and felt her stomach churn as she waited until she was told to start. All she could think was, why hadn't her sisters told her there were so many tests, and then at least she'd have known what she was in for. Next it was about putting coloured cards into matching boxes, and then came a set of puzzles to solve. After this, somebody took her temperature and felt how cold her hands were. This, she was told, was to see if she would be able to use a chocolate piping bag, as if her hands were too warm the chocolate would go white once cooled. Molly's head was spinning when at last she was asked to pack shapes into a box. The shapes were made of plaster of Paris and the tester smiled as Molly's face fell when she realised that they weren't edible.

'Pack them in exactly the same way as you see in the completed box just there and make sure each one is contained in a frilly paper cup. When I say go, the gentleman over there will time you,' the instructor said, and watched as Molly stood at the table and waited, a determined expression on her face.

'GO.'

Molly felt her hands sweating and her brain tried to calculate where each chocolate should go. Could she do it quickly and correctly enough to get into the chocolate packing department along with her sister Annie? She had told her how fast they all worked in there, so she knew her hands had to be nimble and her mind sharp.

Suddenly she dropped one of the pieces and it landed on the floor, causing her to lose precious seconds. She did not dare to look at the inspector's face as she hurried to finish the task and at last heard the man click on the stopwatch as the last shape was given its allotted place. She sighed and stepped back; surely that was all the tests over.

'Thank you, Miss Freeman, if you could go and take a seat out in the corridor we will come to a decision and let you know.'

Molly's legs felt like jelly as she walked back into the corridor and sat down with relief on one of the leather seats. There was no sign of Connie, she was either still taking part in the tests or she had already left, Molly thought as she clenched the palms of her hands together and just hoped that she would not be going home with disappointing news. Had she put the coloured cards in the right boxes, and would dropping a pretend chocolate count against her? It was too late now, the instructors would have made their decision and there was nothing she could do. Her heart beat wildly as the door opened and the instructor stepped out and smiled.

'Providing that you pass your medical, I'm pleased to say that we would like to welcome you to employment with Rowntree's, to work in the Card Box Mill, making and printing the various chocolate boxes that we have for our products. Well done, Miss Freeman.'

Molly sighed. She had passed the test, and that was the bit that she had been most worried about, but she had really wanted to be a part of the chocolate icing team. 'Thank you,' she said, trying to smile. Perhaps she would eventually get there if she proved herself. She would try and ignore what her sister Annie had said about the Card Box Mill, she always did exaggerate slightly.

'Don't thank me yet, let's get you through the medical and then you can. Follow me,' the instructor said, and walked a little further down the hallway, stopping to open a door with an 'Occupational Health Department' sign on it.

Molly walked into the room. It was large and airy and smelt of carbolic soap, and she was greeted by a man in a white coat.

'Ah, you must be Miss Freeman, please take a seat and I will then examine your eyes and ask you to read from the board over there as far as you can, then my colleague Nurse Jenkins will ask you a few questions and will ask you to undress for a full-body examination.'

Molly sat down in the chair and looked up towards the light that the doctor shone into her eyes, and then once he had made notes she was asked to read a series of letters that got smaller line by line.

'Excellent! Now you just have the nurse to see and then on to the dentist.'

Dentist – she had seen a doctor before but never a dentist, and she didn't want to undress in front of somebody she didn't know. She was acutely aware that her knickers were patched and worn and was embarrassed by the state of them as she stood in front of the nurse and answered question after question about her health before being asked to strip off to her underwear.

'Hold out your hands. Now turn them over so that I

can see both sides.' Molly held her hands out and noticed them shaking as the nurse ran her hands down her spine and legs and then parted the hair on her head. 'Just looking for nits,' she said, 'and then we will measure your height and weight.'

Standing under the wooden measuring stick and then being weighed, Molly felt thankful that her ordeal was nearly over.

'You are a bit thin for your height but it's something and nothing. Tell your mam to give you a slightly bigger portion at dinnertime,' the nurse said, and smiled as she wrote her notes down.

'I don't think she'll do that, there's not that much to go around anyway,' Molly said, and wondered why her weight was so important.

'There will happen to be a bit more, once you have started working for us, every penny counts,' the nurse said, and then walked her to the door once Molly had pulled her clothes back on. 'Next door down, just knock and enter, the dentist is waiting for you.'

'Thank you,' Molly said, and felt a tingle of excitement and fear as she left the nurse and walked into the dentist's surgery.

'Ah, Miss Freeman, welcome, come and sit in my chair and let me examine your teeth.' The dentist, dressed in white, ushered her into his chair and pressed a pedal to make it recline as he hovered over her with a dental mirror in one hand and a steel thing that Molly had never seen before in the other. 'Now this should not hurt, but if it does, then let me know.'

The smell of the surgery and the all-new experience frightened her and if she could have got up and run away she would have done, but Molly knew that she needed the job too much to show how scared she was and to leave. So she closed her eyes tight, blocking out the dentist's face as he prodded and poked about in her mouth.

'Ow!' Molly yelped as the steel probe hit a nerve in a decaying back tooth and then wished that she had said nothing as the dentist pushed the pedal to bring the chair upright again.

'I'm afraid, Miss Freeman, that back tooth is very badly decayed and will have to come out immediately. We will do that right here and now and have you home in no time.'

Molly felt the blood drain from her face. 'I've never had a tooth out before, will it hurt?'

'No, you'll not feel a thing, I'll give you some anaesthetic and some gas, and it will put you to sleep for a short while, just until I extract the tooth. Now when did you last eat?'

'I didn't have any breakfast this morning, I was too nervous,' Molly said and felt like crying, but if a tooth was stopping her from making money for the family then she would have to put her faith in the dentist.

'Excellent. I'll get my nurse just to place you in a white gown, we don't want you walking home with blood on your clothes now, do we?'

Molly felt like crying as the nurse prepared her for the tooth extraction. She watched as clinical devices were put into an enamel tray next to her chair and finally, a stand with two bottles of gas and gauges was wheeled up, to which a mesh mask was attached. The nurse checked that the white gown was tight around her neck and then the dentist loomed over her.

'You won't feel a thing, my dear, you will only be asleep for a short while and when you wake up we will take you next door into the nurse's room where you can recover.'

Molly looked at the dentist and noticed every vein and blemish on his face as he placed the mask over her nose. It smelt of rubber and something stranger that she had never smelt before and she wanted to run as she heard a hissing sound and her mouth went dry and her head went dizzy and she felt slightly sick as the gas did its work and she slipped off into sleep.

Molly had no idea how long she had been asleep when she heard the nurse speaking. 'Molly, Miss Freeman, are you back with us?' She felt a gentle hand on her shoulder and then tasted the horrible irony taste of her blood in her mouth as she tried to sit up and leave the chair. 'Not so fast, you will be dizzy and disorientated for a while. Take your time,' the nurse said as the dentist came back over and asked her to open her mouth for a final check.

'Everything looks fine, now don't wiggle your tongue in the cavity, else it will start to bleed, don't eat anything until teatime, and remember to brush your teeth twice a day and then you won't have to return to me in a hurry, hopefully.' The dentist indicated that the nurse should help Molly back into her room.

'Oh, and no toffees or chocolate,' the dentist added as

Molly found her legs with the aid of the nurse and made her way to a chair to wait in until her full senses returned.

Molly felt groggy as she took the nurse's arm. Toffees or chocolate, she never had either except at Christmas, and was he supposed to say that to someone when after all he worked for a chocolate factory? She'd never go back and sit in his chair ever again if she could help it, she thought, as she spat a mouthful of blood into the clean white hanky that her mother had made her bring.

After a short while the nurse looked across at her and smiled. 'Feeling better now? Do you think you can stand and walk all right?'

Molly nodded, she had to get away from the smell that she now knew to be the anaesthetic. She never wanted to smell it again.

'Right then, I'll walk you back to the main office where you took your aptitude test. There are a few things that you will need before you start work in the morning.' The nurse opened the door for Molly and waited for her to slowly gain her ability to walk and for her head to clear from the fumes of the gas.

Work in the morning, she was to start work in the morning, she thought as she sat across from Mrs Spencer, who nodded to the nurse, taking Molly's new dental records for her files.

'Right, Miss Freeman, you start with us tomorrow morning at seven thirty sharp in the Card Box Mill. You will work a forty-four-hour week and will be paid eleven shillings a week. This is a copy of the Works Rules and Regulations: make sure you read them before you start in the morning.' Mrs Spencer hesitated and looked at Molly for acknowledgement.

'Yes, Mrs Spencer, that sounds fine,' Molly said and then realised that school hours had been a doddle compared to the hours she was about to work.

'You need two white turbans and two white aprons that you can buy from various stores in town. I advise that you wear stockings and flat shoes, no high heels, no sandals and no jewellery, other than a wedding ring. You need money for whatever you eat, dinner can be bought and eaten here in the dining block, the food is good and is cheap.' Mrs Spencer must have said the same thing over and over again and had got the patter off to a fine art as she looked across at Molly's pale face. 'Are you all right with all that, Molly, have you heard all that I've said?'

'Yes, thank you. I already know most of that; I have two sisters that already work here, one in the boxing room and one I don't know where at the moment, she isn't allowed to say.' Molly looked across at Mrs Spencer who looked quizzingly at her.

'Oh, you should have told the dentist that you had sisters that already work here; they would have been allowed to stay with you when you had your tooth removed. Would you like me to fetch one from their work to make sure that you are all right?' Mrs Spencer asked, leaning over and looking at Molly closely.

'No, I'm all right now; it was just when I woke up that I felt a little light-headed and queasy,' Molly replied, saying nothing more.

'Now, let me see. When you say you don't know where your sister is presently working in the factory, that must make you Rose Freeman's sister, she is helping us with an exciting new product that is about to be released. She is sworn to secrecy so it is good to hear that she has not discussed her present work. So, that also makes you Annie in the packing department's sister. We like to give employment to full families, so I'm glad to welcome you into our family, Molly,' Mrs Spencer smiled.

'Thank you, yes, I'm the youngest and my sisters have told me how good it is to work here.' Molly wasn't entirely telling the truth: Rose spoke nothing but well of the Quaker chocolate factory, but to Annie, it was just a job to be endured. She would soon be finding out which she agreed with.

'You'll know then to report to the timekeeper each morning and not to be late else you will lose your morning's pay and will be locked out?'

Molly nodded. Annie had been late a morning or two and had come back home to get a good dressing-down by her mother, and she wasn't going to let that happen.

'Right then, seven thirty sharp, report to the time-keeper's office and someone will meet you and take you over to the Card Box Mill, where you will be taught your job.'

Molly made her way home past the larger houses of Hambleton Terrace and the terraced houses of Rose Street, turning onto her home street of Belgrave. She could see her mother standing outside talking to their next-door neighbour, her brush in hand from sweeping the small front path.

'Been sweeping the muck up from the rag 'n' bone man's horse. I've just put it around the rose that's flowering at the back door; waste not want not,' Winnie said.

'Well, how have you done Molly? Do you start work in the morning?' Jenny Campbell asked, showing more interest in her neighbour's daughter than her own mother did.

'I start in the Card Box Mill in the morning,' Molly said. 'But Mam, they had to take one of my back teeth out, they said it was rotten.'

'Only one? You won't remember, but our Rose had three out when she started. We never warned you because we thought you wouldn't go.' Winnie ignored the fact that she had just got a job until she saw the upset on her youngest daughter's face.

'Well done, lass, it will be work in the morning with the other two. You'd better do what you want this afternoon as it will be the last time you will have some time to yourself for a while. I've already bought you new turbans and aprons, I knew you'd get a job there.'

'Thanks, Mam, I might have a walk into town while I've got the chance,' Molly said and thought that she would make the most of having some time away from school and home.

'There's threepence on the kitchen table, you get what you want, my lass, but perhaps not toffees, not until that gum heals over. My treat.'

'Thanks, Mam, that's a real treat.'

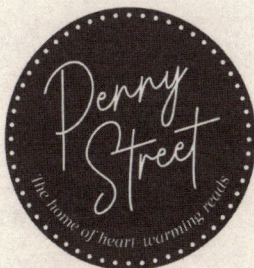

On a station platform, with nothing to read,
and a four-hour train journey stretching ahead of him...

That's where the story began for Penguin founder Allen Lane.
With only 'shabby reprints of shoddy novels' on offer,
he resolved to make better books for readers everywhere.

By the time his train pulled into London, the idea was formed.
He would bring the best writing, in stylish and affordable
formats, to everyone. His books would be sold in bookstores,
stationers and tobacconists, for no more than the price
of a ten-pack of cigarettes.

And on every book would be a Penguin, a bird with a certain
'dignified flippancy', and a friendly invitation to anyone who
wished to spend their time reading.

In 1935, the first ten Penguin paperbacks were published.
Just a year later, three million Penguins had made their
way onto our shelves.

Reading was changed forever.

—

A lot has changed since 1935, including Penguin, but in the
most important ways we're still the same. We still believe that
books and reading are for everyone. And we still believe that
whether you're seeking an afternoon's escape, a vigorous debate
or a soothing bedtime story, all possibilities open with a book.

Whoever you are, whatever you're looking for,
you can find it with Penguin.